She was a sus
Brilliant—perhaps even dangerous.

And he was a government agent.

They had no business even entertaining the notion of a future together. But at the same time, the fact it had even entered his head shook Scott Armstrong to the core. He had not thought about the future this way for the past nine years. Not since his wife and child were killed by his enemy, the Plague Doctor.

The acrid and familiar anger seeped into his throat.

Was this woman sleeping in his arms allied with a dangerous criminal mastermind on par with the Plague Doctor?

Skye murmured in her sleep. He turned, stroked her face. And deep down, a part of him prayed to God he'd find Skye Van Rijn innocent.

Dear Reader,

We keep raising the bar here at Silhouette Intimate Moments, and our authors keep responding by writing books that excite, amaze and compel. If you don't believe me, just take a look RaeAnne Thayne's *Nothing To Lose,* the second of THE SEARCHERS, her ongoing miniseries about looking for family—and finding love.

Valerie Parv forces a new set of characters to live up to the CODE OF THE OUTBACK in her latest, which matches a sexy crocodile hunter with a journalist in danger and hopes they'll *Live To Tell.* Kylie Brant's contribution to FAMILY SECRETS: THE NEXT GENERATION puts her couple *In Sight of the Enemy*, a position that's made even scarier because her heroine is pregnant—with the hero's child! Suzanne McMinn's amnesiac hero had *Her Man To Remember*, and boy, does *he* remember *her*—because she's the wife he'd thought was dead! Lori Wilde's heroine is *Racing Against the Clock* when she shows up in Dr. Tyler Fresno's E.R., and now his heart is racing, too. Finally, cross your fingers that there will be a *Safe Passage* for the hero and heroine of Loreth Anne White's latest, in which an agent's "baby-sitting" assignment turns out to be unexpectedly dangerous—and passionate.

Enjoy them all, then come back next month for more of the most excitingly romantic reading around—only in Silhouette Intimate Moments.

Yours,

Leslie J. Wainger
Executive Editor

Please address questions and book requests to:
Silhouette Reader Service
U.S.: 3010 Walden Ave., P.O. Box 1325, Buffalo, NY 14269
Canadian: P.O. Box 609, Fort Erie, Ont. L2A 5X3

SAFE PASSAGE

LORETH ANNE WHITE

Silhouette®

INTIMATE MOMENTS™

Published by Silhouette Books

America's Publisher of Contemporary Romance

If you purchased this book without a cover you should be aware that this book is stolen property. It was reported as "unsold and destroyed" to the publisher, and neither the author nor the publisher has received any payment for this "stripped book."

SILHOUETTE BOOKS

ISBN 0-373-27396-7

SAFE PASSAGE

Copyright © 2004 by Loreth Beswetherick

All rights reserved. Except for use in any review, the reproduction or utilization of this work in whole or in part in any form by any electronic, mechanical or other means, now known or hereafter invented, including xerography, photocopying and recording, or in any information storage or retrieval system, is forbidden without the written permission of the editorial office, Silhouette Books, 233 Broadway, New York, NY 10279 U.S.A.

All characters in this book have no existence outside the imagination of the author and have no relation whatsoever to anyone bearing the same name or names. They are not even distantly inspired by any individual known or unknown to the author, and all incidents are pure invention.

This edition published by arrangement with Harlequin Books S.A.

® and TM are trademarks of Harlequin Books S.A., used under license. Trademarks indicated with ® are registered in the United States Patent and Trademark Office, the Canadian Trade Marks Office and in other countries.

Visit Silhouette Books at www.eHarlequin.com

Printed in U.S.A.

Books by Loreth Anne White

Silhouette Intimate Moments

Melting the Ice #1254
Safe Passage #1326

LORETH ANNE WHITE

As a child in Africa, when asked what she wanted to be when she grew up, Loreth said a spy…or a psychologist, or maybe a marine biologist, archaeologist or lawyer. Instead she fell in love, traveled the world and had a baby. When she looked up again she was back in Africa, writing and editing news and features for a large chain of community newspapers. But those childhood dreams never died. It took another decade, another baby and a move across continents before the lightbulb finally went on. She didn't *have* to grow up, She could be them all—the spy, the psychologist and all the rest—through her characters. She sat down to pen her first novel…and fell in love.

She currently lives with her husband, two daughters and their cats in a ski resort in the rugged Coast Mountains of British Columbia, where there is no shortage of inspiration for larger-than-life characters and adventure.

To JoJo, Pavlo and Marlin
for being my sounding boards.
To Mu for believing.
And to Susan for keeping the bar raised.

Chapter 1

Scott Armstrong drove off the ferry ramp with a clunk. He felt like he'd just been spat from the belly of a vibrating metal beast.

He was back on Canadian soil. A bloody island of it—trapped on all sides by the placid, steely waters of the Pacific Northwest. He couldn't feel more claustrophobic if he tried.

He glanced at the golden-haired dog at his side as he maneuvered the truck through congested ferry traffic. The retriever grinned foolishly at him with a lolling tongue, thunking its tail on the seat.

What in hell had Rex been thinking, giving him a dog as part of his cover? He didn't need the stupid hound any more than he needed this lame-duck mission. He was being put out to pasture and he damn well knew it. Scott clenched his teeth. He'd bloody well show them he still had what it took, blown-out knee and all.

He tightened his hand on the wheel, shifted gears sharply, wincing as an all-too-familiar shaft of pain shot up his leg.

He swore, turned onto the coast road and followed the exit signs to Haven.

The sun was dipping behind the mountains of Vancouver Island, throwing farmland into evening shadow. Beyond the fields the sea shimmered like beaten silver. The bright light made his head hurt.

Scott wound down the window, letting the crisp spring wind whip at his hair, clear the fog in his brain. Honey wriggled closer toward him along the cab seat, chomping her jaws, testing the breeze, dribbling with excitement.

"At least one of us is happy," he muttered, elbowing the dog back over to the passenger side.

Honey's tail stilled for an instant. Scott felt a pang of guilt. "It's okay, girl," he muttered. "You do what you gotta do." The wriggling and rhythmic thunking resumed. A warm splotch of drool seeped through the denim of his jeans. Scott sucked air deliberately, deeply, into his lungs, straining for an elusive sense of calm. This might just end up testing him to his limit. And Lord knew, he was pretty much out of tolerance for life in general.

He ignored the wet drool on his thigh and tried to focus on the task ahead. Apart from skimming the facts and checking for directions to his rental house, Scott hadn't had the time or the privacy on the ferry to study the dossier Bellona Channel boss Rex Logan had handed him the second his plane had touched down in Vancouver.

All Scott knew was that he had to watch Dr. Skye Van Rijn. Some brilliant entomologist geek with *possible* biocriminal or terrorist links to a disease devastating the cattle industry south of the border, one that was rapidly spreading to humans. But the link between Dr. Skye Van Rijn and the Rift Valley Fever currently sweeping the Southwest corner of the United States was tenuous at best. Even Rex had admitted that the bug doctor had pretty much checked out.

Yeah. Lame-duck mission if he ever saw one. He should be where the action is, not in some bucolic village on a vague fishing expedition for a *possible* bit player in a game that had snared global headlines and rocked stock markets.

Scott hit the wheel, swore again.

Surveillance was a junior agent's beat.

His beat was out there, in the international field, in the wilds of the Borneo jungle, under the relentless sun of India's Thar desert, in the hot red sands of Namibia. Not here. Not in the stifling, dripping, cool, gray stillness of a place he'd once called home.

He didn't have a home. Not anymore. But right now he had no choice. He'd almost lost his leg.

And his mind.

It was this, or a desk job, while he recuperated. And he'd rather die than push a pen behind a desk.

He snorted at the irony of his situation. Because his cover was that of a full-time paper-shuffler and pen-pusher. He was to be Scott McIntyre. A writer. A futurist. It would put him at liberty, Rex had said, to ask questions, to get the doctor's views on things like macroeconomics, social trends, globalization, American imperialism.

And Honey, he'd added, would help break the ice.

Yeah. Right.

It was almost dark by the time he found the narrow farm road, picked out the house number on a faded green mailbox. Grass and weeds grew up between the rutted tire tracks that constituted the driveway. The truck jounced up to the front porch. Honey yipped with glee.

"Oh, shut up, dog!" She made him feel like a redneck arriving on the farm in his beater. All he needed was a shotgun behind the seat and load of beer cans in the back.

Scott pulled to a stop, threw open his door. Honey dug claws into his thighs and scrambled over him, promptly relieving herself in the grass. Scott scratched his head. "Okay. Sorry, pooch. Guess you gonna want food, too, huh? Let's see what Rex has packed for supplies."

He grabbed his old, gnarled walking stick, hesitated, fingering the ancient knots in the smooth, durable wood as if they'd somehow yield an answer. A reason for it all.

The dog yipped again, jerking him back to the present. Scott shrugged off the sensation of buried memories scratching at locked mental doors, climbed out of the truck and tentatively tested his leg on the ground. It felt okay. Better than it had in weeks. He could almost put all his weight on it. "Small mercies," he muttered as he limped up the porch steps, pushed open the front door.

He flipped on the lights.

Honey's paws skittered over wooden floors as she explored the premises, butt wiggling in a crazy hula of excitement.

Scott checked out the rooms. More than he'd ever need. The kitchen was big and airy. And the windows looked out onto Dr. Van Rijn's neighboring property.

"Sweet," he told Honey. "I can wash the dishes and watch the Bug Lady at the same time. Ain't life grand. Come, let's see if we can find you some doggy chow before it gets too dark out."

Scott counted five large cardboard boxes in the back of the truck. One was marked Computer, another Books. Yet another was marked Kitchen. He sliced the tape on the kitchen box with his army knife and tore back the cardboard. In the fading light he could make out a box of cereal, some tins, and a humungous bag of dog kibble.

Then he cursed Rex.

How in hell was he supposed to carry all this crap with a walking stick in one hand?

His buddy had probably done this on purpose. Just to make sure he turned to someone for help. Just to make sure he met some locals.

"There's no way I'm going to be reduced to begging someone to help me carry a couple of boxes," he mumbled. Honey circled his feet with excitement.

Scott dropped the tailgate with a clunk, maneuvered the

kitchen box to the end. Dropping his cane, he used both hands to grab the box. He flexed his knees, slowly lifted the box, trying to transfer most of the weight through to his core ab muscles, shoulders and thighs and onto his good leg. He closed his eyes, took a deep breath and took a few steps toward the porch.

Pain sparked out from his knee, seared down his calf, shot up his thigh. He swallowed it. Jaw clenched, he made his way, step by painful baby step. And in his mind he heard the heavily accented voice of Dr. Ranjit Singh from the Mumbai hospital, rattling off dire warnings about what could go wrong with his leg if he didn't follow the recuperation procedure, if he didn't keep his weight off his new, fake knee. Pain, swelling, slippage, infection. He could cope with those. It was the risk of breaking the bone below the new joint on which his knee was anchored that concerned him most. Or the threat of a blood clot.

But it was not enough to stop him from carrying the box. Minute beads of perspiration pricked through the skin of his forehead as he stepped through the front door. He made it a few more paces and slumped to his haunches with a grunt of pain.

He hunched over the box, rested his forehead on the cardboard, letting wave after nauseating wave of pain flow over him. His heart thumped against his chest from the exertion. ''Oh, sweet Mother Mary,'' he whispered to no one in particular.

But Honey heard. She quivered, licked his face, sat beside him, watching, her liquid brown puppy eyes almost level with his.

''You know, Honey, you actually look like you understand. What is it about dogs that—'' He saw the change in Honey.

She stiffened. The fur on her neck rose.

It stopped him dead.

Scott was so used to living in the wild he'd almost developed an animal's sense of a presence himself. He could feel the hair on his own neck prickle with that awareness now.

"You drop this?"

He swiveled the instant he heard the voice.

His hand shot instinctively for the knife at his ankle. In another heartbeat he'd have thrown it.

But he froze at the sight in front of him.

The most striking woman he'd ever seen. At his door.

He swallowed.

Her stance was wide, her muscles tensed, knees flexed. She held his wooden cane across her body, one end in each hand, as if to deflect the knife he held in midair.

As reflexive as his reaction had been, hers had been more so.

Scott stared, realized he had his knife aimed at her heart.

Shaken, he slowly lowered the arm that held the blade. He slipped the knife carefully back into the sheath at his ankle, his eyes never leaving hers.

Honey snarled, head low, hackles raised.

But the woman didn't flinch. Not even blink. Her jaw remained clenched. She stared straight at him with penetrating silver eyes.

Scott could almost see her mind computing, trying to second guess, to figure out what had just happened. Lord knew, he sure was.

She made the first move, the muscles of her shoulders visibly relaxing as he moved his hand away from the knife, safely back in its sheath.

She stepped forward, held his wooden cane out to him as if an offering of peace. "I think you dropped this." Her voice was low, like smoke over the desert, and it came from lips that invited sin.

He stared at his cane in her hands.

Then he looked up into her eyes. They were set above strong cheekbones and they were shaped like almonds.

Large and light with impossibly thick, dark lashes. There was a wildness, a recklessness, that lurked there. Something he recognized. Something that reminded him of vast spaces and untamed tribes.

The shape of her face was exotic. Foreign. Her skin was a soft olive tone. Her hair, lush and dark. It fell below her shoulders in a soft wave. The image of her burned into his brain, in the way he had trained his mind to capture the tiny details of each new face he encountered on a mission.

She wore a cream-colored sweater that caressed the curves of her breasts in a way that should be declared illegal. And her legs, in dark blue denim, were long. And slim. He noticed she wore heavy black motorcycle boots.

She had the advantage of height over him. She took another step across his threshold, into his new home.

A growl rumbled low in Honey's throat.

"Honey, quiet." He tried to push himself to his feet, buckled under a hot wave of searing pain, "Damn!"

"You all right?" The woman stepped further into his life.

"Yeah." He clenched his teeth. "Fine."

"Here, let me help." She bent to take his arm and her hair fell across his cheek. The spicy, female smell of it sent an unbidden and long-forgotten wave right through him.

He shook her off. "Just hand me that stick. I can manage."

She raised a dark brow, passed him his cane.

"Thanks." He swallowed a curse, another surge of pain, and forced himself up onto his feet. She was tall, but this way he could still look down at her from his height of two inches over six feet.

He held out his hand. "Hi."

She looked down at his hand, laughed. A smoky laugh, like sex and smooth whiskey. He could almost feel the sound of it in his gut.

"Seems a little trite after you almost killed me." She

held out her own hand. It was cool, soft to the touch. "My name's Skye, I live next door."

"You're..."

The Bug Lady?

"Your neighbor." Her lips curved into a smile that made his stomach churn.

Scott found his voice. "I'm Scott...McIntyre. This is...this is Honey." Christ, he'd blown it. He hadn't had time to go through the damn dossier.

"You always attack when surprised?" She stared him straight in the eye.

"You looked pretty primed for a fight yourself."

Her eyes flicked quickly away, scanned the room. "You startled me. Where're you from?"

Scott leaned heavily on his cane. He was supposed to be the one asking questions. He should be controlling the flow of information.

"I'm from...out east." Damn. He'd thought he'd have plenty of time to go through the file, familiarize himself with his cover, before running into the doctor. But this woman with the silver eyes had him cornered.

"East? As in Ontario? Or farther east?"

Scott attempted a laugh. "Even farther. I've been traveling for a while." A long while.

"Business?"

"Research."

"You've come home then? Back to Canada?"

There was that word again. Home. "I don't have a home, neighbor."

"Hey, home is where the heart is. So they say."

"Yeah. Like I said, I have no home. Now, you tell me something, do you subject all newcomers to Haven with the third degree?"

Something flickered through her eyes. Then it was gone. She smiled a full smile, revealing strong white teeth and a sharp twinkle in her eyes.

"I'm sorry. Naturally curious nature, I suppose. Goes with the territory. I'm a scientist. You?"

He cleared his throat. "Writer."

"Is that what brings you to Haven?"

"Pretty much. Thought it might be a nice, quiet spot to work on my book. Close to the sea, not too far from the city, lots of space for Honey."

Skye Van Rijn bent to pet Honey. "You're a real pretty thing, aren't you?" She looked up at Scott. "She still a puppy?"

"Pretty much."

"What kind of book you writing?"

Damn. "Some call me a futurist." The words did not come easily over his tongue. He felt anything but a futurist. Mostly he thought about the past. "I look for global trends. Economic. Social. That kind of thing."

"You widely published?"

Hell if he knew. He'd just have to wing it. "Nope. Mostly small university presses, academic journals, that kind of thing."

She frowned. "You'd enjoy talking to my fiancé then. He's all into big-picture economic trends and futures. Stock market, import-export business is his thing."

Her words blindsided him. He blinked.

"Fiancé?"

She smiled a slow smile, looked down at the dog. If he wasn't mistaken, it was a sad, resigned smile.

"Yes. I'm getting married day after tomorrow."

Scott couldn't begin to identify the strange little slip he felt in his chest, the hollowness in his gut. He liked the idea of the doctor being single. Rex hadn't told him about a fiancé. It was probably also in that damned dossier.

"Congratulations." The word sounded inane. It hung between them.

She stepped back. "Yeah, well, I should be going. I'm really sorry to have barged in on you like that. There's been no one in this house for a while. I thought you were the caterers. I'm expecting them. I thought they'd come to the wrong address."

She turned. Scott watched the sway of her ass as her long legs carried her to the door.

She stopped, spun suddenly back to face him. "By the way, how'd you hurt your leg?"

Images shot through his brain. The bullet smashing his knee. The terrorist group in the Thar. The suspicious disease he'd been investigating. Scorching heat. Pain. The hospital in Mumbai. His old life gone.

"Skiing accident," he said. "Torqued my knee."

"Oh." She ran those exotic eyes over him slowly. "Well, you've got an exquisite cane. Don't think I've seen wood like that before."

"Picked it up in Africa years ago. It's mukwa wood, a gift from a Venda chief. Never thought I'd end up needing it in this way, though."

"I'm sorry." She turned to go, hesitated, turned back. "Would you like to join us for the reception Saturday? We're having the caterers set something small and simple up at my house for after the church ceremony. I really didn't want anything fancy."

There was something about her demeanor that made him ask, "Why not?"

She shrugged. "Jozsef wanted to have the wedding brought forward for a number of reasons. This was the best option at such short notice."

Scott's curiosity piqued. "What short notice?"

She laughed. "Now who's giving the third degree? Good night, Scott McIntyre."

She slipped out into the dark and the house felt suddenly empty.

"Nice to meet you, Dr. Skye Van Rijn," Scott whispered to the black night that had swallowed her.

* * *

Scott spent the rest of the night pouring over the dossier. Suddenly this mission wasn't looking so lame. The bug doctor was not what she seemed. He sensed it in his gut. She was too quick with her reflexes, primed to react to physical threat in the way of no ordinary citizen.

And behind her smooth, smoky voice, her bold, unflinching gaze, she was guarded, hiding something. He knew it. Scott had spent years reading slight gestures, nuances of movement. He'd lived with tribes who communicated by tuning in to nature. He'd survived only because he was constantly poised for the slightest hint of danger, the mere intuition of imminent attack. Scott had lived the life of both hunter and prey. And there was something about this woman that made him feel she knew exactly what it was to be both. But which was she now?

And which was *he?*

He flipped over a page in the dossier, new energy humming softly through his system. And he told himself it had nothing at all to do with female curves that invited sin.

Skye pushed a button and her computer screen crackled softly to life. She scanned her e-mail before punching in her code and logging into the Kepplar lab system. She opened her work files, then rubbed the heels of her hands into her eyes. She couldn't concentrate. Couldn't sleep, either. An edginess zinged through her veins. Maybe it was wedding jitters. But deep down she knew it was more than that. It was the man next door. He'd unnerved her. She didn't like the knife strapped to his ankle, his gut reaction to surprise.

She didn't trust him.

There was something wild about him. Something she recognized. Something that had slipped past her guard and made her ask him to her wedding reception.

She stood, paced over to her window and stared out across her yard. The light was on in his kitchen.

His shadow moved momentarily against the shade.

She jerked back in reflex, told herself he couldn't see her through his closed blinds. She edged forward, studied the shape of his silhouette as he moved around his kitchen.

Scott McIntyre. She tested the name in a whisper over her tongue, found she liked the feel of it.

He dressed like a writer in that knobbly wool sweater with leather patches at the elbows. His body, however, did not belong to a man who spent his life hunched in front of a computer terminal. She'd seen the way his jeans were faded in the most eye-catching places, how the worn fabric strained over the thick muscles of his thighs. She'd noted the power of his wrists, the latent strength in the shape of his broad shoulders, the arrogance in the line of his wide and defined jaw. A jaw that needed a shave. His face was rugged, rough, but with an air of intelligence, a hint of compassion.

And his lips. They hadn't escaped her notice, either. Sculpted. Almost harsh.

She laughed at herself. Yeah, as if a writer had a certain kind of lips.

Yet, as she watched the hulk of his shadow in the kitchen next door, she couldn't pull her thoughts away from the hot image branded into her mind. He certainly looked as though he'd traveled recently. His skin was sunned a rich brown that contrasted startlingly with the deep jewel-green of his eyes. And his hair, thick and mahogany-brown with sun-bleached tips, needed a trim. But she liked the look of it. She liked the look of him. Wild. Dangerous.

And there was something about his eyes that made her want to look into him. To find out more about him. Not only because she was intrigued, but because knowledge was strength.

It could mean life over death.

She yanked her drapes shut, turned to her computer, her mind ticking over. He said he was published. A futurist.

She sat in front of her terminal. With a few quick clicks she logged into the Internet and pulled up a search engine.

She punched in the letters of his name and a few keywords.

Scott sipped his second mug of tea, flipped over another page in the dossier the Bellona Channel, the international nongovernment agency dedicated to researching and fighting bio crime and bio terrorism, had prepared on Dr. Skye Van Rijn.

According to the file, Bellona's Canadian headquarters had received an anonymous tip that Dr. Van Rijn, research and development scientist with Kepplar Biological Control Systems, had recently traveled from Kenya to Mexico where she'd crossed the border into the United States. Within weeks of her visit the first cases of Rift Valley Fever were being reported in Texas cattle. Devastating news. International borders had shut instantly, killed the American beef industry. The stock market reeled.

And then came worse.

Human infection.

And panic.

So far all the deceased were employees who had contracted the disease via slaughtering livestock at a Texas abattoir. RVF occurs naturally in Africa and is spread by one of three ways: mosquitoes, physical contact with the blood or secretions of infected animals, or inhalation of the airborne virus.

But no one had yet managed to identify the source of the U.S. outbreak.

Scott whistled softly through his teeth, set down his mug. Apart from an episode in Saudi Arabia and Yemen two years ago, there had never been a documented outbreak of RVF outside of Africa. Could this RVF strain have been brought in accidentally through commerce? Or had it been purposefully introduced? And if so, how? By contaminated animal products? Insects?

His thoughts turned to Skye. Insects were her field. She certainly had the expertise. She had been in the area after a visit to Africa.

But it was all so circumstantial.

He stretched his leg out, removed his makeshift ice pack, massaged his knee gingerly. Honey stirred at his feet. He reached down, scratched absently behind her ear.

Agro-terrorism, thought Scott, was easy to execute, low risk and often almost impossible to trace. It could instil mass panic, especially if there were human deaths, yet not generate the kind of backlash a direct civilian hit would. It was the kind of terrorism that had the additional value of being a powerful blackmail and extortion tool.

It had the potential, he figured, for use by organized crime and terrorist groups to raise huge sums of money by manipulating the U.S. agriculture future commodities markets. An astute player could simply invest in competitor's stock before carrying out an assault with pest or pathogen.

Scott made a mental note to ask Rex to check into recent stock market trades. Bellona may have already done so but there was nothing in the dossier.

Scott turned to the next page, his interest in Dr. Skye Van Rijn now thoroughly piqued—in more ways than one.

Bellona had combed through Skye's background. Born in Amsterdam, she immigrated to Canada ten years ago at the age of twenty-two. The dossier contained copies of her immigration papers, birth certificate, social security number, driver's license along with transcripts from the universities she'd attended and details of her scholarships.

She now worked for Kepplar, designing and developing biological control measures for the agricultural and horticultural industries. Rex and his boys had been pretty thorough. Everything had checked out.

She looked clean.

But Bellona still wanted to keep an eye on her. It was part of the organization's mandate to do so. And Skye Van Rijn was on record as having expressed controversial views on American imperialism, globalization and blow-back.

Scott raked his hands through his hair.

Maybe this gig wasn't going to be too painful. Watching Dr. Skye Van Rijn's wickedly sexy body, listening to that mysterious smoky voice...things could be worse.

He rested his head back on the sofa. Honey shifted again at his feet. Scott found himself smiling. He was kind of enjoying the dog's company. He prodded Honey with a toe, scratched her belly. "Well, dog, looks like the doctor's got something to hide. And we're gonna find it." He drifted off into a dream of wild spaces and liquid warmth.

Some time later, he woke with a jump.

He blinked, momentarily disoriented. Then his brain identified the sound. An engine growling. Low and throaty. Next door. His eyes flicked to his watch: 3:00 a.m.

He jerked to his feet, lunged to the window. His knee protested violently. White pain flashed through his skull. He swallowed it, forced his eyes to adjust to the dark shadows outside.

He was just in time to see the sensuous shape of Skye Van Rijn, clad in black leather and straddled over a sleek motorcycle, purr down the driveway.

Refracted yard light glinted like liquid on her black helmet. She kicked the mechanical beast into gear and growled down the pastoral street.

"Honey!" he barked as he grabbed his jacket and keys. "She's on the move!"

Chapter 2

Scott cut the engine, crawled silently to a stop in the peripheral shadows along the outside of the compound.

He watched Skye park her gleaming bike under harsh sulphur lights that flooded the fenced parking lot of the Kepplar lab complex on the outskirts of Haven.

Honey remained motionless at his side. Scott stroked the dog's head, watched Skye remove her helmet, shake out a wave of dark hair. Even under the flat whiteness of industrial lights, her hair shimmered, alive with burnished highlights.

He watched as she strode openly, confidently, up to the main entrance of the building, helmet tucked under her arm.

He checked the glowing digits of his watch. Three-fifteen. What in hell was she doing here at this hour?

A security guard stepped out from under the portico. Scott saw him exchange words with Skye. The guard nodded. His teeth glinted as his smile caught the lights. Skye laughed at something he said. She slotted what Scott imagined was a coded identity card into a panel. The building doors opened. They slid smoothly shut behind her. The guard retreated to his cubicle under the portico. All was still.

Scott shifted his throbbing knee into a more comfortable position and settled back in his seat to wait. This surveillance business was crap.

A movement caught his eye. He tensed. So did Honey. The dog peered intently out the window. Another vehicle. Silver Mercedes. It crawled down the road toward the fenced lab compound, turned into the gates, cruised quietly to the far end of the parking lot and came to a stop.

Then nothing.

Scott noted the plates, reached for his sat phone and punched in the code to activate the scrambler. The red LED indicator showed voice encryption had been initiated. His satellite communication was secure.

"Logan," Scott rasped into the piece.

"Jeez, you have any idea what time it is, Agent?"

"Desk life making you soft, buddy?"

Rex ignored the gibe. "What's up?"

"I need a plate run."

"Couldn't wait until morning?"

"It *is* morning."

"Don't tell me...you're pissed with the job."

"The plate?"

"Okay, okay," he mumbled. "Let me find a pen here somewhere... All right, shoot. Oh, and next time, call Scooter direct."

Scott chuckled inwardly. This would teach his boss for making him report to *him* direct. "Sorry. Haven't got Scooter's home number." He gave Rex the plate number, flipping the phone shut as the door to the Mercedes opened.

A man stepped out. Dark, well over six feet, and tough-looking. He strode to the entrance. There was something threatening in his movements.

Scott's knee-jerk instinct was to get out and follow the

guy into the building, to make sure Skye was okay. But he forced himself back against the truck seat. His brief was to watch. And she was a suspect.

Not a victim.

Skye hadn't been able to shake the deep sense of unease that pulsed low in her core. Sleep had remained elusive. She'd tried. Tossed and turned. But her thoughts had scrambled over each other like wild, hungry, teething puppies.

Work, she'd decided, was her only salvation. It was the only thing that kept her going forward. The only thing that made her forget the past.

The only thing that dulled her latent fear.

She placed the minute beetle carefully under the microscope, adjusted the focus. It was so tiny. So perfect. So very beautiful in its own way. If everything went according to plan, these little bugs would lead an army and conquer the enemy blight in its path. She adjusted the scope, bent closer.

A sound at the far end of the darkened lab crashed into her thoughts.

She jerked back, knocking a petri dish off the counter. It clattered to the floor, the sound disproportionately loud in the deserted laboratory.

Skye peered into the night shadows.

Her heart thumped a steady beat against her chest wall. Nothing. No movement.

She chided herself, turned back to her beetle. The Kepplar labs were perfectly safe. Even at night. Still, more than ten years down the road and she hadn't stopped looking over her shoulder. She was still seeing ghosts in shadows. Hearing sounds in the night. Afraid he'd find her.

Then she heard it again.

She froze. "Who's there?" She could hear the brittle edge of panic in her own voice.

Neon light flooded the lab, exploded into her brain.

She blinked against the brightness.

Jozsef stood beside the light switch, a wide grin on his face. "What you doing working in the dark at this ungodly hour, Dr. Van Rijn?"

Skye sucked her breath in slowly, trying to steady her popping nerves. "Good grief, Jozsef, you startled me. What in heaven are *you* doing here? When did you get back?"

He walked forward, arms behind him. "I thought I'd find you at home. I didn't. So I came looking here."

"You could've tried my cell."

"I wanted to surprise you." He grinned broadly. "What are you working on so late...or should I say so early?"

"My beetles," she snapped defensively, anger edging out fear.

"The ones for the whitefly epidemic?"

"Jozsef, how did you get in?"

He laughed, held up an access card.

"That's mine. That's my spare." She reached for it.

Jozsef held it playfully out of reach. "You left it at my place, sweetheart."

"I thought I'd misplaced it. Besides, you still had to get by security."

"When's that ever stopped me." He smiled warmly, slipping the card into his back pocket.

Skye frowned.

"C'mon, Skye." He lifted a hand, brushed a tendril of hair from her cheek. "Marshall Kane gave me the all-clear with security. They know I'm with you."

She hesitated, suddenly strangely unsure of the man in front of her. The man she was going to marry. "I bet Marshall didn't think you'd be trying to get in here after hours."

Jozsef shrugged. "Enough of this already. You're way too jumpy." He stepped closer. "Besides, I got a surprise for you. Guess." His words were warm against her ear.

Skye forced a smile. "What?"

"I said guess."

She sighed. "A rose?"

"Nope."

"Chocolate?"

"Come on, Doctor, I'm a little more original than that. You got one more guess."

"I give up. Look, we should go. You really shouldn't be in here—"

Jozsef Danko raised a finger to her lips. "Shh." He winked. "I won't tell if you don't." With his other hand he brought a small box out from behind his back. It was a deep burgundy-red. He set it on the lab counter, a smile playing around his dark eyes. "Open it, Doctor."

The light in the man's eyes was infectious. Skye relented. She peeled off her latex gloves, picked up the box and lifted the lid. Nestled in shiny black satin was a tiny gold bug with glittering emerald eyes. It hung from a gold chain.

She looked up at Jozsef. "You get it in Europe?"

"It's a little token to celebrate the completion of your big project."

"I'm not finished yet. They'll only be ready for release in another two weeks."

"Yes. But the bulk of your work is done, not so?"

"I guess." She lifted the chain and pendant from the box. "It's so unusual. Where'd you find it?"

"I had it made. Here, I'll put it on for you."

Skye lifted her hair, bent her head forward as Jozsef fastened the clasp behind her neck.

She turned to face him. "What you think?"

"Take a look in the mirror."

"There isn't one."

"There is, in the washroom. Go on. Humor me. I'll wait here."

Skye made her way to the bathroom, pushed open the door. She stared at her reflection under the harsh washroom lights. It was certainly a perfectly proportioned little bug.

And knowing Jozsef, the gold of the carapace nestled at the hollow of her throat was as real as the glittering emerald eyes of the beetle. It really was perfect. But it wasn't her. It didn't go with her coloring. She preferred silver.

She shrugged. So what? It showed he cared. It showed he'd gone to the trouble of finding something tailored specifically for her.

When had anyone ever done that?

But a little niggle of doubt ate at her as she headed back down the empty corridor to her lab, the heels of her boots echoing in the empty gloom. It summed up her relationship. Jozsef Danko seemed so perfect, but everything about him was always just slightly off center. It hadn't worried her before. But today it did. Maybe she was making a mistake. Maybe she just needed a holiday. The stress of this project had been getting to her.

Or maybe she'd just been unsettled by the mysterious man who'd moved in next door.

She shoved open the lab door, gasped.

Jozsef had the lid to the box of larvae open. She rushed forward. "What are you doing?"

He glanced up, smiled that nonchalant smile of his. "Just peeking at your babies."

"You shouldn't—"

"Oh, come on. It can't hurt. So, do you like your pendant?"

"Yes." She moved over to make sure the lid to the larvae was properly secured. The ugly little grubs, her pride and joy, represented a fortune to Kepplar Biological Control Systems. And there was stringent protocol on secrecy. A leak could spell the loss of millions. She couldn't understand why Marshall would clear anyone with security. Even her fiancé. It just didn't make sense.

"Come." She turned to Jozsef. "Let's get out of here before you ruin me."

Jozsef chuckled. "Now that would be the last thing on

my mind.'' He lifted his hand and brushed her cheek softly with the backs of his fingers. ''Come, let's go grab some breakfast. My place or yours?''

Skye hesitated. ''Actually, Jozsef, I'm really tired…and I've got a meeting with Marshall in a couple of hours.''

He studied her face. Then he nodded. ''Sure.'' He took her arm. ''It's okay, I understand.''

Skye felt everything but sure. Or okay.

Jozsef halted at the door, grasped her shoulders, turned her to face him. ''Skye—''

The sudden severity in his eyes startled her. ''What?''

''Promise me you'll wear that beetle *always.* No matter what happens. Can you promise me that?''

She reached up, fingered the gold carapace. ''Why? What's going to happen, Jozsef?''

''Just make me that promise.''

She tried to read his eyes. Couldn't. ''All right,'' she said tentatively. ''I'll wear your beetle…no matter what happens.''

Scott's phone beeped. He flicked it open. ''Yeah.''

''The plate's registered to a Jozsef Danko.''

''That was quick.''

''He's in the system. Landed immigrant, a Hungarian national. Investor, stockbroker, importer-exporter, all-round international businessman. Travels a lot. Works from an office out of his residence. Wonder why an international player like him has set himself up in a place like Haven.''

''He found something to keep him here. He's getting married morning after next.''

''What?''

''He's the fiancé.''

''What fiancé?''

''Dr. Van Rijn's.''

Silence. ''We didn't know there was a fiancé.'' There was a new bite in Rex Logan's voice.

Scott felt a wry smile tug at his mouth. The Bellona boss was suddenly taking this mission a little more seriously. "Well, there *is* one. And do me a favor. Have someone check into Danko's recent investment history."

"Why?"

"A hunch. I think these two may be working together." Scott flipped his phone shut as two figures emerged from the Kepplar lab building. Danko and Skye.

Jozsef Danko walked her over to her bike. Scott noticed his arm around her slim waist. Something in his stomach tightened.

Danko leaned down as if to kiss her but she moved abruptly, positioning her helmet on her head as if she hadn't noticed his intention. It gave Scott an unexplained jolt of satisfaction.

Danko's vehicle exited the Kepplar compound, turned left. Skye, on her Harley, turned right. Scott followed the bike.

The doctor rode home at a ridiculous speed. Scott turned down a side road and approached his house from the opposite direction as pale gray fingers of dawn reached over the distant sea.

He had just fed Honey, sunk down onto the sofa with a mug of coffee and fresh ice pack when he was jolted by a banging at his door.

He sat up, winced. His knee felt like a bloody water-filled balloon after the box-carrying episode last night. He dragged his hands through his hair, reached for his cane, pushed himself to his feet.

The banging got louder.

"All right, already!" He limped over to the door, threw it open.

And froze.

Dr. Skye Van Rijn stood there in a soft pale pink sweater, fresh as a freaking daisy after her night of sneaking around in the dark. She smiled up at him with those lightly glossed lush lips. Her eyes were as pale silver and lambent as the monochromatic dawn sky.

Something shifted in his belly. He pulled the door closer to his body, hiding the dossier, her personal details scattered all over his living room coffee table.

"Mornin'," he said slowly.

Her eyes flicked over him, taking in his rumpled clothes. "Doesn't look like *you* got much sleep."

He shrugged.

She waited.

He said nothing.

"Your truck wasn't here early this morning."

"I work odd hours. Needed to chase my muse this morning. Went for a drive."

She bit her bottom lip, studied him with those crystal-clear eyes. "I see."

He shifted slightly, held the door closer.

"I thought you might need that." She turned and pointed to a dolly she'd left alongside his truck still loaded with gear. "I had one in my garage." She angled her head, looked back up at him, a twinkle playing in the silver of her eyes. Amusement tugged at one side of her mouth. "I had a hunch you weren't going to ask anyone for help unpacking."

She'd floored him. Again. He scrambled for composure. "Thanks." He said no more. Waited.

"Well, I'm off to work, then. You coming tomorrow, around eight?"

"Tomorrow?"

"My wedding reception."

"Oh. Yes. Of course. I'll be there."

"Well, have a good day, then." Her top lip twitched slightly as if at some secret joke. "Happy writing."

Was there mockery in her tone? Challenge in her voice?

"Happy doing whatever it is scientists in Haven do," he answered.

She halted, as if unwilling to leave just yet. She turned back to face him. "I do research and development. I work mostly with insects and design biological control measures for the agriculture and horticulture industries."

"You mean, you create assassin bugs?"

She laughed that deep, smoky laugh. "That's cute, McIntyre. Yes, I find and develop little predators."

"I see." He allowed his eyes to walk slowly, obviously, over her utterly amazing body. "I'd never have pegged you for a bug lady."

She laughed again, a little less sure. "A bug lady? What's a 'bug lady' supposed to look like?"

Scott smiled, holding her eyes. "Not like you."

For a moment their gazes locked. A silent, primal current swelled, surged between them.

Then she broke the moment. "And there *I* was, wondering what a typical futurist looked like." She turned in a fluid movement and strode down the rutted driveway. Scott couldn't help but watch the way her firm buttocks moved under the denim fabric of her jeans, couldn't help the soft pulse of warmth in his groin.

"Oh." She stopped suddenly and swung round.

He braced.

"I meant to tell you, nice Web site."

Scott closed the door deliberately, quietly.

And blew out a stream of breath he hadn't realized he'd been holding. Thank God. Rex's boys must have placed some cyber-litter for his cover. It made sense that a woman like Skye would check him out on the Internet. *Especially* if she was hiding something.

He leaned heavily on his cane, looked down at the dog waiting patiently at his feet. "We'd better use the doctor's dolly to unpack that computer gear and get connected." He limped over to where his jacket hung across the back of the sofa. "That is, once we've made sure work is where she really is headed this morning." He picked up his keys, bounced them once in his hand. And he couldn't help grinning. The woman was a challenge he didn't mind right about now. She was up to something, sure as hell. And he'd find out what. He'd prove Agent Armstrong still had what it took. This little game was gonna buy him a ticket back out into the field.

The *real* field.

The jitters in her stomach were still there. And her neighbor wasn't helping matters. Skye pulled into the Kepplar parking lot, dismounted, yanked off her helmet. She should never have taken him that dolly. But seeing that big pile of boxes still in the back of the truck this morning had tugged something inside her. She'd wanted to reach out, to help. She'd also been curious. Because when she'd come back from the lab in the dark hours of dawn, his truck had *not* been there. And that only added to the strange cocktail of anxiety skittering through her system.

But taking him that dolly was definitely a mistake. Because seeing Scott McIntyre at the door, ruffled, sleepy, and all get-out sexy, in the same clothes he'd worn the night before, had stirred something else deep within her.

Something that manifested in a potent fusion of basic female desire and a maternal need to care. Both were parts of herself she'd locked away more than ten years ago.

In a few short hours Scott McIntyre was digging them out. Scratching at her veneer. And she knew what lay beneath was too raw and malignant to ever be exposed.

Besides, she couldn't afford to be distracted now. Her beetle project was close to completion.

And she was getting married in the morning.

Skye shoved her emotions aside, pushed open the lab door and shrugged into her white coat. She was early, but Charlotte, her assistant, had arrived even earlier and was already busy at her microscope.

''Hey, Charly, getting a head start?''

The blond woman looked up, smiled. Skye had allowed herself to get close to Charly, closer than she really was comfortable with. A part of her craved the kind of open, genuine and honest friendship so many women shared. The other part of her was afraid she'd let something slip. She wished, at times, she could let her guard drop, her hair loose and just be free to share. Staying vigilant required energy. Concentration. Sometimes she just got tired.

Very tired.

Maybe that's why she was marrying Jozsef. She could be with him, play the part of a regular woman, without opening up. He was like that. And marrying him would help seal her cover. Help her hide.

"What're you doing here, Skye? Working right up until the day of the wedding? You should be pampering yourself at the spa, hon. Not poking at beetles and grubs."

Skye made a face, motioned with her eyes to the ceiling. "Marshall wanted to meet with me this morning, discuss the project. Besides, I need to check on their progress."

"The critters are doing just fine. You've worked magic again, Doctor. There's nothing more for you to do but wait for the first shipments to mature."

"Let's hope they can stand the cooler temperatures."

"That little gene seems to have done the trick. The control group is still thriving."

The phone on the wall rang. "Yeah," said Skye, reaching for the receiver, "but the ultimate test will be in the field. Dr. Van Rijn," she said crisply into the receiver.

"Marshall, here. You ready to meet?"

"I'll be right up."

She hung up, rolled her eyes heavenward. "God has spoken."

Charly grinned. "Have fun…oh, I almost forgot, Jozsef was here earlier."

Skye stopped dead in her tracks. "Jozsef?"

Again?

''Why?''

''Looking for you.''

Skye frowned. ''He knew I was home.''

''He probably forgot. The guy's excited. Give the poor man a break. Tomorrow he gets a wife.''

Skye turned, started to push the lab door open but stopped midway, her mind racing. ''What time was he here?''

''Jozsef?''

''Yes. Jozsef. Who else?'' She heard the snip in her voice. So did Charly, from the look on her face.

''I don't know. He was already in the lab when I arrived. Security let him in like always.'' Charly stood. ''What's eating you?''

Skye shoved the door fully open. ''Nothing. Wedding nerves.'' But that little niggle was back, biting, probing deeper into the dark depths of her subconscious. She forced it down. She had work to do. An agricultural epidemic to halt. She strode down the corridor to the elevator.

The director of Kepplar Biological Control Systems was waiting.

Chapter 3

Marshall Kane stood at his office window, heavy brow crumpled down low over small dark eyes. Skye noticed the lines on the sides of his mouth were etched deeper than usual.

"Dr. Van Rijn, come in. Take a seat."

Skye sat, noting the formal use of her title.

Marshall remained standing, a hulking silhouette in front of the gray morning light. "Thanks for coming. I know this is a busy time for you what with the wedding and all."

Skye nodded. "What's up?"

He rubbed his jaw. "Last year this was a purely Canadian problem. Now it's a bloody international one. I got word last night that the whitefly epidemic has found its way into southern Washington greenhouses. And this morning, I'm told it's been detected in Northern Oregon. Inside *and* outside the greenhouses. It's like a goddamn army marching south. It's like nothing I've seen."

"It's nothing any of us has seen, Marshall."

"It'll be hitting the U.S. produce basket before we know

it. If California takes a hit, the whole damn nation will take a hit.'' Marshall moved from the window, seated himself behind his massive glass desk. ''Think a minute about the financial implications, Dr. Van Rijn. A Japanese-only embargo of California fruits and vegetables could cost more than 6,000 jobs and over $700 million in lost output. An international embargo of California fruits would cost the state maybe 35,000 jobs and more than $3.8 billion in revenues.''

Marshall leaned forward, elbows on his desk, hands spread flat out in front of him on the glass. ''But a total quarantine of California fruits, in which shipments and sales within the United States are embargoed, would result in hundreds of thousands of jobs lost and up to $20 billion in lost revenues.''

''You're forgetting the hit the Canadian greenhouse industry has already taken, sir. And with all due respect, we are not responsible for the spread of the whitefly to the U.S.''

''No. We are not.'' He raised his hand, leaving a steamy imprint on the glass. ''But just think about the implications for Kepplar if we are successful in halting the little bastards.'' Marshall had a greedy gleam in his small dark eyes. Beetle eyes, thought Skye. He was like a fat hungry bug himself. He picked up his silver pen, punctuated the air as he spoke. ''There's a lot riding on your project, Dr. Van Rijn. The U.S. Department of Agriculture is watching us. Our first beetle shipment goes out to Agriculture Canada for mass dispersal in two weeks, right?''

''Correct. We're on target.''

''Good, because the U.S.D.A. is waiting to see how effective we are. If they like what they see, there's another big contract in the works for Kepplar. A U.S. contract. We'll make headlines, Doctor.''

Skye nodded. She liked the money that came with success. It helped her buy freedom. But she shunned the publicity. That could cost her dearly. She shifted to the edge of her seat, leaned forward. "Marshall, I don't need to tell you I'm still unhappy with the early target date. And I know I don't need to warn you no project is without risk, including this one. Ideally, I'd like more field trials."

"Nonsense. The contained trials had excellent results. We haven't got time for more. The risks are minimal. I've read your report."

"Any time an alien species is released into an ecosystem there's a risk the new bugs could become pests themselves. Or worse, become a vector for another disease."

"Dr. Van Rijn, you are a pessimist. This bug was bred in our labs. It's clean. There's minimal risk of transmitting new disease."

"I'm no pessimist, Marshall. I'm a pragmatist. Yes, we bred the bug here. Yes, it's clean. But we started with a bug imported from Asia—"

"It went through the requisite quarantine process."

"There's always risk when meddling with nature."

Marshall rolled his silver pen tightly between his thumb and middle finger. "But you have a fair degree of confidence in this project?"

"I do."

"And the first colonies will be ready in two weeks?"

"Yes. But as I said, I'd like more—"

"Good. Because the last thing our southern neighbor needs right now is this army of whitefly marching south from Canada and heading straight for their produce basket. They're already scrambling with the damned cattle plague. Now this. It's straining diplomatic relations and they're looking for scapegoats."

"I've seen the papers. The Americans figure we should have moved earlier to control the epidemic in our own backyard. But these things know no borders."

"Well, neither will our predator bug so it better damn well work." Marshall slapped the pen onto his blotter. "If it does, Kepplar is made. If not, we go under.'' His beetle eyes bored into her. ''This is make or break, Doctor.''

''I read you, Marshall.'' Skye felt anger starting to bubble. She had no doubt it would be her who took the fall should the project fail. Not Marshall. Not Kepplar Biological Control Systems. Not Agriculture Canada. She'd be the one hung out to dry. Held out to the media as the pathetic scapegoat who failed to avert an economic crisis.

She stood. ''Anything else?''

''No. Thank you, and, um, congratulations, with the wedding stuff and all.''

It took all of Skye's control to walk quietly out of Marshall Kane's office, to close the door gently. But once shut, she stormed down the corridor. No elevator for her. She needed to work out her adrenaline on the stairs.

For Marshall, it always came down to the bottom line—cold hard cash. Personal acclaim. For her, it was the satisfaction of making something work. For finding a way to kill a parasite. To stop a blight from spreading.

And this whitefly had certainly become a blight on North America's agricultural map. Skye knew of about twelve hundred different species of whitefly, but this was not one of them. It was a new species. A voracious species that could withstand extreme temperatures. And as yet, no one knew where it had come from and no one had isolated a natural predator to counteract it. So she had set out to create one, adapting a tiny black Asian beetle and breeding it in her lab. Her work was so promising that last year the feds had started taking a keen interest. And early this spring, the Canadian department of agriculture had ordered a massive beetle shipment from Kepplar for large-scale release across the country.

Marshall was still basking, gloating, shareholders patting him on his back for *her* hard work. Now it looked as though he had set his sights on U.S. contracts. He had even bigger fish to fry. More shareholders to woo. Damn him.

Skye couldn't care less if Marshall took credit for her work. It helped keep her out of the media, below the radar. But now he was rushing this project. He was running risks she was uncomfortable with. The margin for error was too great.

And failure would make headlines, place her in the international spotlight. She couldn't have that. She couldn't let the last decade go to hell in a handbasket now.

She ran down the stairs, working off her fury with physical motion. It always boiled down to this. One way or another she was always running from her past, the threat of exposure. By God, she wished she could stop running.

By the time she got back to her lab she'd found a measure of outward control. She snapped on her gloves and got back to work, avoiding Charly's questioning eyes. By the time Skye looked at the clock again it was after five. She flipped the switch on her microscope. "That's it. I'm done and I'm outta here. I need my beauty sleep tonight."

Charly got up, gave her a kiss on the cheek. "There's my girl, clocking out at a decent hour for a change. I'll be at your place at the crack of dawn with champagne and croissants."

Skye laughed. "That's all I need, a loaded maid of honor with croissant crumbs down her cleavage. I'll be happier if you make sure those adult beetles get packed nicely into those bottles with vermiculite while I'm away."

"We're on it. No worries. That first shipment will be gone and released before you get back from your honeymoon."

"Yeah." She mumbled to herself as she slipped out of her lab coat. "That's *exactly* what worries me."

Scott washed and rinsed the blue cereal bowl for the third time. The kitchen sink was the best vantage point. From here he could watch the early morning wedding activity next door, and keep an eye on Honey in the yard.

He couldn't remember the last time he'd adopted such a domestic pose. It was in another life. When he was happy. When Leni cooked and he cleaned up and little Kaitlin chattered from her high chair.

Before the "accident."

The old pain began to pulse at his temple. He pressed two fingers hard against the throb and for the billionth time cursed Rex...himself...the whole bloody world.

The damned wedding next door was bashing on bolted doors to memories. The woman next door had woken the sleeping monster within him, and it thrashed like a caged beast.

Scott slammed the cereal bowl into the drying rack, picked up a glass, rubbed viciously with the dishcloth.

It was nine years ago his wife and baby girl had been blown up in their car. The Plague Doctor's men had done it. Scott's family had died because of his job.

Because of *him.*

Because he hadn't backed down from hunting one of the world's most wanted men. He'd helped Rex take down the Plague Doctor in White River just over three years ago. But the global significance of their victory had rung hollow in Scott's soul. It hadn't brought his family back. It had done nothing to quell the desire for vengeance that pumped through his veins, or to fill the bitter, aching void in his heart. Nothing to dull the sharp edge of guilt that sliced at him. And seeing Rex so happily reunited with Hannah, the mother of his son... It had burned a hole clean through him.

Rex had saved his family.

Scott hadn't.

The failure couldn't be more stark.

And he couldn't stand to have his face rubbed in the sharp gravel of that reality. So he'd taken one job after another out in the field, in the far wild corners of this earth. Anything to keep him away from a place that had once been home. Anything to keep him from looking in the mirror, facing himself.

Scott's jaw clenched as he watched a cab pull into the driveway next door. A trim blonde climbed out, paid her fare and trotted up the steps to Skye's front door. He watched the door open in welcome, Skye's dark head appear. This morning the doctor wore a soft yellow robe. Cinched at the waist. Bare feet. He saw her laugh, hair falling around her face. The happy bride-to-be.

Scott crushed the glass in the reflexive power that surged through his hands and swore at the sharp pain. That bride-to-be wasn't going anywhere but the chapel today, of that he was certain. He was wasting time washing dishes, watching her house, thinking of the past.

He glanced down, slightly bemused at the fresh dark blood welling from his hand. He flexed his fingers, testing his injury. The pain in his flesh was nothing compared to the twisted mess in his chest.

He chucked the dishcloth into the sink.

He'd go check out the town, buy some supplies. And when it got closer to wedding time, he'd go wait at the church, see who was arriving. He'd had enough of peeking through drapes. He wrapped a handkerchief roughly around his bleeding hand, grabbed his cane and keys, stepped out onto the porch and whistled for Honey.

To his surprise, the dog bounded instantly to his side. It gave him an unexpected stab of satisfaction. He ruffled the fur on her head. "Come, you silly pooch. We're going to get some supplies then we're gonna head on down to the church and watch a wedding."

Shopping done, Scott and Honey drove to the only chapel in town and pulled into a parking space across the street, under the boughs of an old cherry tree frothy with pale pink blossoms. Scott opened his newspaper, turned to the business pages, took a bite of dried sausage, and began to read. And wait.

A wet splotch of drool hit the far edge of the business section. Then another. He looked slowly up from the newsprint into pleading brown eyes and doggy breath.

"Jeez. Okay, you have the sausage then."

Honey inhaled the piece whole, tail thumping down on the front seat.

"You didn't even blink, Honey. Was it worth it?" Scott wedged the business section onto the dashboard, opened a bottle of water. "Okay, Honey, this is your car water." He held up the bowl they'd just bought at the Haven General Store. "And it goes in your new car bowl. Got it?" Scott sloshed water into the bowl, set it on the floor of the truck. "Careful now, don't knock it over."

The darn hound was hard work. He'd gotten used to caring only for his own needs. Hadn't had to think about making anyone else happy for a long, long time.

Not even a dog.

He watched as Honey lapped up the water. And suddenly he was seeing a black Lab. Merlin—the dog he'd owned when he was eleven. The dog he and his dad used to take on fishing trips. And that made him think of the times he had gone fly-fishing with Leni, before Kaitlin was born.

Scott blinked, rubbed his face. Guilt bit at him. He hadn't seen his dad or his mum since the funeral. He'd cut everyone out. Everything that made him think of Leni and Kaitlin, of the role he'd played in their deaths. He'd sliced out the very core of who he was.

Scott cleared his throat, retrieved the business section and glanced across at the chapel. He had to focus.

But there was still no action. He turned his attention back to the paper, scanned the headlines.

There was another article on the devastating U.S. beef crisis. And a smaller one about the whitefly epidemic sweeping south. His eyes widened. "Hey, look at this—Kepplar has been contracted to develop a predator bug for this whitefly thing. Our Dr. Van Rijn is in charge of the project.''

Honey burped. Scott looked up, frowned. ''You know, Honey, it's a conspiracy. Rex figures by giving you to me, you'll make me go fully nuts. Soon I'll be talking to myself. Then they can happily institutionalize me. Zero guilt for Bellona.''

Honey perked up, but not because of Scott's scintillating conversation. Her interest was captured by sudden activity outside the church. Cars started arriving. Small groups of people were entering the chapel.

Scott closed the paper, folded it, watched the action across the street. Two men in suits climbed out of a red convertible parked directly in front of the church. Scott studied them, but he couldn't see the groom.

Then a Harley, identical to Skye's, rumbled into one of the parking spaces behind the convertible. Another man in a suit. He carried his helmet under one arm, entered the church.

The activity seemed to die down a little. Scott glanced at his watch. It was almost six-thirty now. By his count there were at least forty wedding guests already waiting inside the church for the bridal party to arrive.

Then he saw it.

A sleek, white limousine cruised down the street, pulled to a stop in front of the chapel. It had no adornment. No silly paper flowers. No ribbons. For some reason, Scott thought this was appropriate and in keeping with the direct and no-nonsense nature of the woman he'd recently met.

A photographer snapped the scene as the driver's door opened. An elderly gentleman stepped out, dapper in a crisp gray suit. Scott recognized him from the general store. The man walked around the vehicle to open the passenger door. A slim blonde stepped out, the same one Scott had seen at Skye's house this morning. A long dress the dark blue of midnight skimmed the curves of her body. It was draped in a way that reminded Scott of ancient Greece. She was followed by a miniature version, maybe six years old, with wild fair curls. The little flower girl clung to a simple basket of petals.

Then came the bride.

Dr. Skye Van Rijn stepped out of the bridal vehicle and took the old man's arm.

And she clean stole Scott's breath.

She was an ancient Greek goddess. An Aphrodite. A high priestess in virginal white. She stood tall, elegant, strong, the simple yet exquisite fall of her dress in the style of old Athens. Her rich dark hair was loosely piled upon her head, held with a tiny silvery-white wreath of leaves. Loose, smoky tendrils curled down, teasing her shoulders. Her arms were bare. Behind her the small stone chapel was silhouetted against the evening sea and a spring sky turning pale violet as the faraway sun set. Scott could think only of white doves and peace offerings and the gods of Mount Olympus. The bug lady looked like she should be marrying Zeus, for Christ's sake. Not some guy called Jozsef. The woman was a dream. Brains. Beauty…

And a suspect.

Keep that in your confounded brain, Agent.

But he couldn't tear his eyes from Skye as the blond woman helped her with the back of her dress. He watched as she climbed the stairs, passed through the chapel doors.

He watched the double doors swing shut behind her. And he imagined her walking down the aisle. "Lucky bastard," he muttered, resting his head against the truck window.

Honey thumped her tail.

"Not you, you hairy mutt." Scott eased his aching leg into a more comfortable position and closed his eyes. He took himself back. Back to his own wedding all those years ago. In his mind he saw Leni walking down the aisle. Toward him. A spectral, shimmering vision of white. But he couldn't see her properly. He strained to make out her face, her features, to call out to her. But she was gone. In a searing flash of white flame. His eyes snapped open. His hand clenched on the door handle. Perspiration pricked along his brow.

He was dwelling again where he feared to tread. This mission was going to drive him clear over the edge. The sooner he unearthed the bug lady's secret, the better. Then he was outta here. And out of the damn country. He had to get himself back into the field. The international one. Not this domestic crap.

"You look beautiful, Skye. What made you go for the Greek theme?" Charly fidgeted with the train of Skye's dress for the umpteenth time.

Skye sighed, exasperated. "I've told you a hundred times. I just like it. Quit trying to distract me." They'd been waiting in the little antechamber way too long. The organist was going through her repertoire yet again.

Charly's little niece, Jennifer, sat patiently on a stiff wooden chair, swinging legs that didn't reach the ground, wilting faster than her basket of petals.

Mike Henderson, the owner of the Haven General Store, a long-time local and dear acquaintance of Skye's who'd been more than delighted when asked to give her away, opened the door a crack, peeked into the chapel. "He's still not here."

"What's keeping him?" Charly asked.

"Damned if I know," Skye snapped. She thought of Jozsef. Of his recent behavior. His hesitation when she asked questions. His unusual appearances at the lab. The increasing frequency of his trips abroad. His growing self-indulgence. Her own insecurities. Her incomprehensible, primal feelings for her new neighbor. And suddenly Skye couldn't take any more. Anxiety, the likes of which she hadn't felt in a decade, swooped down on her, clawed at her heart.

The urge to run swamped her.

She took a deep breath, stepped forward. With both hands, she threw open the antechamber doors, glared at the rows of pews filled with her close acquaintances. Not friends. Acquaintances. Colleagues. Dear people. But not family.

Not friends.

Everyone turned to stare at her.

She read shock, pity, on their faces. Skye took one tentative step into the chapel. The organist broke into the strains of the wedding march.

Here comes the bride.

Skye took another step, then another and another. The organ music sped up to match her increasing pace.

All dressed in white.

Skye lifted her dress up about her knees, stormed down the aisle, heart pounding, vaguely aware of Charly running after her.

A murmur rippled through the guests like storm wind through a forest of trees. Some jumped to their feet as Skye marched past them. The crazy organist madly beat at the wedding march tune, trying to match Skye's pace. She finally gave up in a discordant thrash of keys as Skye reached Jozsef's best man, who stood patiently near the altar.

Silence now hung thick, anticipatory, under the dark curved beams, the stained glass.

"Where is he?"

"Skye, I'm sorry, I don't know. We tried calling his home, his cell—"

"For chrissake, you're the best man, Peter. Isn't your job to see that the groom gets to the damn church on time?"

"I'm sorry, I—"

"Forget it. I made a mistake. Give me the keys." She held out her hand. It trembled violently.

"They're my bike keys."

She dropped her voice to a harsh whisper. "You gonna

humiliate me further or are you going to give me those keys?''

Peter fumbled in his pocket, extracted the keys. ''Skye, I'm pleading with you. Let's take the limo. You're in no state—''

''You expect me to leave in the *bridal vehicle?* You're nuts. Just give them to me.''

Peter reluctantly held them out. She snatched them.

Charly tried to take her arm. ''Skye, please—''

She shrugged her off, hoisted her dress up with one hand and turned to face the small crowd. ''That's it, folks. Party's over. Thanks for coming. Maybe next time.''

But there'd never be a next time, another wedding, not as long as she lived.

Skye stormed down the aisle, heading for the massive arched chapel doors, a chorus of shocked murmurs flowing in her wake.

The chapel doors flung open. Scott jerked to attention.

He realized with a shock that he'd dozed off.

He squinted, trying to make sense of the vision in front of him.

The Greek goddess stormed out of the church, down the stone stairs, dress hiked up about her knees. He rubbed his fist in his eyes. Maybe he was still asleep.

He watched in numb fascination as the bride lifted her dress, straddled the motorbike and kicked it viciously to life.

Tires screeched as she pulled out of the parking space and smoked down the road, hair, ribbons of white fabric fighting in the wind behind her.

''Oh, sweet Mother Mary.'' He snapped into action, fired the ignition.

''Buckle up, Honey. Looks like we got us a runaway bride.''

Chapter 4

Scott floored the gas, swerved out onto the coastal highway in hot pursuit of the bride bent low on the Harley. Honey skidded across the seat, bashed against the passenger door as the truck hugged a corner.

"Sorry, bud. Hang ten."

The road grew narrow, climbed, hugged cliffs that dropped sheer to the ocean. Skye veered to the right, following the curve of the twisting tar ribbon.

His hands tensed around the wheel.

She leaned low into the bend, naked knee almost skimming the tarmac. Scott winced, prayed her long dress wouldn't catch on anything. If she wiped out at this speed, she'd be grated to shreds. And that laurel garland on her wind-whipped tresses was nowhere near a helmet.

But by God, the woman could ride. She looked as though she'd been born with a machine between her legs. She was one with it. And it looked as if nothing else but speed mattered to her right now. Speed and escape.

From what?

He matched her pace.

She veered sharply off onto a dirt track.

He rammed on the brakes, skidding sideways onto the shoulder.

He could see a plume of dust as she followed a rough switchback down to the sea.

"Hold on to your teeth, Honey!" Scott gunned the gas, kicked up dirt, fishtailed back onto tar and swerved onto the rutted track.

It was pocked with small craters, rock. He squinted into the dust. He'd have to slow down if he was going to make it down alive. Damn, he'd lost sight of her.

By the time he reached the isolated cove at the base of the dirt track, the bike was propped on its stand alongside a gnarled arbutus tree.

Scott opened his truck door and stepped out into a cloud of settling dust. Honey followed, staying close at his feet. She seemed to sense this was no time for play. "Where is she, girl?" he whispered to the dog at his side. Then he saw her in the dim evening light, across the white sand of the cove near a rock at the water's edge.

She was frantically tugging at her clothes, shedding layers as though she was yanking and discarding parts of her life. She tore at the garland in her hair, tossed it to the sea. Wild wind-knotted curls fell loose below her shoulders.

Scott swallowed.

Her back was to him. She had nothing on now, save for a scrap of lace cut high away from the graceful curve of her buttocks. And she wore a white bra, the strap thin across the olive skin of her back.

"Sweet Mother Mary," he whispered to no one in particular. Then he saw the lacy wedding garter around the top of her lean thigh.

What happened, Doctor? What happened to your wedding?

He watched, immobile, as she rubbed her hands through

her hair, shook it free. Then she stepped into the water. Even from this distance, he could see the shiver that ran through her body. Then she took another step.

And another.

And she didn't stop until she was waist deep. Scott watched as she dived, sleek, into the steel-gray water. He held his breath as the calm ocean swallowed her, leaving nothing but ripples where she'd last stood.

Then he saw her head come up yards away. She struck out with a strong, smooth crawl. And she was going.

Going.

Straight out to sea…

Scott came to his senses in that instant.

The woman was suicidal.

She had no intention of coming back.

He started to run down to the water, buckled in pain. He turned back, hobbled to the truck, grabbed his cane. He might not be able to run with his crippled leg, but by God, he could swim. He knew once he hit the water he'd get to her in no time.

But when he looked again, he saw her dark head over the gentle swells. And he saw that she had turned and was swimming back to shore.

The relief was overwhelming. He stopped, held back, retreated to his earlier vantage point under cover of the orange-skinned arbutus, heart beating wildly.

He gave her the space she seemed to need. But still he watched. He could leave. But he told himself it was for her own safety.

He told himself this was his assignment.

These were his orders.

To watch the doctor.

But never, not once in the course of his undercover work, had he ever felt so much like a voyeur. He was looking into some very naked, private and anguished moment in this exquisitely beautiful woman's life. He felt both privileged and dirty. As foul and titillated as a damn Peeping Tom.

He wiped the back of his hand hard across his mouth, realized his heart was still hammering in his chest. He sucked down a deep breath of salted sea air, strained for calm. She was emerging from the water, a spectral vision in the dusk. He could see now how her bra was cut low against the firm swell of her breasts. Water shimmered down her flat belly. The garter was gone. Left to the sea. Her hair was slick as a seal's. She ran her hands up over her face and over her head. Her chin was held high and she was breathing the night air in deep. He could see her chest rise and fall from the exertion of her swim, her ride…whatever had made her flee.

She sat on the rock, upon the remains of her wedding gown, facing the ocean, her back to him.

She sat like that for a long time, until it got dark. There was pale light from a fat gibbous moon. It shimmered like silver sovereigns scattered in a path over the bay. Scott could see Skye's silhouette against the water. Honey made a plaintive little noise at his side. It was getting cold. Still the doctor sat, damp, on her rock, wearing nothing but her underwear.

Scott crouched next to Honey, spoke softly in her ear. "Wait for me in the truck, pooch. I think the lady out there needs some help." Either that or she was going to get pneumonia.

Scott let Honey back into the truck, grabbed his old brown leather jacket, made his way slowly over the sand of the cove. She didn't seem to hear him approach. She was shivering, holding her hands tight over her knees.

"Skye," he whispered behind her. A jolt cracked through her body at the sound of her name. But she didn't move otherwise.

"It's okay, Skye." He carefully positioned his jacket over her shoulders, lifting her wet hair away from her back.

A small noise escaped from somewhere deep in her throat at his touch. It was so primal, so basic a sound of need, it sliced clean through to his core.

"Skye, I'm going to take you home. You need to get dry. Warm."

She turned then to face him.

He sucked in his breath.

Her face was pale as porcelain in the moonlight. Her eyes dark and big. Mascara traced sooty trails of tears and salt-waterdown her cheeks.

She looked like a broken doll.

"Oh, Skye..." He didn't plan it, just did it. Gathered her into his arms. It was the right thing to do. The only thing. And he held her like that, under the moon, wondering what in hell he'd gotten himself into.

"Skye, I'd carry you if I could, but I can't, with this bloody leg. Lean on me and I'll lean on my crutch and we'll both get there. Together."

She did as he asked. In silence.

Honey's face was eager in the truck as she saw them approach. Scott helped Skye into the passenger seat. She climbed in, grasped on to Honey as if for warmth, for tactile comfort.

"Is that your bike?"

She shook her head.

"Okay. So we'll leave it here. Is there someone I can call to come and fetch it?"

She nodded.

"Fine. I'll call whoever it is when we get home."

Scott pulled into Skye's driveway, heater still cranked.

"No!"

It was the first time she'd spoken since the beach.

"Not here. Not my house...please."

He looked at her. She was still shivering under his leather jacket, arms still wrapped around Honey. "Where?"

"Anywhere but here." She looked away, out the dark window. "The wedding stuff. The caterer's stuff…it's all in there. In my house."

"I see. Is there anywhere else, anyone you want to stay with?"

She shook her head.

Scott backed slowly out of Skye's driveway, turned down his. He couldn't think of another plan. The woman was in shock. And if she didn't get some clothes on, her core temperature up soon, she'd be dealing with hypothermia, as well. If she wasn't already.

Scott ran a hot bath, then fished around in his closet for something for her to wear. It all looked foreign to him. Rex had provided him with a "writer's" wardrobe. Scott found a pair of sweatpants, a T-shirt and a fleece sweatshirt. She would swim in them, but they'd keep her warm.

While she bathed, he built a fire. He heated soup and poured a large brandy. This he pushed into her hands when she walked into his living room.

"Here. Want some soup?"

She looked deep into his eyes, as if seeing him for the first time. "Scott, thank you. I—I don't know what to say…"

"It's okay. Come, sit here by the fire." He pulled the sofa up close to the warmth of the flames. She sat. Her hair hung in damp, dark waves, her silver eyes were wide, startling against her impossibly thick dark lashes and pale skin.

She took a deep sip of the brandy, swallowed, coughed, eyes watering. Honey settled at her feet, curled into a ball. Scott watched the blush of color creep back under those high cheekbones, into that lush mouth.

He tore his focus from her lips, seated himself in the chair on the opposite end of the hearth. "What happened? Why'd you run?"

She didn't look at him, just stared into the flickering flames, shaking her head.

''Skye?'' he said softly.

Her eyes looked slowly up into his. He swallowed sharply. What he saw there was vulnerable, raw. She'd dropped the veil. She was all naked emotion as she looked at him. It threw him completely.

''He...he didn't show.'' Her voice was thick. ''Jozsef left me at the altar.'' Moisture pooled along the bottom rims of her eyes, making them glimmer like quicksilver in the firelight. It spilled over onto her cheeks into shimmering trails.

Something snagged in his chest. He took a shallow breath, came quickly over to her side, put his arms tentatively around her. ''It's okay, Skye. Take it easy. You don't have to talk now.'' He lifted a hand, hesitated, then let it gently stroke her dark hair. His breath caught in a ball. It was soft. So soft under his palm.

''I—I should've seen the signs...'' A soft sob jerked through her body. Tears spilled softly over her face.

''Shh.'' He pulled her close, enveloped her in his arms. Her scent surrounded him, a clean freshness mingled with the sophisticated scent of brandy and the faint saline of seawater. He held her a little tighter, stealing her fragrance with a flare of his nostrils.

She relaxed slightly, rested her dark head against his chest. It was a movement so innocent, so trusting. He couldn't seem to breathe normally. He allowed his cheek to brush softly against her head, to feel the sensation of her hair on his face.

And something swelled painfully inside him, brought a sharp prick of emotion to his eyes. He hadn't held a woman like this in a long time. Not since his wife.

His jaw tensed.

Sure he'd held women in that time—but not like this. Not like it mattered.

He'd fought hard against this very feeling, this aching sense of vulnerability. He'd gotten himself out of civilization. He'd left home, family, friends—anyone who reminded him. He'd blocked it all out by fighting. Fighting against bio crime, terrorists, the world, himself, his guilt…against finding himself in a moment like this.

His heart beat a wildly increasing pace against his ribs.

And now he was here.

He felt afraid—of himself, of feeling. But the instinct was overpowering. He gave in to it furtively. He closed his eyes, allowed the sensation of her body, warm against his, to sink into him, through him. He nestled his nose softly against the top of her head, drank in the silkiness of her thick dark hair, of the little breaths that shuddered intermittently through her body as she fell asleep in his arms. He held her, listening to the pop and crack of flames in the hearth, to the sounds of the night outside.

He didn't want to think of anything, only of how it felt to hold a woman in his arms. A woman who needed him.

Honey gave a little whimper. Scott's eyes flickered open. The dog watched him with her liquid brown pools.

God, he'd fallen asleep with her. The flames were faint glowing embers, the cool night air creeping in as their quavering watch against the cold dwindled.

Shocked, Scott edged out from under Skye's weight, careful not to wake her.

She murmured.

"Shh. Sleep," he whispered.

She stirred. "The…the bike, Peter Cunningham's bike—"

"Shh. Not to worry. I'll call him. Get some rest. I'll get you a blanket."

She nodded, snuggled deeper into the sofa.

Scott covered her with a blanket, stoked the fire, flicked the living room lights off, leaving only the shimmying copper flames and dancing shadows on the walls. He stared down at her. She looked like something unreal. So exotic, so striking…yet fragile, vulnerable.

How, wondered Scott, could anyone in their right mind ditch a woman like Skye Van Rijn? How could a man leave a woman like this at the altar?

Then with a rude jolt, he remembered his mission. He dragged his hand hard through his hair, reached for his cane, went to look for the phone book.

He called Peter Cunningham from the kitchen.

"Thank God she's all right."

"Yeah. Your bike's fine, too." Scott told him where he could pick it up.

"*Who* did you say you were?"

"Scott McIntyre, her neighbor…a…a friend."

"You weren't at the church?"

"I was late. Caught her bolting, so I followed her."

There was a moment of silence on the other end of the line. "The cops are out looking for her."

"She's okay, Peter. She's sleeping, but I can wake her if you want…or you're welcome to come 'round. Send the cops, whatever."

Peter hesitated. "I'll get Charly to come 'round. I think she'd prefer that."

"Fine. Any idea what happened to her fiancé?"

Peter cleared his throat. "After the church, when I got home, I checked my voice mail. There was a message from Jozsef. He's gone."

"What do you mean, gone?"

"Skipped town. Vamoose. Decamped—"

"I got it. Why'd he go?"

"Lord if I know. I thought I knew this guy…thought he loved her. I thought—"

"He say where he was going?"

"No. I went to his place to see if I could catch him, but he'd already cleaned out. I mean totally." He hesitated. "We're all terribly sorry for Skye. I just can't believe this. We were worried sick. Thank God she's all right."

"Yeah."

"I'll let the cops know you found her...and thank you."

"Sure." Scott hung up, then checked to make sure Skye was still sleeping. He closed the heavy kitchen door, activated the scrambler and called Rex.

The Bellona boss picked up on the first ring. "Hey, I was just about to call you. Bloody good hunch on Danko, old chap."

"Meaning?" Scott spoke quietly.

"He's linked with several offshore companies who've made a killing from this U.S. beef embargo. And get this, they're companies Bellona has suspected of having financial ties to the Anubis group."

Scott's fingers tightened around his sat phone. "You're kidding." Heat pulsed through his veins. Images seared through his mind. The Anubis cell in the Thar that he'd been hunting. His blown-out knee when he'd gotten too close. "These links," he said. "Anything proven?"

"Not yet. Working on it. But it appears we're not the only ones interested in Danko. The U.S. Securities and Exchange Commission is nosing around. These particular companies Danko is aligned with also happen to have a vested interest in seeing the North American produce market go down the tubes."

He whistled softly. "You think Danko and these companies are tied somehow to the Rift Valley Fever *and* this whitefly thing?"

"Hell knows, but I'm joining the dots and it's shaping up to be a pretty darned interesting picture, especially when you throw Dr. Van Rijn into the mix. If the whitefly get much further south, Danko and his bunch stand to make another killing from investment into the stock of U.S. competitors."

"Danko must have gotten wind of the S.E.C. probe."

"What do you mean?"

"He's split. Left town."

Silence. "What about the wedding?"

"He left our doctor high and dry at the altar."

"And where is she?"

Scott glanced at the kitchen door. Behind it the broken bride lay sleeping in front of the fire. He cleared his throat. "She's still here."

"You getting close?"

Too close.

"Close enough. She took it pretty bad, the whole wedding thing."

Scott could hear the hesitation on the other end of the line. It wasn't like him to get personal. Rex knew that. "Yes. Well, good…and keep me informed."

"No worries. I've got my eye on her." *I've just got to keep my hands to myself.*

Scott flipped the phone shut, shoved his feelings brusquely into a dark corner of his brain, ran through the cold facts. This possible Danko-Anubis tie threw everything into stark new light.

How was Skye connected?

He shoved open the kitchen door, limped slowly into the living room. Soft amber light glowed from the dying embers in the hearth. But the room was still a cocoon of warmth. Honey was having little doggy dreams at the foot of the sofa, her paws quivering in imaginary chase. Skye was curled like a child on the couch, dark hair soft across her face, blanket falling to the floor.

Scott lifted it to cover her properly. As he did, he caught the scent of his own soap. Then he caught something else.

A tattoo.

He stilled.

His baggy gray track pants had slipped low on her slim hips, exposing a tiny image on the smooth olive-toned skin near her hipbone. He bent closer.

His breath caught in his throat.

It was the stylized head of a jackal on the body of a man.

Black and angular. Egyptian style. Bared teeth. Long, pointed snout. Ears like horns.

Anubis!

Scott's heart thudded hard and quiet against his chest. This was too much to be coincidence.

Dr. Skye Van Rijn bore the ancient Egyptian symbol hijacked by La Sombra the mysterious mastermind behind the vast and growing shadowy Anubis organization. A group that had begun colluding with international organized crime.

But instead of a staff, the Anubis on her hip was depicted with a long, slim sword.

Scott gritted his teeth, yanked up the blanket, dropped it over her, spun around and grabbed the heavy iron fire poker.

He dropped to his haunches and jabbed the poker at the glowing logs. He thrust more fuel onto the rising flames, yanked the fire curtain shut, then slumped into the armchair beside the hearth.

He stared at the mysterious woman asleep on the sofa opposite him. Calm and innocent in repose. But who would she be when she woke?

One of La Sombra's soldiers?

He flopped his head against the back of the chair, closed his eyes. Little was known about La Sombra apart from the code name given him when he trained under Castro's regime on the Isle of Pines.

Authorities did not know his real name. Nor his nationality. And no one knew where The Shadow was based. It was believed he moved around, adopted different identities, and only those in his closest confidence knew it was he who called the shots. His cells, stationed around the world, were so tightly structured that none of the members knew who delivered the orders and who controlled whom.

La Sombra was the genius who'd stepped into the confusion created by the demise of the Soviet Union and the dissolution of the Warsaw Pact. He began to consolidate a loose net of international terrorist groups that were spawned during the 1960s and 1970s. Groups that were left retarded or disenfranchised and directionless with the collapse of the Soviet empire. No matter the religion or ideals of these various groups, La Sombra had reinstated a flow of funds and given them common cause, a reason to unite and co-operate in a massive international web...to fight what he called the American Evil, or Western Imperialism.

And he'd kicked into gear aggressive and sophisticated training programs.

La Sombra had theatrically dubbed this network Anubis, after the ancient Egyptian god who judged the souls of the dead and guided them to the underworld.

Scott pulled a face at the notion. It suited La Sombra to see himself as the ultimate judge. But there was little doubt in Scott's mind that the philosophies he espoused were purely Machiavellian. It was power that drove the man.

Not ideals.

Possession. Power. Ruthless control. That's what La Sombra got off on. He had no soul. And that's what made him infinitely dangerous.

Harsh images flashed into Scott's brain. He flexed his leg, flinched. Sometimes it still seemed like it had happened yesterday. But it was almost a year ago that he'd been tracking an Anubis cell in the northern reaches of the Thar desert. A cell comprised of rebels who had been flirting with a suspicious zoonosis, one that had already killed several children in Mumbai. But Scott had been ambushed. His guides, tipped off earlier, had fled with camels and supplies. There'd been nothing but him against the rebels.

But they hadn't killed him.

They'd fired a bullet into his knee, shattering the joint, turning cartilage into gelatinous mash. And they'd left him to die a slow, tortuous and certain death under the merciless Indian sun, hook-beaked vultures circling up high.

He'd had time to think as he'd begun to die, tongue thickening, cracking with thirst in his mouth.

Visions of mercurial delirium had shimmered in front of him with the waves of heat off the sand. He'd seen Leni and Kaitlin, spectral figures, wavering, calling to him. He'd tried to call out to them, but no sound had come from his parched throat. He'd reached out for them to take his hand.

The insects had come to his bloodied knee.

The vultures had come closer.

The desert would have eaten him alive if it hadn't been for that lone Jawan soldier.

That man had taken him back to his camp. The Jawans had nursed him under a white canvas tent, eased him back out of fever and delirium. He'd eventually been carted off to Mumbai. And there he'd spent many months under the care of Dr. Ranjit Singh.

He'd survived, and he'd vowed revenge. Not against the rebels—he wanted La Sombra himself. It was men like him who'd taken his family, his life.

Could this job be giving him another stab at his nemesis?

Scott opened his eyes, studied the sleeping form in front of him. *If* Skye was involved with the Anubis group, it was most likely she didn't know the man.

She stirred, moaned softly in her sleep, rolled over.

His heart stumbled.

And for a second he wanted to believe the image on her hip was sheer coincidence. He couldn't begin to mentally align the broken bride, the raw pain he'd seen in her silver eyes with the calculating cold of an Anubis terrorist.

He cursed.

He was deluding himself. She had the moves, the secrets in her eyes, the gritty edge. He'd recognized that the instant she'd stepped across that threshold and into his life.

And she had connections. But *if* she was in partnership with Danko, why had he left her? What was their game?

Scott took in a deep breath, filled his lungs to capacity, blew out slowly.

Questions. Lots of questions.

And he'd get answers.

He'd play her.

He closed his eyes, allowed the tired, rhythmic throb of his knee to pulse through him. He strained to find mental space.

Like the wild, hot emptiness and endless horizons of the desert.

He took his mind there. But instead of numb space, he saw only a bride, a broken Aphrodite shivering on her rock, overlooking a sea as mysterious and silver as her eyes…and a snarling jackal-headed beast.

He awoke with a start.

The fire was dead. Cold. Gray fingers of dawn searched through the blinds.

His eyes flashed to the sofa.

Nothing.

Just a pile of blanket.

Skye was gone.

He jerked to his feet, threw back the blanket.

Damn. She'd sneaked out under his trained nose while he'd dozed in front of her. She'd cut under his highly tuned radar. *Only a bloody expert operative could do that.*

Then he heard it.

The unmistakable deep-throated growl of a powerful motorcycle engine.

He hobbled quickly over to the window just in time to see Dr. Skye Van Rijn pull out of her garage astride her bike. Her hair hung in a thick dark braid down the center of her back. And, Scott noted, she was wearing his old leather jacket.

She roared into the street, spun her tires and disappeared in a cloud of dust and fumes.

A brown sedan, parked across the street, pulled out behind her.

Chapter 5

Skye *had* to find Jozsef.

She intended to demand an explanation. She wanted to hear it come from his own lips, to watch his eyes when he gave it to her. Because not only was she burning from rejection, she was flat-out scared. Things weren't adding up right. She needed to try to make sense of it all, to put her mind at ease.

She flicked her wrist, opened the throttle, fed speed and life into her engine. She bent low, headed for the coast road that would lead her to town, to Jozsef's penthouse.

In her mirror she caught sight of a dun-colored car behind her, matching her speed. An edge caught in her throat. Skye barely hesitated at the intersection, cutting sharply in front of a logging truck. The driver swerved, blew his horn at her stupidity. She fed her bike more gas, accelerated. The brown car tucked in behind the truck.

She went faster, put distance between the car, the truck and herself. She watched the tail of road grow like string spooling out behind her. Sea air pummeled her face.

And she smiled.

It was only with speed that she felt free. Truly free. If fleetingly. Skye knew she used speed as just another way to try to outrun her past, her fear. But right now she didn't care. She wanted distance. And fast. She wanted space. Lots of it. Between herself and a life that was becoming more convoluted by the hour.

She fed the engine more gas. It gobbled hungrily at the spurt of fuel. The wind pulled at her cheeks. She crouched lower, raced away from her house and the wedding cake that sat, uncut, on her dining room table. Away from the sight of the wilting hors d'oeuvres and the unopened bottles of champagne and the clean, empty glasses.

Away from the writer next door.

Not because he'd stepped out of the wilds of nowhere into her life. Not because he knew how to use a knife and his deep green eyes held even deeper secrets.

But because he'd cared.

He'd reached right through her fortress, touched her at the very core in a way no other man had.

And that scared the hell out of her.

Not once in her relationship with Jozsef had he even come close to touching her soul. Her real self had always stayed safe, hidden. Jozsef had never known the real woman who cowered, lonely, inside a prison of lies and secrets. A prison she'd built for herself.

To keep safe from Malik.

Skye shot even more power into the engine with another flip of her wrist. She swerved dangerously close to the edge of control. Still, the feeling of Scott McIntyre's strong, tanned arms around her, his male smell, chased her. And even as she fled, a part of her knew she couldn't run from this.

Even in her flight, something in her had reached back for the comfort of his leather jacket, taken it with her as protection against the elements. And deep, deep down, that told her she was in serious trouble.

She slowed briefly at a stop sign, glanced down the road, accelerated. She knew once she stopped, life would again catch up with her.

She cut onto Haven's main road. The dun sedan stayed with her. Her breath snared in her throat. She thought she'd lost it. Her heart thudded against her ribs. She slowed her bike. The car was still behind her when she came to a stop in front of Jozsef's waterfront apartment building.

She didn't turn to stare. Too obvious. She dismounted, removed her helmet, bent as if to fix her nonexistent makeup in the bike mirror. She could see the car reflected there. Two men in it. Too far away to make out any distinctive features. Her heart skittered, skipped up a few more paces.

But outwardly she remained calm, walked casually up to the entrance of the apartment complex.

Scott pulled into a parking space a block down from the brown sedan and watched Skye saunter up to the entrance of a swanky apartment building. She was still wearing his leather jacket.

He turned his attention to the car. Who in hell was on her tail? He punched Rex's number into his sat phone, watched Skye open the front door with a key.

"Rex, I need you to run another plate for me."

Skye used the key Jozsef had given her to enter the plush lobby. She took the stairs, then strode along the corridor to Jozsef's suite. She didn't knock. She wanted surprise on her side now. Skye slipped the key quietly into the lock, turned, edged the door open.

And stopped dead.

Jozsef had cleaned out.

There was nothing.

She felt her mouth drop, her hands begin to tremble. Every last little piece of furniture was gone. The photograph of her on the mantel was gone. The big TV screen he loved was gone. The sofa…gone.

Skye walked on numb legs into the kitchen. She yanked open the refrigerator. Empty. She put her hand inside. It wasn't even cool. The power had long been turned off. Dazed, she entered his office. Nothing. Computer, files, all gone.

She moved faster now, from room to room, frantically yanking open cupboards, drawers, bathroom cabinets, searching for a sign. Some damn little sign. Anything. Any little thing that might have shown he'd actually cared, been here, a part of her life.

Then she heard a noise. She froze. She'd left the front door open.

"Hello, anyone here?" It was a woman's voice.

Skye peeked cautiously out from the bathroom into the hall. Jozsef's landlady.

"Oh, Mrs. Tupper. Hi. I—I'm…" She didn't know what to say. How did you tell your fiancé's landlady you were looking for the man who'd ditched you at the altar?

Hettie Tupper shuffled forward. "Dr. Van Rijn, I'm glad you came. I tried to call you, but you weren't home." She fished in her pocket as she spoke, pulled out an envelope. Skye saw her name on the front, written in Jozsef's distinctive bold hand.

Hettie held it out. "He asked me to look out for you…to give you this."

Skye stared at the white envelope, not taking it.

"He said he had to leave in a hurry. He didn't have time to give this to you personally."

Skye reached out, snatched the envelope. "Thank you." Her throat felt tight.

"He was a good tenant."

"I'm sure he was."

But Hettie Tupper made no sign she was leaving.

"Thanks, Mrs. Tupper."

"Um, if it's all right with you—" she cleared her throat "—may I have the keys? Jozsef said you had the other set. I have a new tenant moving in next week—"

It dawned on Skye then. She'd lost her right to be here. It really was over. "Oh, I'm sorry." She felt for the keys in her pocket. But she wasn't ready to let them go yet. "Do you mind if I lock up and drop them off in the box downstairs. I, ah, lost an earring, somewhere on the living room carpet. I'd like to try to find it before I leave."

Hettie reached out, touched Skye's arm. "It's okay, dear. I understand. Take your time."

Skye waited for Hettie Tupper to close the door behind her. Then she ripped open the envelope. He'd typed it. On the computer. Impersonal.

My dear Skye,

I have no words to say what I need to say. But I can't go through with it. I think it best I leave immediately. A clean cut will be easier on both of us. Please do not try to locate me or contact me. I wish you all of the best in life.

Jozsef.

Bastard!

He could have told her before the wedding. She crumpled the note tight in her fist, hurled it at the floor, clutched her arms tight into her waist, trying to hold in the emotion bubbling, roiling up from her core.

She couldn't.

It surged in a confusing wave of hot angry pain up through her chest. She sunk into a heap to the middle of the living room floor. She clutched her knees and she let it all come out. Racking, aching sobs. She cried where no one could see her. Until she was dry. In the empty apartment of the man who'd abandoned her.

Then she sat, spent, staring out drapeless windows. She told herself she'd be fine. She'd get over it. She'd gotten over way worse. She hadn't really loved him. She never wanted to love anyone. She'd wanted Jozsef for other reasons. For a semblance of normality. For comfort. She had human needs, even though she'd been taught to shun them.

Her whole childhood had been about denial, sacrifice for the Anubis cause. She'd been born into an Anubis camp, sequestered in the children's compound, schooled daily in Anubis dogma. She'd been trained to fight, to think like a soldier. She'd been taught not to feel, to kill in cold blood. But she *did* feel.

She had emotions she'd never managed to subdue in spite of all her years of training. That's what had gotten her into trouble in the first place.

That's why she was here now.

Skye stood, dusted herself off mentally. If she'd learned anything in that camp, she'd learned how to survive. Alone. In a foreign environment. She walked over to the window, stared blindly out across the ocean, trying to make sense of it all.

Because it *didn't* make sense.

Why had Jozsef left so suddenly? Why had she felt so unsettled around him lately? Why were there men following her? Why were they waiting outside for her right now?

A talon of panic gripped her heart.

Malik had found her.

Her past was coming to get her. She must have slipped, gotten too complacent. The claw of fear squeezed. Skye's hand shot automatically to her belly. She hadn't done that in more than ten years. But the pain…the fight with Malik when he'd discovered her trying to leave the camp pregnant with his child. She closed her eyes tight. She could almost feel the black heat of his fury again, the brutal beating he'd given her. She'd managed to escape, bleeding. She'd lost her baby. The pain…it was suddenly all so real, so raw again.

She pressed her hand harder on her abdomen, felt once again that unfathomable, aching loss. She blinked back hot, bitter tears.

An overwhelming sense of claustrophobia swamped over her. She didn't understand how. Or why. But things were closing in on her. And she couldn't afford to take chances. She smudged the tears angrily from her face. It was time for her to get out of Haven. Go somewhere, lay low, figure out what was happening. Plan her next move.

She'd hide out at Henderson's cabin in the mountains. It was totally isolated. He'd said she could use it anytime. And the alpine snow would have receded by now. No one would be going near that place until the summer. Henderson only used it for fishing during the warm months.

She could make it up there with her bike.

Scott followed the dun car as it pulled out behind Skye's motorbike. He kept his distance well back, tailing the tail.

Skye headed into Haven, pulled up in front of the general store. She wasn't in the store long. She came out with a backpack, a bedroll and food supplies.

Scott turned to the dog beside him. "Well, Honey, looks like the doctor is leaving town."

The brown sedan followed Skye back home, parked under a tree down the street. Scott cut down a side road, approaching his house from the opposite direction. He noted her tail was still there.

This was getting real interesting.

Skye lifted the blind slightly with the back of her hand. It was getting dark, but from her living room window, she could still see the sedan with the two men. Damn. How was she to get out without them seeing her?

Anxiety swamped her. She took a deep breath.

Calm yourself. You'll screw up if you panic. Think this through.

She forced herself to relax.

She dropped the blind, lit a candle. She wanted to keep the interior dim. Then she double-checked her backpack, her supplies. She had enough to keep her going for a couple of weeks at Henderson's place. She rolled her sleeping bag tight, punched it down into its sack, secured it to the bottom of her new backpack.

She wanted to be gone before sunrise. It would take about six hours to reach the cabin. And if she could, she wanted to take one last look at her beetles before she left. She was still queasy about Marshall's desire to rush the project.

Once she checked on the control group, she'd leave a note for Charly, tell her she planned to be away for a couple of weeks. They'd understand. No one would look for her for a while. She was booked off for a two-week honeymoon anyway. Some honeymoon.

But first she had to figure out how to shake her tail. She had an uneasy sense whoever was in that car might try to make some kind of move on her tonight. Once it got dark.

She'd best be ready.

Skye sank down onto her sofa, trying to think, to come up with a plan. But all she could see was the white cake on the table across the dimly lit room. Three layers with two little figures positioned on top.

One a bride.

The other a groom.

Mocking her from the shadows.

Scott's sat phone rang the minute he opened his front door. He let Honey in, closed it behind him.

It was Rex.

"Scooter ran that plate for you."

"And?"

"You ready for this?"

"Surprise me."

"The vehicle belongs to the feds."

He gave a derisive snort. "Shoulda made them for cops. What do our Royal Canadian Mounted Police want with the doctor?"

"I've set up a meeting with our RCMP contact for tomorrow afternoon. I'll know more then. I suspect it's got something to do with Danko. We might have to let them know we're working an angle on this case, as well."

"Great." A possible turf war. He needed that like a hole in the head. Scott flipped the phone shut and stared out the window at the car. So the doctor was in trouble with the feds. It was time to pay her another visit. His brain ticked over. He could actually use this to his advantage. A "good cop, bad cop" kind of routine.

A smile tugged at the corners of his mouth. Yeah. He'd play this one for what it was worth.

Scott and Honey climbed the two stairs to Skye's porch. It was fully dark out now but no lights blazed from Skye's home. Just a faint flickering glow. Candle, he assumed.

He lifted his hand to knock, realized the door was slightly ajar. He edged it open, motioning Honey to be quiet.

He peered into the dim light, catching sight of her in the living room. He bit back a chuckle.

Dr. Van Rijn was slouched on a sofa, her long legs propped up on a coffee table, one ankle crossed over the other. Her feet were still shod in heavy black biker boots. In her right hand she held a wrist-braced slingshot. Yellow light quivered from a candle on the mantel over the fireplace.

Fascinated, Scott watched as she took a metal bead the size of a large marble from a leather pouch resting at her side. She fitted it against the powerband of the slingshot, drew it slowly, steadily, back with her left hand.

She aimed, right arm extended fully. And released.

Before he could blink, the silvery-white wedding balloons hanging in the far corner of the living room exploded into tattered rags.

Scott's hand shot down to muzzle Honey.

Skye reached for another bead. Scott watched, intrigued as she repeated the process. But this time she aligned her weapon directly with the wedding cake on the table in the dining room.

He held his breath.

She pulled.

Released.

The silver bullet whizzed, slamming the tiny groom dead in the heart. It shattered, flew back with a crack against the wall.

Scott swallowed.

The woman was an astounding marksman. And what she held in her hand was a deadly serious weapon. Stupefied, he stood motionless as she positioned another bead, stretched the yellow surgical tubing back taut.

She raised it slowly, aimed at the heart of the little white bride standing lonely on the cake.

But Honey could stay quiet no longer. She whimpered.

Skye spun.

Before Scott could breathe, the lethal bead was trained on him, aimed straight at the center of his forehead.

He froze.

Skye didn't move. Her face was totally expressionless. That above all spoke volumes. He'd seen that kind of control before. He had little doubt she could kill.

He cleared his throat. "You could hurt someone with that, Doctor."

Still she didn't move. "That's the idea, *Mr. Futurist.*" Her voice was steady, smoky.

"Who do you plan to hurt?"

"I can think of a couple of people off the top of my head."

"I'm one of them?"

"Should you be?"

"Perhaps."

She slowly relaxed tension on the slingshot, lowered her weapon, her expression still deathly serious. "What, exactly, is that supposed to mean, Mr. McIntyre?"

"Damned if I know. It sounded right. You scared the spit out of me. I don't think straight when I'm scared," he lied.

She laughed, mirthlessly. "Sorry. Come in. I thought you were someone else."

"Oh, really. Who?"

Her eyes flicked to the window and back. "No one. Doesn't matter. Come in."

Scott felt as if he'd been invited into a lair. Wary, he stepped over the bags at the door. He nodded toward them. "You planning on going somewhere?"

She stood as he entered the living room, stared him directly in the eye, her back straight as a rod. "What's it to you?"

He raised both hands. "Hey, I'm sorry if I've come at a bad time. I can come back later."

She studied him carefully. Her eyes cut briefly back to the window. Then she spoke. "No. My apologies. I've had a bad day. I could do with some company. Take a seat. Help yourself to food." She gestured to the table. "Sorry the champagne's warm."

By the way her eyes kept flicking to the window, Scott figured she'd noticed the tail parked across the street.

And he figured she was worried. She didn't want to socialize with him, she wanted him around for protection from whomever she thought was following her.

And that suited him. Because he wanted information.

He moved over to the table laden with wilted wedding

hors d'oeuvres. A sad sight. He looked up from the table, at the jilted bride. Something snagged in his heart.

He quickly glossed it over. Resting his cane against the table, he reached for two glasses, pulled a bottle of champagne from the silver tub of melted ice.

Without speaking, he limped over to the coffee table, set the two glasses down, popped the cork with a muffled burst and poured frothing warm liquid into the glasses.

Skye watched in silence.

He straightened, held a glass out to her. She took it, fingers softly brushing his as she did, her touch leaving a wake of sensitized nerves.

Scott swallowed his reaction, raised his glass. "I propose a toast."

Skye's mouth pulled sideways in a grimace. "Yeah." She raised her glass. "To being dumped at the altar." She pressed the glass to her lips, took a slow sip, eyes locked steady with his over the rim.

He noticed her lips were full as they rested on the champagne glass rim, moist with the drink. Scott felt sudden thirst, took a deep sip from his own drink.

Still her gaze didn't shift. Silence hung heavy, thick.

He felt a prickle of unease, tore his eyes from her stare. *Focus, dammit.*

He set his glass carefully down on the coffee table.

"Why'd you come over tonight, McIntyre?"

"I...wanted to see if you were doing okay. You were in a bad way last night." He attempted a smile. "And I want my jacket back."

Confusion pulled at her brow. She glanced at the leather jacket slung over the backpack by the front door. "I'm sorry. I was going to bring it back. Thank you, once again, for taking care of me last night. It's not my style to crumble like that."

"That, I can believe." But despite her efforts at outward control, Scott could see the woman was jumpy. Maybe even flat-out scared. He decided to put his theory to test. "Well, you seem to be doing fine. I'll just grab my jacket and be going now—"

"Wait." She grabbed his arm, eyes wide. "Have some food. Stay. Someone's got to eat that stuff. Maybe Honey wants some. There's plenty more champagne."

Scott could feel the urgency in her fingers. He was right. She was petrified. He pulled a face. "Got any ice?"

"Plenty." She made for the fridge, returned with a bucket of ice and set it on the coffee table. She moved quickly over to the hors d'oeuvres, started loading the lifeless snacks onto two plates. She brought them over to the coffee table, set them next to the ice bucket.

She hesitated. "Did you see those guys outside, in the brown car?"

So she *had* seen them. "Nope, why?"

"They seem to be waiting for something. I thought maybe you might know them."

She was fishing. "Never noticed them." He popped a cracker into his mouth. "More champagne?"

She held out her glass. He poured.

"Thanks." She sat on the sofa, sipped, shivered slightly as she swallowed. She looked so drained. Cold.

"Can I light your fire?"

Her eyes snapped wide, startled by his gesture. "I...yes, thank you...I'd love some warmth."

He eased himself down onto his haunches and started to build the fire in her hearth.

She picked at the food on her plate. But he could feel her eyes on his back, watching him as he coaxed tiny flames to life. Tongues of fire grew, licked, crackled around the kindling.

With the fire fully engaged, warmth emanated quickly from the hearth. Honey moved near, flopping down beside him. Skye leaned a little closer. "Come join me on the sofa, McIntyre." Her words were soft, her voice rich. It had an almost opalescent quality that rolled smooth, rounded and low through his gut.

He looked up into her face. Her lids were low, sultry over the silver of her eyes. She reminded him of an animal who prowled, lean and hungry in the shadows. One not to be trusted.

What game was she playing now?

Scott tried to push himself to his feet, winced as fresh pain sliced through his knee. He dropped back down to the floor, choked a curse.

The dangerous smoke wiped instantly from her eyes. Instead, concern etched into her features. "You okay?"

"Nothing I can't live with." He breathed shallow, waited for the tide of pain to ebb.

She reached out, tentatively touched his leg. "What's the prognosis for your knee?"

He shrugged. "I had a joint replacement. If I'm a good boy and rest enough, I should be fine. If not, I'm in trouble." He blew air out slowly through pursed lips. "It'll always be a thorn in my side, though. Just when I thought I was on the mend it's all swelled up like a bloody balloon again."

"Let me see." She dropped down beside him onto the hearth.

"See what?"

"Your knee. Let me see it."

"Why?"

"Maybe I can help." She reached down, started to roll up the leg of his jeans. Her braid fell over her shoulder. He could smell her shampoo. He jerked back, shocked at the hot reaction in his gut.

Her hand halted in surprise.

Her eyes slid slowly up to his, held. "Take it easy, McIntyre. I don't bite."

Yes, you do.

She turned her attention back to rolling up the cuff of

his jeans. Scott sucked air in sharply, braced against the sweet, wicked electrical pulses that shot up the inside of his thigh as he felt her hands, cool and soft, against his ankle.

Her eyes shot back up to his. "That hurt?"

He swallowed, met her gaze. "Not exactly."

She touched the inside of his calf.

He gasped. Nerves, already hot and sensitized from pain, zinged raw under the coolness of her touch. He gritted his teeth, flinched at the kaleidoscope of sensation.

Her eyes held his. The air between them grew thick. Surged. Her lips parted slightly. She moved her hand slowly up the inside of his calf, splayed her fingers over muscle, began to caress with slow, rhythmic undulating movement.

"Tell me what you're feeling, Scott." A carnal smoke swirled through the silver of her eyes. It snaked husky and deep through her voice. His own vision blurred.

"Tell me if this hurts." She pressed harder.

His stomach swooped in reaction. He swallowed, couldn't seem to find his voice.

Her hand moved higher up the inside of his leg toward his knee.

"How does this feel, McIntyre? Tell me." Her voice purled through him. "I want to know what you're feeling."

"Scott, call me Scott." He split the hot tension, grabbed for a sense of normalcy. "Do you know what you're doing here? You a medical doctor, too?" She knew damn well what she was doing to him. He was sure of it.

"I know some stuff." Her voice remained low, undeterred.

Her eyes dropped to her hands as she worked the denim carefully up, exposed his knee. She sucked her breath in sharply at the sight of it. Her eyes flashed up to his. "That looks painful."

"You see, looks like a balloon."

"God, that's one angry scar." She traced the puckered,

puce line of flesh softly with her fingers, following it around to the tender underside of his joint.

Scott jerked back. Shocked. Not from pain but from the burning thrill of her cool hand on his hot, sensitive skin. It cracked a jolt clean through to his groin.

"That hurt?"

"You don't want to know how it felt." He heard the thick, heavy edge in his own voice.

A faint, sultry smile tugged at the corners of her mouth. Her lids drooped over her eyes, her voice went even lower, like smooth, hot mist over a desert well.

He swallowed, his throat dry.

She stroked the inside of his feverish knee with languid, rhythmic movement. He felt himself grow thick. "Does that feel good?"

His loins answered, pulsed, hot and heavy between his thighs, aching for the languorous touch of her hands. By God, she was seducing him. And he was utterly powerless.

She moved closer. He could feel the sweet warmth of her champagne-kissed breath. "Stretch that leg out in front of you."

He obeyed, his brain ticking over, too slowly, trying to find a way to take back charge.

Skye took an ice cube from the bucket on the coffee table. She bent her dark head over his chest, touched the cube lightly to his skin.

He gasped.

She let the cube linger as his skin adjusted to the sensation. Melting water dripped around to the inside of his thigh, ran down toward his groin. She slid the cube over his knee, lightly.

He couldn't take any more, had to snap the sexual tension that simmered between them before he lost every last inch of his control. "Skye—"

Her eyes darted up. "Am I hurting you?"

"No...it's just—" He knew what she was doing. This

was her way of making him stay the night, of buying a form of protection against whoever waited for her outside. And by God, his body was willing to sell even if his brain screamed stop.

The light from the fire danced silver in her low-lidded eyes. Her lips, so lush, so full, were open. And it was obvious, despite her ploy, that she was as turned on as he was.

The knowledge was intoxicating. He felt himself lean in, drawn to that mouth of sin.

She moved even closer, her lips almost touching his. He could feel her breath, warm against his mouth. Fire spurted to his loins, seeped molten through his belly. Her lips touched gently to his.

And he drowned in that instant, engulfed by a blinding, raging wave of scarlet pleasure.

What was left of the tiny ice cube fell with a chink to the floor. She moved one leg over him, straddled him, her braid spilled down over her shoulder onto his, and she took his bottom lip firmly between her teeth, a throaty, almost imperceptible growl emanating from somewhere deep in her throat.

The fear she would bite down on his lip, draw blood only fuelled his desire. She bit a little harder. He moaned. The swollen weight between his legs ached with hot, delicious pain. Screamed for release.

She eased her pelvis against his.

His control snapped.

Chapter 6

Scott grabbed the back of her head firmly in his hand, yanked her mouth down hard onto his. Her lips splayed open to him under the sudden pressure. Her legs split wider as she was pulled down over his groin.

A groan rose from deep in his belly. He thrust his tongue into her mouth, deep, roughly exploring. She was hot. Sweet. Slightly fruity with the taste of warm champagne. His tongue slipped over hers. Danced. Mated. And he felt as though his loins would explode without the same hot, slick sweetness.

Her pelvis rocked slowly against his, forcing rhythmic pressure onto the painful swollenness of his need. His vision went black. Red.

And he felt her hand, sliding up the inside of his thigh. Then he felt her fingers, deft, undoing his buttons, working to lower his zipper.

He couldn't breathe.

He felt himself swell out of the confines of his jeans into her soft hand.

He snapped suddenly to his senses, jerked back, pushed her away. ''Skye...no!''

She jolted back. Shocked, lips swollen and hot-pink. Confusion clouded eyes dusky with silver and lust.

He reached for his zipper, fumbled to contain his blatantly obvious male need.

She watched his hand. Said nothing. But the question was raw in the set of her features.

He reached up, touched the side of her face. ''I'm sorry, Skye. I can't—''

She jerked out from under his touch, looked away, hiding naked hurt. And something else. He could see it in the faint blush that crept up her neck into her cheeks.

Embarrassment.

Scott cursed himself. He'd just rejected a woman who'd been ditched at the altar. He couldn't begin to imagine how she was feeling. But that was precisely why he couldn't do this. As much as he wanted, needed, to. As much as he needed to strip her naked, expose her deepest, innermost sweet secrets. As much as it might help him get to know her better. He couldn't take advantage of her like this.

''Skye, talk to me, look at me.''

She did, turning her head slowly back to face him. When she did, she was an absolute study in self-control. Those silver eyes didn't flinch. Instead they lanced into his. But she said nothing. She waited for him to speak.

''Skye, you're one of the sexiest, most damn desirable women I've ever laid eyes on. But I just can't do this to you. You're bouncing like a bungee on the rebound, for heaven's sake. I don't think it's me you want.''

It's protection from whatever waits outside that you want.

Anger flashed in her eyes. ''You think I need some kind of self-affirmation? You think I need to prove I'm still a desirable woman? Is that it?''

''No.'' He reached out to touch her. ''I'll stay the night

Skye, if that's what you want, if you want someone just to be here.''

She lurched to her feet. ''Get out.''

''Skye—''

''I said get out, McIntyre. You and that wretched dog. Leave me alone.''

He got to his feet, hobbled over to get his cane. She watched, unmoving.

''I'm next door if you need me, Skye.'' And he meant it.

''You think I'm *that* pathetic? I don't need your *pity.*'' She spat the words at him.

''Fine. Honey!'' The dog raised herself grudgingly at the command in his tone, left the warmth of the fire.

''We're outta here.'' He limped to the door, shoved it open.

''Here.'' She thrust his jacket at his chest. ''Take this with you. I don't need you. I don't need your damn jacket.''

He took it, stepped out into the dark with his dog.

Skye slammed the door behind him. Only then did she realize she was shaking. The room was suddenly cavernously empty. And dark. Save for the quavering apricot glow of the flames he'd built in her hearth. And her belly.

She slumped against the door.

She'd gambled. And lost. She'd tried to seduce him to get him to stay the night. And she'd lost. Control.

Dignity.

She'd thought she could handle it. But nothing could have prepared her for the explosive energy she'd unearthed in him. It had blown her apart like a wooden shed in a tornado. Consumed her. Blinded her.

And then he'd rejected her. Because he was too much a gentleman. Confusion warred in her brain. She'd sent him away in a surge of fury fuelled by humiliation, but all she really wanted right now was for him to hold her again. Like he had last night. And tell her it would all be all right.

No one had *ever* held her like that.

She touched her fingers to her mouth, still hot and swollen from his aggressive kiss. That would teach her to play Russian roulette with a man like McIntyre, with her own libido. That would teach her to open doors she didn't know how to shut.

She pushed away from the door, moved quickly to the window and lifted the blind with the backs of her fingers. She watched the large dark shadow of Scott McIntyre and his dog make its way across her lawn.

The moonlight was pale gold on Honey's fur. The man leaned heavily on his cane as he moved with a wide, angry gait. In spite of his injury, he was sheer male. Rough. Hard. Even the emerald glint in his eyes held the coldness of stone in unguarded moments. She'd glimpsed a calculating man in those eyes. She was profoundly unsure about him.

But by God, he made her feel as no other man had.

He had the dark sexual power of Malik. He had the same hard edge. But Malik's eyes were black like a demon's heart. Not deep green like Scott McIntyre's. She'd glimpsed hints of hidden laughter in Scott McIntyre's eyes. Maybe even pain that went beyond his knee, beyond the physical.

It made him strangely vulnerable, accessible.

Malik's raw energy was about power, control. It was destructive. Negative. It had near killed her.

Might yet kill her.

She tore her attention from Scott's dark form to scan the road for the brown car. It was still there. In the shadow.

Skye dropped the blind, spun on her heels. She had to get out. *Now.* She checked her bags. She was ready. She would wheel her bike quietly out the back of the garage and over the lawn at the rear of her house. She'd try to get it through the thick brush at the back of her property and onto the adjacent farm field. From there she could make her getaway.

But she had one more task—she had to e-mail Jalil. Her only friend in this world. He was the only one who knew the truth about her. He was the only one she kept in contact with. Because she owed him her life. He'd risked his own to get her out.

Skye pulled out the chair, sat in front of her computer, clicked the screen to life. She was careful what she said in her e-mails to Jalil, for both their sakes. It was always behind a veil that they spoke. They never mentioned the escape. The deception.

She tapped the keys. She told Jalil her wedding was off, that the project she was working on was still a go and that she wouldn't be writing for a while. She was going away, into the mountains, because she needed a break from things. She needed to reassess her life.

Skye moved the mouse to click Send.

But as an afterthought she highlighted the part about going into the mountains, deleted it, then clicked Send.

It would be early morning in Amsterdam. Jalil would get her message soon. And she'd be long gone when he did.

From the bridge of the *Esmeralda,* he could make out the distant, misty green ridges of the Queen Charlottes. He adjusted the telescope. They were almost in position, in international waters off the Pacific Northwest Coast of North America. From the "cargo" ship he often used as a base, he would orchestrate the final stages of Operation Vector.

"A message came through." His assistant's voice sliced into his thoughts. "For Jalil."

He jerked upright. It was always with the e-mails for Jalil that he got his most valuable information. They had stopped coming for a while. But that was all right. Jozsef had been in place. Then he'd received word Canadian authorities were onto his man and he'd had to extract him. Right before the wedding. Still, he was unconcerned the project would be compromised. Operation Vector was far enough along to hold the pieces together. And Jozsef had ensured the tracking device was in place. Two more weeks and all would be accomplished.

He made his way to the cabin that served as his office, seated himself at one of the computer terminals, reached for the mouse, hesitated.

He looked up at the massive oil painting that dominated the one wall of the plush cabin. It was a study of a woman. A woman so regal, so beautiful, she looked like a Greek goddess.

She'd had so much potential. He'd had her painted wearing white, holding her symbol. The sword. At her side was a massive jackal-headed beast in a white Egyptian loincloth.

Anubis. *His* symbol.

The ears of the jackal were like the gold horns of a devil. The black canine head bared jagged teeth to a world that lay at their feet. Theirs for the taking.

Until she'd crossed him.

He turned abruptly to his computer, clicked open Skye's message.

Scott lay naked on his bed, sheets twisted around him. The glowing red symbols on his digital clock taunted. He'd watched them flip from 2:00 a.m. to 3:00 a.m. to 4:00 a.m.

He threw off his sheets, kicked his feet over the side of his bed. He'd screwed up. He should've taken her lead. She'd opened the door, shown him a way in, and he'd freaking shied away.

Because he couldn't take advantage of her?

He snorted. Yeah, right.

He rubbed the heels of his hands hard into the grit of his eyes. He really *had* lost it. He should have used her. Impartially.

But that was the problem. He couldn't find that impartiality within himself. As much as he tried to deny it, he felt something for the woman.

It was lust. Pure and simple.

But he was lying.

Something had hooked into him when he'd held her in his arms on the night of her failed wedding.

That simple act of holding a soft woman in his arms had cracked open something deep within him. Something that went beyond the haunting pewter of her untamed eyes, beyond the way her seductive curves set every primal nerve singing, every red-blooded male cell in his body screaming with need to bed her hard and fast and long.

He rubbed the back of his hand over his mouth. *Get a grip, Agent.* The one rule in this kind of game was that you held the reins of control at all times, that you called the shots, each and every goddamn one of them. Slip and you gave your opponent power.

He stood, limped over to his window. Dawn was barely a hint on the horizon as the sun crept in from far-off lands.

He watched as the first pale rays infused the dark sky with soft blue-gray. He had a job to do. And he better make good of it if he ever wanted to get back out there, over that horizon, into those foreign lands. And that meant keeping any feelings for the doctor in check.

That also meant using any opportunity she handed him.

Dr. Skye Van Rijn was a suspected bio-terrorist. The feds were after her. She was hiding something.

And he was going to get it from her. One way or another.

He was going to show Rex, Bellona, the whole bloody world, that he still had it in him. La Sombra's men had blown out his knee, not his balls.

He clenched his jaw with fresh determination, reached for a shirt and jeans. The first step was to find out exactly why the feds were tailing her.

Once dressed, Scott limped to the kitchen, clicked on the

kettle, poured biscuits into Honey's bowl and punched in Rex's number. He stared out at his neighbor's house as he waited for Rex to pick up.

A sudden movement in the doctor's yard caught his eye. The men from the brown sedan were marching up her driveway.

Uh-oh. Looked as if he was going to find out firsthand what they were after. He flipped his phone shut as the men climbed the stairs to Skye's door. They hadn't even waited until daybreak. They were going for the shock factor.

Scott grabbed his jacket. As his hand touched the leather, he heard a soft rapping at his kitchen door.

Honey yipped.

Scott unlocked the door, started to open it…but before he could register what was happening, Skye barreled through the crack, into his kitchen, knocking him off balance. She dumped her pack on his floor, swiveled, quickly locked the door behind her. Her movements were sharp, controlled. No emotion showed in the set of her features. Only her eyes. They were wide and pale with fear.

She turned to him. "You've got to help me."

"Skye." He took her shoulders in his hands. "Slow down. What's the matter?" He knew well enough. Undercover RCMP were banging on her door and she was running for her life. He had her now. *Exactly* where he wanted her.

Her eyes darted to the window, then back to him. "I've got to get out of here, out of Haven. Can you help me? With your truck?"

"Hey, take it easy." He pulled a chair out from the kitchen table. "Sit. Talk to me."

"Could…could you pull those blinds?"

Scott reached for the cord. "Sure." He dropped the blinds. "Better?"

She nodded.

He took a seat opposite her. Honey milled at their feet, wiggling her butt, sensing adventure.

"Now tell me what's going on."

She bit down on her lower lip, studied him. He could see her fighting mentally, deciding what she should dish out to him.

"Those guys in that car, they're following me."

"You sure?"

"*Dead* sure."

"Why? Who are they?"

"I—I don't know."

She was lying. She *had* to know it was the cops. "Why're they after you?"

"I told you, I don't know."

Scott made a face.

"Honest to God, I don't know. You've got to believe me."

"You must have some idea. Otherwise why are you running like this? Maybe they just want to talk to you."

"Get real. They've been outside my house since yesterday. They followed me to Jozsef's apartment and back." The brightness of urgency burned in her eyes. "I need to get out of town. I need a ride. If you can't help me, I'll find another way."

Scott studied her. Her outward control was slipping in front of his eyes. She was a bundle of nerves. He definitely had the upper edge now. He called her bluff. "I can't help you. You're not being straight with me." He got up. "Want some coffee before you go?"

She jerked off her chair, grabbed his arm. "Scott, please. Just a ride out of town. I'll pay you."

Scott carefully set the coffee mug back down on the counter and turned to look into her eyes. "You're serious, aren't you?"

She nodded.

Yes. He had her exactly where he needed her. "Where do you need to go?"

"I need to go to the lab, to Kepplar Biological Control Systems. I need you to wait outside for me while I check on something. Then I need you to drive me north, to some place where I can rent a bike or a truck. I can go the rest of the way on my own."

"Where are you going?"

"I—I can't say."

He turned his back on her. "Forget it. If you can't trust me, I can't help you."

Silence stretched, thick and heavy.

"Scott."

He turned.

"I don't know who those men are. I hate to admit it, but yes, I am afraid. For my life. And I'm begging you to help me."

He pressed the advantage. "But why? What makes you think those men mean you harm?"

"I—I don't really understand what happened to Jozsef. He's cleaned out his apartment. I think those men may have something to do with his disappearance. Some weird stuff has been happening in my life. I just need to lay low until I figure out what is going on."

She was one hell of a liar. If Scott didn't know for a fact those were undercover officers banging on her door this very minute, he might even have believed her.

"Tell me where you're going or I can't help you."

She hesitated, eyes probing his. "To the mountains."

"Where in the mountains?"

She gritted her teeth, anger dragging her brow down, forcing the glint of steel into her eyes. "Jesus, McIntyre."

He shrugged. "Take it or leave it. If I'm in, I'm in all the way. Because whoever those guys are, if I help you, I become a target, too."

She studied him, eyes wary.

"You owe me that much, Skye. You want my help, the least you can do is trust me."

Her features shifted. "What's it to you anyway?"

He stepped forward, lifted his hand, moved a smoky tendril that had fallen across her eye. Her breath caught. She backed up, was stopped by the kitchen table, trapped. Scott stepped in, bent his head, his lips almost touching hers. He dropped his voice to a low whisper. "I like you. That's what's in it for me."

Her top lip quivered. Her breathing became ragged around the edges. "Last night—"

"What I said last night still holds. I don't take advantage of women on the rebound." He dropped his voice. "Doesn't mean I wouldn't like to."

She swallowed. Her eyes darkened. The thick fringe of her lashes fluttered low. But the instant was fleeting. There was a crash next door. The officers had broken in.

She grabbed control, made her decision fast. "There's a cabin in the mountains. Up north."

"Fine. I'll take you there."

"It's far."

"I'm mobile. No sweat."

She stared at him blankly.

"I'm a writer, remember? I can work anywhere. Go on, get in the truck while they're still inside your house. Cab's open. Lay low. There's a blanket in there. Cover yourself until I get there."

She said nothing, hoisted her pack onto her back in one fluid movement and made for the front door, biker boots clunking on the wood floor.

Scott rummaged in the closet for his own backpack. He quickly threw in some gear, including a sleeping bag. He checked his knife, his gun. Honey did whatever she could to trip him up. "Calm down, girl. I'm not leaving you behind. Where the doctor goes, you and I go." He slipped his satellite phone into his jacket pocket, grabbed Honey's lead and flipped the light switch.

He stepped out onto the porch, closed the door quietly behind him, locked it. He scanned Skye's yard in the pale dawn. The feds were nowhere to be seen outside. But inside, lights blazed from every visible window. The cops were probably going through Skye's things. That told him they had a warrant. That in turn meant they had sufficient evidence she was up to no good.

In the criminal sense.

And he was helping her run from the law. He smiled inwardly. It put him in a mighty strong position. Just the way he liked things. About time something went right with this mission.

He hobbled over to the truck, threw his cane and his pack into the back, yanked open the driver door. Honey bounded in.

A jolt shot through Skye as the cab door opened. She peered out from under the blanket just in time to reach out and stop Honey from sticking a paw in her eye. The dog scrambled over her, confused, looking for a place to put her hairy butt. Skye realized she'd taken Honey's spot in the cab. She fought off the blanket and struggled up into a sitting position, making room for the dog.

Scott's heavy hand shoved her right back down to the seat as he fired the ignition. "Keep down, dammit."

She cowered back down under the blanket, felt the truck jounce down the driveway and onto the road.

She was in one tight spot. The static of the blanket made her hair cling to her face, she had dog fur in her mouth, dog claws in her back. But that was the least of it. She was being forced to trust this man. This enigmatic man around whom she couldn't even trust herself.

"Okay, you can sit up now, coast is clear. Which way to the lab?"

Skye shoved the blanket aside and sat up. Honey maneuvered quickly into the space between her and Scott. "Take a right on the Coast Road," she said, trying to smooth her hair down, straining for some form of composure.

Other than giving directions to the Kepplar labs she said nothing. Neither did he.

She stole a glance at his profile. His granite features told her nothing, either. But she saw the way his eyes kept flicking up to the rearview mirror, watching for a tail. He seemed adept at this kind of game. Way too adept.

She had to get away from him as soon as they were far enough north.

Scott drove through the gates of the Kepplar compound and pulled into the lab parking lots. They were deserted apart from the vehicles used by night security staff.

"Not here," she said. "Go around back. There's an entrance I can use there."

He followed her instructions, drove around a shed and a hangar to the back of the building and parked the truck near the rear door.

"Wait here."

"How long?"

"I'll just be a few minutes."

"You got a cell phone?"

"Yes, why?"

"Might need you in a hurry. Make sure it's on. What's the number?"

She gave it to him. He was making her real nervous. She opened the passenger door, glanced back at him.

His eyes tunneled into hers. "Be quick."

Two simple words. Yet they tripped her up. It was the way he looked at her when he said them. Something in the deep emerald of his eyes spoke of compassion. It caught in her throat. "Thank you, Scott."

He nodded.

She shut the door, ducked into the Kepplar building as the sun broke, feeding gold light over the horizon.

Fred Ryan was on security detail. Good. He seldom wanted to chat. Skye nodded, smiled at him, slotted her ID card into the system, strode briskly down the corridor to her lab. The sound of her boot heels clacked hollow, echoed off walls.

She was taking a risk coming here. It was costing precious time. But she'd invested too much in this predator beetle project to let Malik get the better of this, too. She would see at least this thing through.

And if she was going to have to disappear again, she needed to know the project would go ahead safely.

Skye snapped on her gloves and checked the boxes containing the control samples. The larvae looked healthy. But her practiced eye sensed something different. She peered closer. The heads of the little grubs were light brown, but the bodies seemed a little lighter than usual. More creamy-white than grayish. Or was it just the effect of the gold morning sun streaming in through the lab window?

She moved on to the pupae. They looked fine, already turning reddish brown, a sign the adults were about to emerge.

Skye moved on to the next control sample. She hesitated. Was she imagining it? The newly emerged beetles were a rich chestnut in color. But the older ones should be glossy black by now.

She frowned, flicked on the fluorescent overhead lighting. They *were* the wrong color. It was so subtle a variation, most probably wouldn't notice it. But she did. Her mouth went dry. Something wasn't right. Perhaps they were at an earlier stage of the life cycle than indicated in the log. She moved quickly to check Charly's notes. Nothing. No mention of changes.

Skye wiped her sleeve across her brow, thinking. She was

running out of time. But she couldn't leave. Something was amiss with her project. She needed more trials.

She reached for a small tweezer-like tool, quickly plucking an adult beetle from the sample. She flicked on her microscope, placed it beneath the lens. Her pulse kicked into high gear. This was something she'd never seen in her previous samples. Minute red speckles scattered over the black-brown shell of the beetle, invisible to the naked eye.

Panic gripped her throat. Perhaps the gene had mutated. She needed to check the hundreds of newly emerged adults that would be shipped within two weeks. She needed to see that this aberration was only being demonstrated in this small control sample. And she needed to know why, what in hell it meant. She reached for another beetle. But the shrill ring in her pocket snapped her back. She fumbled, pulled out her cell.

"What?"

"Get out now! They're coming around the front."

Adrenaline squeezed at her lungs. Her eyes shot to the lab door, then back to her beetles. She had to make a choice.

The security alarm sounded. Someone was trying to get into the building.

Fear kicked Skye into action. She raced for the lab door, shoved it open, sped down the corridor. Fred Ryan was not at his security post. She flew out the back exit, alarm bells clanging in her ears.

Scott had the truck waiting, engine running, door open. She threw herself into the cab. He spun tires, her feet barely off the ground. He floored the gas, gunned through the parking lot.

And Skye could see why. The two men had seen them and were running for their car. She tried to duck down into the cab.

"Too late, sweetheart, they've seen you. And me. We're in this together now."

She clenched her teeth as he swerved out of the Kepplar gates and onto the road.

"Buckle up, we're on the run."

She turned to him. His face was pure granite, a study of self-control. Not an edge of fear.

"You've done this before."

He yanked on the wheel, cut down a side road. "That an accusation?"

"Who *are* you?"

"Just a guy with a sense of adventure." He grinned, pulled on the wheel again, spinning her and Honey hard up against the passenger door. "I told you to buckle up," he yelled.

Skye pulled herself upright, grabbing for the seat belt as Scott turned again, veered down a narrow farm lane and suddenly slammed on the brakes. She lurched forward, belt cutting into her neck.

Scott peered into the rearview mirror. "There they go."

She spun around in time to glimpse the brown sedan speeding down the road they'd just left. She slumped back into the seat, heart pounding a staccato beat against her ribs. "God, that was close." She pushed the hair out of her face, realized she was still wearing her latex gloves. She stared at them. "What now?"

"Now you tell me the truth. Now you tell me what you're running from."

She opened her mouth to lie, saw the hard green glint in his eyes, shut it slowly.

"Well?"

She studied him, weighing her options. "Why should I trust you?"

"Because right now I'm all you've got, sweetheart."

She swallowed under his keen scrutiny. He was right. At this moment he was all she had. And she had little doubt that if she didn't satisfy this man, he'd ditch her. Right here on this dirt road. And it would be mere minutes before those men realized they'd ducked down one of the lanes.

Think fast, Skye. Skirt the truth. It'll be easiest that way. She pulled her gloves off as she spoke. "I—I had a possessive boyfriend once. I think he's come after me."

Scott McIntyre threw back his head, laughed loud and long. Then he stopped suddenly, anger pulling the ledge of his brow low and threatening over eyes that had turned to cold, green stone. "Get real, Doctor. You think I'm buying that one?"

"You have to, because it's the truth." She heard the edge of desperation in her own voice. "He was violent. I had a restraining order slapped on him. It was many years ago."

"Right. Now you're asking me to swallow the fact that he's in that brown sedan with some other guy, chasing you?"

"No. Like I said, I don't know who those two men are. But I wouldn't put it past my ex to hire two goons to come after me."

"Sweetheart." She heard the warning bite in his tone. "You're pushing it. And I'm losing my patience."

She placed her hand on his forearm. "Scott, like you said, you're all I have right now. Why would I lie?"

"You tell me." He stared at her hand on his arm.

"You're so pigheaded."

"Give me reason not to be."

"Okay, okay. My ex had criminal connections. Mob." She swallowed. Her throat felt as dry as the Greek hills she'd been raised in. And what she was telling Scott McIntyre wasn't that far from the truth. Just thinking about Malik turned her stomach to water.

Something shifted in Scott's eyes. He pulled his arm out from under her hand. "Why do you think these men had something to do with Jozsef's disappearance?"

"I don't know. Honest. Maybe they paid him off or something."

"Come on, Skye. You want me to believe your fiancé, the man who loved you, took cash over a wedding?"

She looked down at her hands. "I didn't love Jozsef," she said softly. "And I don't think he loved me."

Scott was silent for a second. He cleared his throat. "Where is this ex-boyfriend of yours now?"

"Don't know. The last I knew he'd gone into hiding."

"When was this?"

"It was years ago. I was young. Very young. I really don't want to talk about it."

He tapped his hand on the wheel, thinking. "How young?"

"Nineteen. Please…can we go now?"

His eyes flicked to the rearview mirror. "Here they come…hang on to Honey!" He shifted gears, floored the gas. She grabbed the dog, the momentum kicking them both back, her head cracking against the rear cab window. Skye screwed her eyes shut. She couldn't look. She felt suddenly exhausted. The pain in the back of her head thumped along with the panicked rhythm of her heart.

She'd told him too much. In her desperation she'd skirted too close to the truth. Her world was closing in on her and she had no clue why. She clung to Honey with both arms, taking comfort from the dog.

And she said a silent prayer in her mother tongue as the truck ripped through the farm fields.

Chapter 7

The sunny morning gave way to an afternoon with heavily bruised skies and spitting rain. Scott clicked on the windshield wipers and cranked up the heat in the cab. He cast a glance Skye's way. She was still asleep. Honey, too, her head resting on Skye's lap. His eyes flicked up to Skye's face. The strong and wary woman was gone. Sleep had stolen her defences. She looked, instead, like an innocent child cuddled up with her pet.

She looked as vulnerable as the night he'd held her in his arms. The thick fringe of her dark lashes stark against the paleness of her skin. Her lips parted slightly, her breaths soft and regular.

Why are you running, Doctor?

He'd find out sooner or later.

He turned his attention back to the road. He'd shaken the tail, left the two cops good and stuck in the freshly ploughed earth of a farmer's strawberry field.

Scott turned down another narrow farm road. He was making his way south down the Saanich Peninsula, using a network of tiny backroads. Skye had said she wanted to go north. But to do that, he first had to cut back around the Saanich Inlet. He'd wake her for further directions when they reached the Malahat pass.

The highway started to climb up the Malahat. Thick mist closed in a shroud around them. Scott frowned. With temperatures like this there was a real threat of snow in higher elevations. He wondered just where in the mountains the doctor wanted to go.

But he had her right where he wanted, under his watch 24/7.

Sleet started to click and spit against the window as they reached the summit of the Malahat, but he didn't have the heart to wake her yet. He decided to wait until they reached Duncan. They'd stop to refuel and he'd touch base with Rex from there.

He checked his rearview mirror. Good. Still no sign of the brown sedan. He started the descent.

And as he did, he had an odd sense the two of them had just entered uncharted territory.

"The GPS alarm has sounded."

Every muscle in his body strapped tight. "She has crossed out of bounds?"

His assistant nodded.

He seated himself in front of the terminal and stared at the tiny red dot blinking on the screen. The tracking device showed she had indeed strayed out of the boundary they'd set. She was out over the Malahat, headed north.

Why?

"Alert our operatives to the coordinates. I want to know the instant they have a visual."

Skye jolted out of her sleep, out of her dream, panic tearing at her jugular like the rancid yellow teeth of a jackal. Disoriented, her hand flew to her throat. She frantically scanned her surroundings. And breathed deep. She *wasn't* in the dry hills of Greece. She *wasn't* buckled over in searing pain, running for the Albanian border.

She was with Scott McIntyre, in his truck, with his dog, surrounded by soft gray mist and gentle rain. But they *were* on the run. She sat bolt upright, eyes wide. They were entering some town. "Where are we?" she demanded.

"Welcome back, sleeping beauty."

"Where the hell are we?"

"Yeah, you're back all right. We're entering Duncan."

"Oh, God, I should've gone back to the lab. I don't know what came over me."

"I beg your pardon? I thought you were running for your life back there."

"My project." She rummaged in her pocket, pulled out her cell phone. "I've got to make a call."

"What project? Your assassin bugs?"

She ignored him and punched in Charly's number. It rang. And rang. No answer at Charly's Kepplar extension. Skye killed the call, dialed Charly's cell number. "Pick up girl. Pick up, Charly. Where the hell are you?"

Nothing.

"Damn." She quickly punched in Charly's home number.

The call clicked over to the voice mail service. "Charly, it's me, Skye. Do *not* let Marshall release those beetles. I repeat, cancel the release. We need further trials. Call me as soon as you get this message. It's urgent."

She flipped her phone shut. Where in hell was her assistant? She should be at work now. And she always carried her cell when she wasn't at home.

"What is it, Skye? What's wrong with your bugs?"

Her eyes jerked up to Scott's face. The real concern she saw there threw her momentarily. "The control group samples don't look right. I need time to check them properly.

And I need to check the adults being prepared for shipment. We can't risk releasing them. Not yet."

"Where is the release scheduled for?"

She gave a soft derisive laugh. "In greenhouses and fields across most of central Canada. The first shipment is due to fly out in two weeks. The West will be next."

Scott whistled through his teeth. "This is for the whitefly epidemic, right? I read about it in the paper."

She frowned at his piqued interest, studied his features carefully before answering. "Yes, that's the one. I designed a bug to target the mutant whitefly. We used gene technology to adapt a subspecies of the black Asian beetle. The ones we release will be sterile so they'll only last one life cycle."

"That'll keep them pretty much restricted to a target area?"

"Basically. But Kepplar is rushing it. Marshall Kane, the director, is impatient. He smells a huge contract from the States if this works as well as I thought it would."

"Now you think it won't?"

"Every indication was there that it should be hugely successful. But I would've liked more time. More trials. Just to be one hundred percent sure. Now, it looks like I was right. There are some subtle anomalies appearing. I detected them this morning. I need to research further—they could mean trouble."

"You want to go back?"

The images from the chase this morning slammed through her brain. And a sinking realization flowed like lead to the pit of her stomach. She might never go back. She might have to disappear again. Forever. If she wanted to live. "I—I can't go back."

"Those men?"

"Yes."

"Maybe I can help, Skye. Maybe we can contact the police—"

"No!"

"No police?"

"Cops couldn't help me before. There's no reason they'll be able to now. Those men will kill me."

His eyes flicked to her face. "You're serious."

"Scott, I can't go back." She'd be no use dead anyway. She rubbed at the grit in her eyes. Dr. Skye Van Rijn would have to cease to exist. She could see no other way. But even so, she had a duty to stop those beetles. She had no choice but to call Marshall. Reluctantly she opened her phone and slowly keyed in the number for the director of Kepplar Biological Control Systems.

"Marshall Kane here."

She swallowed. "Marshall, this is Skye."

"Where the hell are you? There was a security breach at the labs this morning."

"I—I heard."

"And Charly hasn't shown up for work, either. What in blazes is going on, Doctor?"

"I—I'm going to be away from work for a while. I—I'm pretty cut up about the wedding. I need some time."

"I'm sorry about the wedding. I heard. But Charly—"

"I'm sure she'll be in soon." Skye sucked in her breath. "Marshall...the project cannot proceed."

"Nonsense. We can manage without you."

"Marshall—"

"You look after yourself. We'll be fine. The bulk of your work is complete. I've seen your latest report."

"No, Marshall. Under *no* circumstances can it proceed. There are anomalies showing up in the control group. It could be dangerous. We need more research. More time." But she knew now she was clean out of time.

Marshall was silent.

"You've *got* to listen to me, Marshall."

The director cleared his throat. "Dr. Van Rijn, with all due respect, as head of Kepplar, this is my decision. I'll liaise with Charly when she gets in. Thank you for your input. And we'll see you when you get back."

He hung up before she could utter another word.

"Damn." Skye slumped back in her seat. She'd have to count on Charly. But where the hell was she?

Skye could feel the heat of Scott McIntyre's scrutiny. But to his credit, he said nothing. And she sure as hell didn't feel like talking.

They entered the town of Duncan, lunch hour traffic pressing at their sides. Pain pressed at her head. Scott pulled into a gas station, cut the engine.

"Okay, Doctor, we stop here for gas, food, maps. Why don't you wait for me and Honey in that diner next door while I fill up? Order me a coffee, will you?"

Skye reached for her pack, opened the truck door, swung her leg out. Then hesitated. She realized in that instant just how much control she'd placed in Scott McIntyre's large and capable hands this morning. She'd trusted him enough to fall asleep in his truck. She'd relaxed enough to drop her defences, let years of fatigue claim her. And she'd trusted him to get rid of their tail, keep her safe, while she slept.

It was a sensation utterly new to her. But it was a mistake. One that could prove fatal. She couldn't afford to let her guard down like this. She had to get to Henderson's cabin alone. Once she was there she could figure out how to disappear. And she couldn't take anyone along for the ride. She had to cut all ties. Once again, she had to start cold, make the journey into this next phase of her life alone.

Or Malik would find her again.

She had little doubt that it was his men who'd come for her this morning. She'd been expecting this for the last thirteen years. But she still hadn't been ready for it.

"Problem, Doc?"

She jerked back to the present, looked up into Scott's questioning eyes. Caring eyes. The vulnerable child long buried within Skye's psyche wanted to drown herself in those deep green eyes of his, to place her life in those warm, rough hands. This time a part of her really didn't want to run away. She bit her bottom lip. Scott McIntyre was like a thread, holding her back as he was helping her flee.

Then she remembered the knife strapped to his ankle.

She set her jaw. She wasn't a child. Never had been. She hadn't been allowed such luxury. She'd used this man. He'd gotten her this far, but now it was time to split. She had no more use for Scott McIntyre.

"You okay, Skye?"

"Yeah. Fine. I'll go get that coffee."

Determined, she slung her pack across her shoulder, strode over to the diner, shoved the door open and surveyed the establishment. The restaurant part of the business lay to her right. To her left was a general-purpose store complete with maps, candy, soda and anything else a tourist might need. There were phones and washrooms to the rear. The diner was busy, the store empty. She had to make her getaway while she had the chance.

She moved quickly over to the map rack, selected one that covered the northern part of Vancouver Island, headed over to the counter. The male cashier rang up her purchase.

Skye handed over cash. "Can you tell me where I can rent a vehicle? I need something with four-wheel drive capability."

"A four-by-four, huh?"

"Yes." She shifted, uncomfortable under his scrutiny. She didn't want to call any more attention to herself than was necessary.

"Don't know if Barney's has SUVs. Hang on, I'll look up his number, give him a call." The man reached under the counter for a phone book, started flipping through pages.

Skye turned to look out the windows that ran the length of the diner.

And froze.

Parked across the highway, outside a fast-food outlet, was the brown sedan.

She was trapped.

Scott filled the truck, paid for the gas and hopped back into the cab. "Okay, Honey, we're going to park 'round back and call your *real* dad."

He drove around to the parking lot at the rear of the diner, reached for his phone, dialed Rex.

"You shook the feds?" Scott could hear the amusement in Rex's voice.

"You got a better plan? Any word yet from our RCMP guy?"

"He cancelled on me. Complications. We're rescheduled for tomorrow."

"Okay, when you meet with him, check whether Skye Van Rijn has ever had any mob connections. Her story is she's running from two goons her ex has sent to kill her."

Rex laughed. "Right. Good one. She's creative if nothing else."

"She's scared of something."

Rex paused. "You're not buying her line, are you, Armstrong?"

"Hell, no. But this is one tough lady and, for whatever reason, she's afraid for her life. Something, or someone, has gotten to her. Bad."

"What's your destination?"

"Don't know yet. Oh, and check to see if there's any history of a restraining order."

"Against the mobster ex?"

"That's her story."

"Right. Don't disappear on me now, we might have to hand her over depending on what the feds tell me tomorrow."

Scott felt an inexplicable slip in his stomach. "Gotcha."

He pocketed his phone, absently scratched Honey's head. Hell, he wasn't ready to part with Skye. Yet.

Lies or no lies. Feds or no feds. After this morning's chase, a part of him really wanted to know what was making her tick. The woman had spunk. He gave a snort. Yeah, she intrigued him all right. Nothing—no one—had actually engaged him in this way for quite some time.

He reached down under the dash and filled Honey's water bowl from his bottle. "There you go, girl. We'll pick up some dog chow later this afternoon. Wait for me here."

Skye was at the far end of the diner, tucked into a booth. She glanced up as Scott approached, her eyes wide.

Something had spooked her.

He started to slide into the seat opposite her.

She reached out and curled her fingers tight around his wrist. "No. Here, beside me."

She pulled him around the edge of the table, down next to her onto the padded bench. "Away from the window."

"What's up?" He could feel the warmth, the firmness, of her thigh up against his. It stole his concentration. The woman had the lean, hard muscles of a long-distance runner. He resisted the sudden urge to place his hand over her thigh. Instead, he set both hands safely on the Formica tabletop.

She leaned into him, dropped her voice to a smoky whisper. "They're there, across the street. Look."

Scott's mouth went dry as the warmth of her whisper brushed his ear. He could smell the spicy-clean scent of her. It floated up with the warmth of her body from the vee of her shirt.

His nostrils flared involuntarily. He pressed his hands firmly against the cool tabletop, forced himself to look out the window.

There it was. A brown sedan.

Scott frowned. He'd left the feds ankle-deep in farm dirt.

He was sure of it. But he and Skye had wasted precious time traversing the network of Saanich Peninsula backroads before connecting with the Island Highway. Perhaps the cops had second-guessed them, headed straight for the highway.

The sedan was parked outside a fast-food outlet. Empty. Scott turned his attention back to Skye. "Order some food."

"I'm not real hungry about now."

"Just order something." He got up, sauntered casually over to the store end of the establishment. At least that's the image he wanted to project. Sauntering was probably the wrong term for his lopsided gait, he thought ruefully. He selected a pair of birding binoculars, paid for them.

"Want a bag for those?" The cashier asked.

"No, thanks."

"Oh—" the cashier reached for a piece of paper "—I see you're with the lady. Can you give this to her? It's the number for Economy Rentals. They've got SUVs."

Scott took the piece of paper, his expression studiously blank. He tucked it into his pocket. "Thanks."

So the doctor had planned to ditch him.

Until she'd noticed the brown sedan.

He said nothing about the cashier or Economy Rentals when he rejoined Skye. He sat, careful not to touch her leg this time. He lifted the new scope to his eyes, found the vehicle in his sights, adjusted the focus. It was the same model. He dropped the binoculars to the licence plate.

Different plate.

He smiled inwardly, set the binoculars carefully on the table. "It's them all right."

She sucked in her breath sharply, turned to look at the car.

It all happened in an instant.

As Skye turned to face the window, Scott caught sight of a young couple and child. They were exiting the fast-food outlet across the street, making straight for the brown sedan.

Damn.

He needed her to believe the two men were still hot on their tail. It would keep her from bolting.

With one arm he grabbed Skye around the shoulders. He placed his other hand firmly along the side of her face, turned her head from the window, pressed his mouth down hard onto hers.

A small, muffled sound of surprise strangled in her throat as she squirmed under him. She forced her hands up against his chest, tried to push him away.

But he gathered her forcibly closer, tasted the wild sweetness of her mouth.

And just as suddenly he felt her go still, soft and malleable in his arms.

A wild sort of terror gripped him as he realized her lips were opening under his. His stomach lurched as he dipped, slipped over the precipice of no return.

Skye stilled in shock as a hot wave surged through her.

But the demand, the hot hunger in his mouth, was overpowering. It kindled some dormant need deep within. It sparked, flared, tore through her like rampant wildfire.

She could do nothing to fight it. She angled her head, gave him more access. His mouth was salty, male, rough. His tongue flicked hard, deep. She met his voracious hunger with her own feral need, let his tongue twist slick around her own. And every conscious thought liquefied as her world tipped out from under her.

Warmth radiated through her entire body to the very tips of her extremities. She could feel the hot pulse of it in her toes, between her legs, under the sensitive pads of her fingers.

She could no more push him away than stop breathing. Her hands splayed hard against the solid warmth of Scott McIntyre's chest. She melted into him, drawing from his feral strength. She opened her mouth wider, starved for warmth, compassion, care. It was an elemental hunger she'd hidden, denied, for most of her life. It was kin to that deep primal need she'd first tasted more than a decade ago. That need to love and be loved, nurture and be nurtured. It was *feeling.*

Life.

And it had almost ended hers.

The memory stabbed sharp through her brain and jerked Skye to her senses.

She wrenched back, flushed, breathing fast and shallow.

But it was too late.

Something inside had been released and it would tax her to the limits to try to contain it. She looked into Scott's face. Arousal etched his features into a granite study of dark, unleashed desire.

He'd been as surprised at the sudden explosive intensity between them. But she could read something else there. In his eyes. Something she recognized. An anguish. It made her want to reach out, touch his cheek. Ask him.

She held back.

Silence stretched, hung thick, tangible.

Neither could find words to break the density of the energy that surged, pulsed alive, between them.

"Your order."

Both jolted, stared up at the woman as if she were a landed alien in the tight little world that had closed around their booth.

The waitress grinned knowingly, set the plates down in front of them, left without a word.

Skye tore her eyes from his, tried to focus on the plate of food in front of her. "W-what do you think you were doing?"

"I was kissing you." His words were gruff. "The men across the road were leaving the restaurant. I couldn't risk them seeing your face."

Skye's brow dropped down into a frown. She felt an inexplicable pang of disappointment. "*You* couldn't risk it?"

He reached for the burger in front of him, bit into it, then spoke around the food in his mouth. "Yeah. We're in this together, remember. What's that you ordered?"

"Ham and cheese sandwich." He'd thrown walls up. That was a good thing, she told herself as she poked at her meal. But inside her belly she trembled. She was afraid not only of what hounded her in the streets, but of what had been set free inside her very being.

And she knew, despite Scott McIntyre's nonchalance, that whatever it was, had touched him, too.

She lifted the sandwich to her mouth, stopped.

Dammit, she felt emotion pricking at her eyes.

The intensity between them had suddenly made it all raw again. After all these years it was as if he'd ripped open some door, found her naked, exposed. She could feel the ancient pain again. She plonked her sandwich back onto the plate, turned away from Scott, tried frantically to blink back the wetness that threatened her eyes.

My baby. I just wanted a life for my baby. Damn Malik for creating life, then violently snuffing it out. May he rot in hell.

She felt the heavy pressure of his hand on her shoulder. She tensed, didn't turn to face him, didn't want him to see her vulnerability.

"You all right, Skye? Not hungry?"

She whirled around. "I told you I wasn't hungry," she snapped. "You're the one who forced it on me." She was talking about more than the food.

"Whoa, easy. I told you to order. I didn't say you had to eat and enjoy. Besides, I wouldn't have thought you were one to take orders without question, Doctor."

She set her jaw, glared at him. "You got that right. I don't. Never have. Never will. But I've paid dearly for my obstinacy, McIntyre.'' She regretted the slip the minute the words tumbled out of her mouth.

He studied her face, reading something there. The flint in his eyes softened. When he spoke, his voice was low, like mist in a green valley. He reached up, touched the edge of her jaw. ''Who wounded you so badly, Skye? Your ex?''

She jerked out from his touch, motioned with her head to the wooden cane resting on the opposite seat. ''You have your own battle scars, McIntyre. I can see it in your eyes. You need more than that crutch of yours.''

He stiffened. His nostrils flared. His brow pulled low. His mouth setting a grim line across his tanned face.

She'd hit a raw nerve.

He said nothing.

She challenged with her eyes. ''I'm right, aren't I?''

His gaze was implacable. He'd shut down completely.

She pressed. ''I doubt you hurt that leg of yours skiing anyways. I saw that scar. It's not consistent with a twisted knee.''

He was dead silent. She should let that serve as warning.

''Can I get you anything else?'' The waitress's voice sliced into the tension.

''Just the check,'' barked Scott. He jerked his chin toward Skye's plate. ''And can you bag that to go?''

He grabbed Skye's arm. ''Come.''

Chapter 8

Honey bounded out the truck and relieved herself on the strip of lawn fringing the parking lot. Scott unwrapped Skye's uneaten sandwich, crouched, fed it to Honey.

But his focus was not on the pooch, it was on Skye. He watched her long legs pace the length of the parking lot, her arms wrapped tight around her waist. She reminded him of a wounded and dangerous animal trapped in a cage.

Dangerous enough to lash out and cut.

He was rattled by the way he'd lost control the minute his mouth had met her warm, sweet lips, shaken at the way she'd brazenly sliced so close to the bone.

He studied her as she strode, back and forth, back and forth, boots clicking against asphalt.

"She's looking to bolt, Honey," he whispered to the dog. "But she's scared. We gotta play this cool. Don't want to push the lady too far into a corner."

He stood, leaned on his cane as she approached. "So where to now, Doctor?"

She halted. ''Those men, how did they find us?'' she demanded. ''I thought we left them in that field.''

''We did. They must've made an educated guess we'd head north. Nowhere else to go from the Saanich Peninsula except by boat. And the only road north through the Malahat is the Island Highway. Perhaps we wasted time using the backroads to get around the inlet.''

Her eyes flickered from one end of the parking lot to the other. The fine mist of rain was leaving diamond drops in her thick dark hair.

''Why aren't you worried they'll see us now?''

''I figure they headed on north when they left, and they'll keep going for a while, until they see no sign of us. My guess is they'll backtrack.''

She angled her head, her almond eyes narrowed. ''You some kind of expert?''

He shrugged. ''I'm a writer. I have an imagination.''

She glanced down at his leg. ''How *did* you hurt your knee, McIntyre?''

It was a test.

She was pushing him, trying to decide whether to ditch or to trust him. He'd better give her damn good reason to trust.

He sighed, fingered the smooth, hard wood of his cane, buying time. ''I do a lot of traveling to remote places, for research. Some of my work is controversial. I got into trouble with a rebel group in the desert in India. They robbed me, shot me and left me for dead.''

''What desert?'' she demanded.

He swallowed. He hadn't expected this level of inquiry. ''The Thar.''

''Where? Near the Kashmir border?''

His gut squeezed into a ball. Most people didn't have a clue where the Thar lay. ''What does it matter?''

Her eyes flicked down to his ankle, where he hid his

knife, then back to his eyes. "There's a lot of political trouble there, near the Kashmir border."

"Has been for years."

She took a step toward him. "Why were you there?"

"Like I said, research. I write about stuff like that. The conflict between India and Pakistan is of particular interest to me."

She moved closer. "And the knife? The one strapped to your ankle?"

Scott met the challenge in her gaze. "You get into a habit, Doctor. You learn to take care of yourself in foreign lands where a government may be of no help to you. Old habits die hard."

He'd touched something, connected. A link had been forged. He could see it in her eyes.

But her words spoke otherwise. "I find it strange, Mr. McIntyre, that someone with your taste for adventure would find himself in pastoral Haven."

That's where people find themselves when put out to pasture. "My leg, Doctor. I needed rest and medical attention for my leg. I'm trying to heal. And that's the bloody hell truth of it."

She flinched as the sudden heat in his words, reached out, touched his forearm. "I'm sorry."

He pulled away, opening the car door for Honey. "In, girl." He turned back to face Skye. "So, where exactly is this cabin?"

She hesitated. "I—I'm not sure."

"You mean, you won't tell me. That's it, isn't it? Scott McIntyre has served his purpose. Now you want to go it alone."

"No." She ran her hand nervously through her damp hair, crushing the diamond droplets. "It's… I'm confused. That's all."

He decided to take the gamble, roll the dice. He climbed into the cab of the truck. "Well, it's been fun." He started to close the door. "Have a nice life, Doctor. Watch out for bad guys."

She lunged forward, grabbed his door. "Damn you."

"Hey, I got a book to write, a leg to mend. If you need my help, tell me." He leaned forward, dropped his voice. "Just don't treat me like a yo-yo, Doctor. You've jerked me around enough."

Uncertainty wavered in her eyes.

He jerked his chin toward her hand holding his door open. "Do you mind? I'd like to leave now."

"Zeballos." She blurted the word out.

His eyes shot to hers. "What?"

"The cabin. It's near Zeballos."

"Zeballos? As in totally isolated? As in population around two hundred?"

"You know it?"

"I know it well."

"Can you take me there?"

His eyes probed hers. "No more bull?"

She made a wry face. "I'll do my best."

"Hop in."

Scott fired the ignition. Bingo. He'd played her right, scored. But again the win came with an ironic twist.

Zeballos, of all places.

Scott hadn't been there since he was a kid. Since he'd gone fishing up that way with his dad.

This was going to be a trip back in time. And a journey into the heart of the wilderness, into the very core of who he was.

It was a place he didn't want to go.

But Skye was forcing him back down that road.

"We have visual. She's just left a diner in Duncan. There's a man with her. We've got a tail on them."

Relief surged through him, then bottomed out. "Who is this man?"

"No ID yet."

He lurched to his feet. A queer, hot sensation sank through to the pit of his stomach. Outwardly, he showed nothing. He paced the room, his mind in turmoil. She had help? An ally? Someone she might trust with sensitive information? This was a new variable. They couldn't afford to take chances with an unknown.

He'd been prepared to neutralize her at any stage of Operation Vector, but he'd have liked to play her through until the end. Perhaps now was the time.

He halted in the center of the cabin, turned slowly to face his assistant. "When they find her, neutralize her."

"You sure?"

He turned his back on his assistant, stared through the thick salt-encrusted window, out over the sea. "Very sure."

They wound through the streets of Duncan, heading away from the well-traveled Island Highway for the lesser-used coastal road. The rain fell heavier, bringing the heavens growling down with it.

Skye glanced at Scott. The set of his mouth was hard. His eyes kept flicking up to the rearview mirror. She felt a new edginess in him as he shifted gears.

She turned, looked out the back of the truck, eyes picking through cars on the roads, trying to see what he was seeing, what was bothering him.

But the brown sedan was nowhere to be seen.

He swerved suddenly right, veered down a side road, then left. And left again.

"What is it?"

"Our tail." His words were terse.

She swiveled in her seat again. "I don't see them."

He said nothing.

She pulled her hands through her tangle of hair. She felt as though she'd been on the road for days. But it had only been hours. If they drove on through the night, they could still be in Zeballos by dawn.

Scott finally pulled onto the narrow coast road. He put his foot on the gas, drove fast, overtaking cars. The speed didn't worry her—it was the reason for the haste that concerned her. She stole another look at his rugged profile. Despite the firm set of his jaw, in spite of the speed, his large hands were relaxed on the wheel. He handled the hurtling vehicle with the calm confidence and gentle touch of a familiar lover. It sent an unbidden and quirky thrill through her gut. She could imagine this man crossing the burning hot sands of the wild, unending Thar. She could picture him in the untamed places he'd spoken of.

She laid her hand on Honey's soft coat, turned to look out the passenger side window. The dark green conifers whizzed by in a monotonous rain-washed blur. Sometimes she missed the sun, the hot, dry hills of her native land. She wondered if Scott McIntyre missed places like the Thar, if they called to his soul in the night the way her home called to hers.

She knew the Thar. Malik had spoken of it often. He'd been there, on business. The Thar desert stood divided between the Sindh region in Pakistan and the Rajasthan in India. Malik had used it as a base to fund rebels in nearby Kashmir in return for their cooperation.

She sucked her breath deep into her chest, exhaled shakily. Way back, when she'd first come to this country, she'd considered going to the authorities, telling them she knew La Sombra, the man behind Anubis, knew where to find him.

But she hadn't.

Because she knew the depth and reach of the Anubis network. And she knew Malik was smart enough to keep moving, to keep switching identities. Even if the world knew Malik Leandros *was* La Sombra he'd still remain as elusive as a ghost.

And where would she be? She'd committed identity theft. She'd entered the country illegally. She'd trained in an Anubis camp. She bore the mark of Anubis. She'd be captured, incarcerated, interrogated and jailed.

And if she ever broke her cover, he'd find her, come after her, kill her.

She had little doubt of it.

No. She wanted to keep the past buried. She wanted to be free. But was this freedom?

She shuddered. Honey snuggled closer.

Scott's eyes flicked over to her. "You okay?"

"Yeah. Fine."

"We'll overnight in Chemainus."

"Why? Why can't we drive right through?"

His eyes darted once again to the mirror. "We need to make sure we've shaken them. If not, we'll be leading them down a one-way street into Zeballos. We'd be like rats working ourselves into an isolated dead-end trap."

He was right. There'd be nowhere left to run.

"We'll pick up the highway again first thing in the morning and make a run for Campbell River. If we haven't lost them by then, we're going to have to rethink our strategy."

Our strategy. He made her feel as though she had an ally. She hadn't felt like that since Jalil had helped her create a new identity. She reached out, tentatively placed a hand on his injured knee. "Thank you, Scott. Thank you for believing in me."

His eyes shot to hers.

Words hung unspoken. Then he jerked back, his attention once again fixed on the road ahead.

Thank you for believing in me. Bloody hell, it made him *want* to believe.

Scott cruised past several motels, found one that satisfied.

"Why this one?"

"It's got parking out back. Can't see vehicles from the road."

Skye looked at him strangely. "Are you sure you haven't done this before?"

He forced a grin. "I watched too many detective shows when my leg was mending. Hop out."

"What?"

"Get us a room. Use my name. Don't move until I get back."

Her eyes widened. "Why? Where are you going?" The shaky edge in her voice tugged at his male ego. She wanted to keep him near. It pleased something primal within. He told himself it was only the satisfaction at having won his quarry over. He was a little closer to her secrets. And that was his mission.

This was just a job.

And that kiss at the diner... It was pure male physical reaction. Normal for a man who hadn't touched a woman in a long, long time. The hunger she'd awakened in him had nothing to do with the permanent void in his chest. The fear she'd stirred in him when she'd looked deep into his eyes and seen the pain of the past meant nothing.

She was a criminal.

"I'm going to get some dog food for Honey. I'll be back soon."

"I can come and get the food with you."

"It's better you lay low." He needed to get her out of the way and to let Rex know they'd picked up a new tail in Duncan. A tail he couldn't be sure was the feds. He needed to switch vehicles. Just in case.

"Fine." She hauled her backpack out of the truck, swiveled on the heels of her biker boots and strode up to the motel's reception area.

Scott unhitched his eyes from the sight of her rump moving in her jeans, shifted gears. "That's one hell of a package, Honey." He pulled back out onto the road.

Scott found a car dealership not far from the little motel. It had just what he needed in the lot.

An hour later, he and Honey sat in a silver Land Rover. It was the color of Skye's eyes and worth more than the black thing Rex had sent him off in. Scott chuckled. "He's not gonna like the tab on this baby," he told Honey as he punched in Rex's number.

"Hey, boss."

"You sound chipper."

"Chipper? That another one of your pommy tags?"

"Cut to it, Agent. Hannah and I have a birthing class to get to in twenty minutes."

Scott's mind went blank. *Hannah was pregnant?*

"Scott...you there?"

He found his tongue. It was thick when he spoke. "Rex...I—I never knew. I never even asked how she and Danny were—"

"Hey. It's okay. She's due any day now. Danny's doing great. Can't wait until his uncle Scott comes to visit."

Scott rubbed his hand brutally over his face. It had been three years since Rex and Hannah had married. Scott had left for the field immediately after the wedding. As happy as he was for the Logan family, their success had only served to sharpen his pain. Guilt welled bitter inside him. "I'm sorry, Rex. I—I've been...self-involved."

"Yeah, I understand." He paused. "How's Honey?"

Scott reached out, ruffled the Logan family pet's smooth fur. The guilt bit deeper. Rex had been looking out for him, giving him their dog. He'd been trying to bring Scott back out of his shell, his self-inflicted prison. And he was keeping tabs on his progress by making him report to him personally.

"She's good, Rex." He paused. "Reminds me of the lab I had when I was boy."

"You were never a boy, Armstrong."

"Whatever." He cleared his head. "I have a destination. We're heading for Zeballos."

"Where's Zeballos?"

"The boonies. A two-hundred-year-old village on the northeast coast of the island that once produced millions in gold. It's a logging community now. Plenty of abandoned gold mines and limestone caves."

"You know this place then?"

"From another life. My dad took me there for one of our father-son fishing trips. It's nestled right on the Esperanza Inlet. Nothing behind the town but sheer mountains and forest to nowhere."

The remorse was suddenly acute at the thought of his father, his parents. It was all coming down on him, as though some kind of floodgate had been opened to feeling. And he was drowning.

Those trips had been real special. A highlight in his young life.

"Where will you be staying?" Rex was talking to him. He yanked his mind back out of the past.

"Not in the town. I'll send you GPS coordinates when we get there. We're headed for a cabin somewhere in that region. Let me know as soon as you've spoken with our federal contact. I need to know what I'm dealing with here. We picked up a new tail today. Dark green Dodge. Couldn't catch the plates."

"Feds?"

"Could be."

"I'll check with our man tomorrow. Scott, if it's not the feds—"

"Yeah, this adds a new dimension."

"Play it safe."

Scott heard the concern in Rex's voice. He tried to laugh it off, tried to tell himself it had zip to do with the fact he was injured, washed up, supposed to be recuperating with a lame-duck surveillance job. "You worried now it's become a *real* mission?"

"Chill, hard-ass. Let's touch base tomorrow."

"Yeah. Right. Oh, by the way, we've got new wheels. Traded the truck in. Tab is headed your way." Scott hung up before Rex could respond.

He smoothed the fur on Honey's head. So the Logans were having another baby. He shook the odd onslaught of emotion, fished out the piece of paper on which he'd scribbled the address of the theater store.

He had to stay focused. If that was not the cops back there in Duncan, then someone else was after Skye.

He was damn sure he'd lost them. But until he knew who and what he was up against, he wanted to keep her hidden.

Chemainus was an artsy community famous for murals that depicted the history of the valley. It was also full of antique stores and boutiques offering sculpture, pottery and glass. And it had the theater store. Scott had found the address in the Yellow Pages while he'd waited for the dealer to finalize the papers for his vehicle trade.

Evening was edging out afternoon by the time he and Honey reached the shop. But it was still open. He wasted no time in asking for what he was looking for.

"You want a short, medium or long?" the salesclerk asked him.

He thought of Skye's lustrous dark hair. She'd never manage to hide it all under a short wig. "I'm going to have to go with one of the longer lengths."

"Color?" The woman held up a chart.

The image, the sensation of Skye's exotic, smooth olive-toned skin swam into his senses. Too blond and she would look false. Too much red or orange and it would clash with her olive skin and silver eyes.

"That one." He pointed to a dark ash-blond mixed with brownish frost.

"The snowy mink?"

He chuckled. ''Yeah, the snowy mink. And I like this style here.'' He pointed to the head of hair on a mannequin. It would balance well with her height, her stature.

''Anything else?''

''Just these.'' He held up a pair of studious looking glasses for himself. Deception, he mused, was an art.

A little voice niggled inside him, *Self-deception, however, is folly.*

He put his purchase on the Bellona tab.

''What do you mean, it's the *only* room left?''

The motel desk clerk gave an apologetic shrug. ''The art festival's in town this week. Everything's pretty much booked solid. You're lucky to find even this. We just had a cancellation''

''Oh, great. That's just great.''

''Would you like me to make some calls for you?''

Skye checked herself. The poor woman was actually trying to help her. ''No, it'll have to do.'' She grabbed the keys off the counter, spun on her heels.

''If there's anything else I can get for you, Mrs. McIntyre—'' the woman called out after her.

Skye whirled, opened her mouth, shut it again, tried to twist it into a congenial smile. ''Thank you, no. We'll be fine. Could you please direct *Mr.* McIntyre to *our* room when he finally arrives.''

She unlocked the motel room door, flung it open, tossed her backpack onto the one and only bed.

Just great. She was going to have to sleep with the writer tonight. And the thought of it punched her smack in the gut. She felt winded. Terrified, actually. She didn't trust herself to be near him.

She sat on the bed, pried her boots off with angry movements. She was way out of her league when it came to Scott McIntyre, dammit. Other men she could kiss without coming totally undone.

Boots off, she threw herself back on the queen-size bed. It was altogether too small. She stared up at the ceiling. She was running all right. And it wasn't just from Malik's men.

She was running straight into another kind of trap.

And she was sure of one thing. If she opened up, Scott McIntyre might just steal her heart.

And she'd end up paying the price.

It was more than she could afford.

"Quiet, now. One sound and you're back in the car." Scott let Honey out of the Land Rover. He didn't know if they allowed pets in the motel but he wasn't going to chance asking them.

The retriever obedient at his side, Scott unlocked the motel room door and walked in.

She lay on the bed like a sleeping beauty, her dark hair spread over the white of the pillow.

His muscles tightened in a band across his chest.

Then he saw.

There was only one bed.

And she was sprawled out on it. Something dark and hot slipped through his gut. He stepped inside the room, quietly setting his package on the dresser.

But even in her sleep, she caught his movement. Her eyes flashed open. She jerked upright on the bed, hand flying to her chest as if to reassure herself she was fully clothed. He'd awakened her from some deep dream. One that had flushed her cheeks a soft pink.

He swallowed at the intimacy he saw there.

Her eyes darted around the room, as if to confirm the reality of her surroundings.

This was not a relaxed woman.

This was a woman doing one hell of a job hiding some deep-rooted fear.

"Arise, sleeping beauty, I've got a present for you," he said dramatically.

"Where the hell have you two been?" she snapped. "You've been gone more than two hours."

"Relax, sweetheart." He picked up the package. "This is for you." He held it out to her.

She took it, uncertain. "What is it?"

"Open it."

She tore at the wrapping, held up the wig, frowned. "You said you were going to get dog food."

"We did. But we got this for you, too." He took the wig out of her hands, lifted it over her head and positioned it carefully over her tresses. He concentrated on ignoring the sensation of her dark silken strands against his fingers as he covered them with the false blond ones.

He stepped back.

The color he'd chosen was perfect. She looked like a siren. He should've guessed Skye Van Rijn would only stand out more as a blonde. Still, it was a highly efficient disguise. That's what he loved about wigs. They were simple. And, in his experience, they worked.

She threw her feet over the side of the bed, padded to the mirror and adjusted the hair around her face. She made a wry face, pouted at her reflection.

Then she laughed. "What the hell is this for?"

He stepped up behind her, caught the silver of her eyes in the mirror. She looked into the reflection, back into his eyes. The frisson was immediate. Heat swelled between their bodies.

"I thought I'd take you out somewhere quiet for supper tonight. Get to know you a little better."

She turned slowly to face him, her breasts almost touching his chest. His pulse spiked. He swallowed against the tension that gripped at his throat. In the mirror he could see her shapely butt as she faced him. And he saw the unmistakeable stamp of raw desire reflected in his own features.

He knew she could see it, too.

She looked slowly up into his eyes. He could feel the

warmth of her breath against his lips as she spoke. ''Ah, you think they won't recognize me in disguise?'' Her voice curled through his senses. ''Ingenious,'' she mocked.

He smiled, lifted his hand to gently move some of the hair from her face. ''Maybe I just like blondes. Snowy-mink ones.''

She stilled instantly at his touch, like a rodent frozen by a serpent's stare. She was afraid. He could sense it in an animal way.

He, too, was afraid, couldn't move. They teetered silent at the cusp of something. One small move would send them down one road. Another would topple them over, past the point of no return and they'd end up naked, limbs entwined, hot and slick on that single bed.

And Scott was so close to making the wrong move. So very damn close. His hand remained immobile against the skin on her cheek. He couldn't seem to unhitch it.

She couldn't pull away.

That's when he saw it. Light refracting in tiny emeralds, eyes of a gold bug nestled at the hollow of her throat. He hadn't really noticed it before.

He moved his hand to touch the unusual gold pendant, remotely thankful to have found sudden purpose for movement.

''Where'd you get this?''

She jerked back, bumped into the dresser. Her hand flew to the jewel at her throat, focus returned to her eyes.

''Jozsef...gave it to me just before the wedding.'' She took another step back. ''I—I don't really like it.'' She sank down into the chair next to the dresser, as if crushed by the sudden weight of an unwanted memory. She clutched the pendant, covering it with her hand.

''But you're still wearing it.'' Scott didn't know what drove him to say that. It smacked of accusation. He ran his tongue over his teeth. His mouth was dry.

"I...he...Jozsef made me promise to wear this beetle always."

Scott stepped closer, laid a hand on her shoulder. "I'm sorry, Skye."

She looked up into his face. Her eyes were wide. He felt like a brutish bull, trampling over her pain. The woman was still hurting. He had no business feeling what he was feeling. No business using her pain to get inside her head.

It's your job, Agent. Remember that. Just another job.

But it wasn't. Not anymore. This one had taken hold of him. Deep down, he knew this was different. It was getting to him in ways he never anticipated. And if he didn't grab control of himself, real soon, he was gonna blow it, seal his fate once and for all with the Bellona Channel.

And that wasn't a future he was ready to contemplate.

"No, Scott, don't apologize. I'm the one who's sorry to have dragged you into the mess of my life." Her voice was brittle as she struggled for composure. "I'm not usually like this. It's just that...that...everything's going to hell in a handbasket."

He sat on the edge of the bed, faced her. "What do you mean?"

She inhaled a shaky breath. "When Jozsef gave me this pendant, there was something in his eyes. Like an urgency. He said no matter what happened, I must promise to wear this. It was like...like he knew something was going to go wrong. I think he knew when he gave me this beetle that he wouldn't be at our wedding."

Scott reached out for her hand.

She pulled away. "Please, don't touch me."

Her words burned.

He held back, moved his hand, instead, to pet the silky fur of Honey's head. The dog could sense the unease, the emotion that pulsed through the room. She nestled her snout into the crook of Scott's knee, whimpered softly.

"Skye, why do you think Jozsef never showed?"

She was quiet for a while. When she spoke, there was a quaver to her voice. "I don't think he had a choice. I think something happened to him."

"Why?"

"You think I'm in denial, don't you? You think I'm scratching for excuses so that I can cope with rejection. I'm not. Things have been adding up weird. I got this feeling."

"What, exactly, makes you think something happened to Jozsef?" His tone was more demanding than he'd intended.

She shut down.

She yanked the wig from her hair, tossed it onto the dresser, raked her fingers through her dark tresses. "Just forget it."

He softened his voice. "Skye, if you talk to me, maybe I can help."

Her top lip trembled ever so slightly. "I just don't know who to trust."

Scott lifted his hand. He needed to touch, to console. But he restrained himself. "You think Jozsef's disappearance is more than some simple payoff."

She slumped forward, dropped her face into her hands, her hair curtaining him from her features. She shook her head, as if to discard everything in it. Her body jerked with a sob. Then another. Emotion tore through her, racked her frame. Scott could hold back no longer. He dropped to his knees in front of her, took her into his arms. Held her. Just held as she sobbed.

Honey whimpered, tried to edge her snout into Skye's lap. And they stayed like that. The three of them. A tiny vignette.

A misbegotten, temporary family built on lies.

Chapter 9

Skye raised her face to the showerhead, let the water sear her skin. But the piping heat didn't penetrate deep enough, couldn't cleanse her past. Couldn't wash away her present predicament.

She stepped out of the shower, reached for the motel towel, scrubbed it angrily against her body. She'd said too much to Scott McIntyre. She'd crashed. That had never happened to her before. And Scott was no fool. He'd soon start putting the pieces together.

She stopped suddenly, snared by her blurry image in the steamy bathroom mirror. She gave a quiet, derisive laugh. That was her, a blur of person. Out of focus. Not quite real. She reached forward, rubbed a hole in the mist with the back of her fist, stared at her own face. More than anything she wanted clarity, openness, honesty in her life. She wanted to be a real person again. Not an alias. She didn't want to run anymore. The little clearing she'd made in the mirror closed in on itself, blurring her reflection as she watched. Skye frantically rubbed it back.

She wouldn't let Malik do this to her anymore. She had to make it stop. She couldn't get old and die in obscurity, running for the rest of her life. Wouldn't. It was time she fought back. Because right now, she had nothing to lose—apart from her life. And what was that worth? Not much living the way she was. She was hollow. And Scott had shown her just how hollow. He had made her feel human, real. And as much as it hurt, she wasn't ready to give that up again.

But how could she fight back? Could Scott really help her? Could she trust him with her darkest secret? She wanted to. Skye slipped into her yellow terry bathrobe and cinched the belt at her waist. She had to. She didn't have a choice. Because she was not going to let Malik win. Not this time. She would not go back to the way she was. She was prepared to gamble with her life on this. She'd even go to prison.

She stepped out of the bathroom determined, an edgy adrenaline coursing through her veins, a thousand tiny butterflies fluttering in her stomach. But ready.

Scott looked up as she stepped into the room. A smile creased the rough, tanned planes of his face. She could almost read relief in the sparkle of his green eyes as he watched her. She smiled warmly back.

"You look like you feel better."

She rubbed a towel through her hair. "I do. How about that dinner now?"

"Excellent idea." He stood, slipped a pair of bookish spectacles onto his nose, looked at her quizzically. "What do you think?"

She threw back her head, laughed from her heart. "Is that *your* disguise? I didn't know you needed one."

He shrugged. "Thought it might be fun."

"Fun?" The word felt alien in her mouth.

He stepped closer. "Sweetheart, we're running from reality, we might as well enjoy the ride."

She swallowed, raw lust once again unfurling slowly through her veins. "How true." He didn't know just how true. She studied his eyes through the lenses.

"Well, what do you think? How do I look?"

"I—I think you look like a writer."

He wiggled his brows. "But I am."

"Yes. I do believe you are, McIntyre." She laughed again. And it felt good.

Skye gaped at the silvery-gray, four-wheel drive. "What's that?"

"That, my dear, is our new getaway vehicle."

She spun 'round, pinned him with her eyes. Her fake hair was platinum, surreal in the moonlight. "What happened to your black truck?"

"Traded it in. Besides, this one goes better with your new hair."

She turned slowly, stared at the vehicle.

"It'll get us into the Zeballos backcountry," he offered.

"You think it'll fool them?"

"Worth a try."

"You did this…for me?"

"You getting in or what? I've made dinner reservations."

She resisted. "Why? Why are you doing this, Scott?"

He shrugged.

She placed her hand firmly on his forearm. "I need to know why you're doing this for me?"

Guilt raised an ugly sharp head in his chest. He pushed it away. "Is a man being nice to a beautiful woman really such a foreign concept to you, Doctor?"

"In my world, nothing comes free."

He slipped his arm over her shoulder, whispered into her ear, "You must learn to trust, Doctor. With trust comes freedom." That thing in his chest twisted sharply. The words he'd just uttered stuck thick in his craw, the irony catching like thorns. He swallowed.

She angled her chin, looked up into his eyes. "I know." Her voice was soft. Warm. "I know." She stood on tiptoe, bussed his cheek. "Thank you. For everything."

He just nodded and opened the passenger door for her. What did Scott McIntyre know about trust, about fun? Obviously a hell of a lot more than Scott Armstrong did. He walked around the Land Rover to the driver's side and opened the back door for Honey. She hopped in, then he settled into the driver's seat, started the ignition.

Agent Scott Armstrong would do well to heed some of futurist Scott McIntyre's advice, he thought ruefully as he shifted the vehicle into gear. Because right now his alias had a better handle on life than he did.

Scott handed the wine list back to the sommelier. "We'll have the Janus Creek Zinfandel."

The stunning blonde sitting opposite him scanned the room. Scott felt bizarre, as though he and Skye were part of a movie set. Two people playing roles in a fake life. But no one was going to yell "Cut" once dinner was over. They would be playing these roles for days to come. He wondered just what was going to give first.

"This is beautiful, Scott. I thought you were kidding when you said we had reservations."

"It's small. Quiet."

And intimate. But that was for security, he told himself.

The sommelier brought the wine, displayed the label. Scott nodded. The man splashed rich red liquid into the bulb of his glass. Scott raised it to his nose sniffed, smiled.

"Perfect," he told the sommelier who proceeded to fill their glasses. Scott raised his to salute Skye.

She smiled. "Cheers. To new beginnings."

"New beginnings?"

She pointed to the label. "It's a Sonoma vintage, from the Janus Creek vineyards."

"What's that got to do with new beginnings?"

"I know the place. Jozsef and I were there about a year ago. We were traveling up from Texas," she said openly. "The farm is named after the Janus Creek, which runs through it. The source of the Janus is a spring that bubbles up precisely at the summit of two watersheds. It splits into two," she explained. "Gravity forces one part of it to flow south to join rivers that feed into the Pacific ocean. The other part flows north before joining the Pacific."

"Two different directions to the same end?"

Skye nodded. "That's why the spring was named after the Roman god Janus. The god that looks both ways, covers both angles at the same time, guards every door."

"But why beginnings?"

"Ancient Romans sought Janus's help at the start of wars. They believed invoking him ensured their beginnings would have good endings. That's why the first of January is dedicated to him. He keeps an eye on the happenings of the old year while looking forward to the new." She studied him over her glass, took the rich red liquid into her lips.

Scott's eyes dropped to the label. He'd never given the appellation much thought. "I thought Janus was a two-faced liar. God of deception."

She shifted slightly in her chair, bit her bottom lip. It had drawn a faint burgundy stain from the wine. He could imagine the taste of her mouth. "Ever heard of Janus-faced, Skye?"

Her eyes narrowed. "That's more of a modern English thing…that two heads equal a divided self. Janus is thus deemed an appropriate symbol for a self-deceived person. It's not the way I see it."

He took a sip of wine, let it settle around his tongue, feeling the tart bite, the wild fruitiness, before swallowing. "So does this Roman Janus have a Greek counterpart?"

She almost choked. She set her glass studiously down onto the linen tablecloth. "No."

He'd touched something. But what? Something to do with Greece? He leaned back in his chair, assessing. "You know an awful lot about this stuff."

"I—I had an interest. Years ago."

Out of the corner of his eye Scott could see the waitress approaching with their food. He sat forward. "You ever been to that part of the world?"

"What part?" She looked edgy.

"The land of the Gods of Olympus. Greece."

She shook her head. "No. Never." The waitress set their plates in front of them. Skye moved quickly to change the topic.

Scott filed the information away in his brain, turned to the waitress. "Thank you."

"My pleasure. Can I get you anything else?

"Some water, please," Skye asked. She looked suddenly pale.

"Sure thing." The waitress halted, staring at Skye's neck. "Oh, what a beautiful necklace."

Skye's hand shot once again to her throat. "Thank you." She looked away, her tone brooking no further discussion. But the waitress persisted. "My sister collects jewelry bugs. Her boyfriend just gave her a little gold bumblebee. What I wouldn't give to find her a beetle like that for her birthday. May I ask where you got it?"

Scott watched, vaguely amused. Skye continued to clutch the gold pendant. But she looked up at the waitress. "Why does she collect bugs?"

"I know, she's totally nuts. But ever since she was a kid she's had a fascination for crawly things. She wants to study entomology at university next year."

A hint of smile toyed with Skye's mouth. "I think I'd like your sister. Tell her good luck. But I don't think you'll find a bug like this locally. This one was made for me in Europe.''

''Too bad.'' The waitress smiled. She left to fetch the water.

Scott picked up his knife and fork. ''Well, someone likes your beetle, even if you don't.''

Skye fixed him suddenly with her silver stare. She reached with both hands slowly up behind her neck and unfastened the clasp. She set the little gold bug with the emerald eyes on the table in front of them.

Scott raised his brow in question.

''I want her to have it. For her sister.''

Scott set his utensils down. ''The waitress? You serious?''

Skye blew out a breath. ''Yes. Dead serious.''

He reached out, picked up the little beetle, weighed it in his palm. ''Feels like solid gold.''

She tucked into her food. ''Probably is. I never liked gold.''

''And the eyes, are they emeralds?''

''Probably. I like emeralds.'' She looked up into his eyes. ''I like green eyes.''

He swallowed. ''You can't just give it away.''

''I need to do this. To move on.'' She tried to change the subject. ''Food's excellent. Yours is getting cold.''

''What if he comes back?''

She stopped chewing. ''Jozsef?''

''You made him a promise, that you would wear it always.''

''No. I didn't. He wanted me to promise. I didn't say the word.''

''What if he *does* come back? What if there really was a valid reason for him leaving you at the altar?'' Scott knew he was acting like a wretched dog with a bone. But all of a sudden, he couldn't let it go.

''You want to know if I'd take him back.''

"Would you?" He could hear the sharp edge in his voice. But for the life of him, he couldn't keep it out.

She shook her head, and a secret weight lifted from his chest. He breathed deep. "Why not?"

"I need to understand what happened to Jozsef. But like I told you, I never loved him. I think I need to acknowledge that to myself." She glanced at the pendant resting on the white linen. "Taking that off is like removing a weight. It makes it final. I can't explain it."

"Why *were* you going to marry him?"

She set her fork down next to her plate. "I guess you have a right to ask that question."

He shrugged. "Do I?"

She took in a breath, slowly released it. "Jozsef walked into my life one day. And he was so right. He knew all the right buttons to push. We liked the same things, shared the same interests. He was fascinated by my work, wanted to know every little detail." She fiddled with the stem of her glass. "He made me feel wanted. I needed to feel normal, Scott."

Her candor made his brain stumble. "And you thought marrying him would make you feel normal?"

"He asked me. It seemed a logical step to take."

"But you didn't love him," he insisted.

She looked down at the garnet liquid in her glass, spoke softly. "I didn't know if I knew how to love…how to feel. I've been numb. For a long time. A very long time."

He lifted his glass and sipped. "And now?"

Her eyes flashed up to his. Color flushed her cheeks. "I think you know the answer to that."

The wine seeped warm in his chest. He could feel it smolder in his belly. He looked into her eyes. And he wanted to kiss her.

"And you, Scott? What's your story?"

He blinked at the rapid turnaround. "Me?"

"Have you ever felt numb, Scott? You know, when

you've been out in the cold too long and you freeze, then when you find warmth again, you thaw, begin to feel, and it hurts like all hell?''

He didn't know what to say.

''Well, have you?'' she pushed.

He swallowed, still speechless.

She leaned forward, lowered her voice to a whisper over the table. ''You know what? I think you have. I think you were burned once, badly, and went numb, like me.''

He couldn't breathe.

''But you're not going to tell me your story, are you?''

The room was closing in on him.

''You want me to trust you and you won't tell me anything about yourself,'' she said softly. ''You said trust brings freedom. But you won't trust me. You're not free, either, McIntyre. You're just as trapped as I am.'' She lifted her glass, sipped, eyes watching him over the rim.

He felt like bloody two-faced Janus. He was building a web of deceit, trapping this woman. This woman who'd been hurt so bad by something she'd gone numb.

Like him.

It's your job, Agent. What in hell is wrong with you? He reached for his glass, took a deep swig, swallowed the bitter pill, choked as the drink went down. This was way wrong. This shouldn't be happening. He took another swig. Like the Janus creek itself, he had a head pointed in each direction. Armstrong looking one way. McIntyre the other.

But deep down, they were one and the same, flowed from the same source. And into the same ocean.

''Scott?'' Her light silver eyes bored into his. ''Oh. I see… It's double standards.'' She held up her glass. ''You look like you just lost your appetite.''

He had. For this mission. Deceiving Skye Van Rijn suddenly tasted real bad. It wasn't fair. *He* wasn't playing fair. He breathed in deep. ''I lost my family. My wife and my baby.'' He said simply.

She paled.

"And I'm not inclined to talk about it."

Neither of them was able to finish their meal.

Skye felt light-headed, surreal, as Scott led her to the front of the restaurant to get her jacket. His words had shifted her world. She suddenly saw him differently. He shared the pain of a lost child. She felt crass for having pushed him. But in a way she was glad she had. Because with those few words he'd opened a window through which she could suddenly see him. She felt as though she could understand this man. Relate to him.

And she felt something else.

A need to help mend his wound. A need to nurture. It was weird, but it felt as if her breasts were full and swollen again. As if the female part of her that had withered and died with the loss of her child was once again stimulated, full, pulsing with a new kind of life. As though she had something to give.

The waitress was waiting up front to say goodbye. Skye pushed her gold beetle necklace into her hands. "For you."

Her eyes widened. "Oh, no. I couldn't possibly take it—"

Skye closed her hand tightly over the woman's. "Please. I want your sister to have it. It'll make me happy that it has a true home."

"I—I can't thank you enough—"

"Don't. I hope your sister finds her place in her chosen profession. It's a fascinating field."

Skye felt liberated by the simple act. She reached for her jacket hanging on the coatrack just as two burly men entered the restaurant.

They glanced at Skye, stared at Scott.

Skye could swear she sensed his hackles rise in primitive instinct at the sight of the men.

An unspoken aggression simmered in the air around him, like waves of heat from a flame.

It made fear stick like a hard ball in her throat.

Her eyes darted to his, questioning. But he made a slight movement with his lips, his eyes, telling her to be quiet.

He casually edged around her, shielding her from view as he helped her with her coat.

The men brushed past them, heading into the restaurant.

Scott whirled, grabbed her arm. "Quick," he whispered. He yanked her out the door, ushered her smartly to their SUV.

A dark green Dodge truck was parked right outside the front door. Scott swore.

"What is it?" she whispered.

He stared at the plates on the truck as he steered her to their vehicle. "Get in the car."

She didn't resist. She didn't like the razor edge in his voice.

He started the engine, but he didn't gun the gas. He moved smoothly, quietly, out of the parking lot, like a hunter through night shadow. But once he was a block away, he stepped on it.

Only after he ducked down yet another narrow side street did she speak. "What the hell was that about?"

His eyes flicked to hers, his features stark and dangerous under the sporadic illumination of streetlights.

"Our tail just showed up at the restaurant."

"Those men? *They* were our tail?"

"Yeah."

"But the brown car wasn't in the parking lot."

"Different men. Different vehicle."

Skye looked at the dark road ahead. The sides of her throat stuck together. Nerves skittered through her belly. Scott McIntyre had not shown this kind of edge when the brown car was after them.

He knew something she didn't.

* * *

The night sky was clear, the moon high when they crept silently into the parking lot behind the motel.

"Why are we coming back here? Why don't we just drive through?" Skye tried in vain to keep desperation from creeping into her voice.

"We need to lay low."

"What are you not telling me, Scott?"

"We picked up a new tail in Duncan. I thought we'd shaken them."

Fear clawed her throat. "How did we pick them up?" Her voice was hoarse.

"Don't know." He parked right up close to their motel room door. Skye bit back her anxiety, waited in the vehicle while Scott let Honey relieve herself under the trees at the side of the building.

She watched as he and the dog made their way through the night shadows. He unlocked the door, then motioned for her to join them.

And a new kind of dread pooled in her stomach.

She was going to have to sleep in the same bed as this man. This man who knew how to reach right into her and take hold of her very soul.

He held the motel door open for her, flicked on the light. She hesitated.

"Come on," he whispered.

She stepped cautiously into the room, saw it almost immediately. The cot. Under the window. She turned to him, eyes questioning.

He smiled, a gentle look in his features she hadn't seen before. "I had them put it in while we were out. You take the bed, I'll take the cot."

An insane gratitude swelled through her chest.

She reached up, touched the rough stubble of his cheek with her fingertips. "You're a good man, Scott McIntyre." And she meant it.

As much as she'd tasted the raw lust in his kisses, as much as she knew he wanted her, he was giving her this space.

He wasn't trapping her. He wasn't using her. He wanted her to be free. Truly free. And the tenderness of it hurt so bad she felt wetness threaten her eyes.

His hand covered hers at his face. It was rough. Large. Protective. "Don't be deceived, Doctor." A quiet edge snaked through his words. "My intentions belie my actions."

A dark thrill quivered, slithered, to her belly. He was still letting her know he wanted her.

He was giving her the choice.

Eyes meshed with hers, he took her hand from his cheek, turned her palm face up, put his lips there.

She gasped softly.

His breath was hot, his lips firm against her skin. The sensation was painfully erotic. He tested, briefly, with his tongue. And her knees turned to putty.

He lifted the strands of her wig, whispered darkly in her ear, lips barely brushing her lobe. "I really do not have your best interests at heart, you know." He slipped his arm around her, gathered her close.

She could feel the hard bulge in his jeans press up against her thigh. His chest was solid under the swollen arousal of her breasts. Her heart staggered, her breathing became ragged. "Why don't you let me be the judge of what is in my best interests…when the time comes."

He stepped back, his voice dusky with desire. His eyes, dark and wild, looked down into hers. "When the time comes, then."

She angled her head slightly. "You make that sound like a threat, McIntyre."

"Think of it as a promise."

The shrill ring of the cell phone in her pocket knocked them both back to the present.

"Oh…I—" She rummaged in her jacket pocket, pulled out the phone, turned her back on Scott. "Skye Van Rijn."

"Skye, this is Martha Sheldon."

"Martha?" Why was Charly's mom calling? At this hour. "Is everything all right?" Skye yanked at her wig, tossed it onto the bed, waited for Martha to answer.

"It's…it's Charly." The woman's voice cracked.

Fresh panic clawed at Skye's stomach. "What's happened to Charly?"

"She's… Oh, God, she's in a coma, Skye. The doctors don't know what's going on. She developed pneumonia symptoms suddenly. They took her into hospital this morning. I just don't understand. She seemed fine yesterday."

"Where is she?"

"It's no use coming to see her. They're flying her to the mainland tomorrow morning. There are some specialists in Vancouver…" Martha's voice wobbled, trailed off.

"Oh, Martha, what can I do?"

"Nothing. I saw you left a message for her. I just wanted you to know. She would want you to know."

Skye clicked her phone off, sank down onto the bed. Her brain spun. She felt nauseous. She was vaguely aware of Scott watching her.

He locked the door and moved to sit beside her on the bed. "Who was that?" He nodded toward the cell phone still clutched tight in her hand.

"Charly…my colleague…my friend, she's very ill. She's been hospitalized. Doctors don't know what's wrong with her." Skye turned to look at him. "She was my maid of honor at my…wedding."

"Tell me what happened. What are her symptoms?" The bite of immediacy hardened his words.

"Her mother said it looked like sudden pneumonia. Now she's in a coma." Skye forced herself to her feet. "I must get to her."

"No." He grabbed her hand, pulled her firmly back onto the bed. "There's nothing you can do."

"Maybe there is. Maybe she just needs me there."

"She has family, right?"

Skye nodded.

"Let them take care of Charly. The bedside of your ailing friend is one of the first places these guys are going to go looking for you when they can't find you here."

"*If* they can't find me here."

"They won't." He grabbed her by the shoulders, forced her to look at him. "Trust me, Doctor. Believe in me, and they won't."

She didn't doubt it. Not at this moment. Not by the look in his eyes. Not by the dangerous undercurrent in his voice. And more than anything, she needed to trust someone right now, to turn to someone. Because her world was crumbling around her. And a sinister thread of thought was twisting through her brain: What if everything was connected? What if this was all just too big for her?

Chapter 10

Scott held Skye until she finally stopped shaking and fell asleep in his arms.

She'd said nothing as he cradled her.

He'd said nothing.

It was the most comforting silence in his life. He'd only stroked the incredible silk of her hair as she'd nestled into the crook between his shoulder and his neck. And despite the sinister turn of events, Scott felt ridiculously fulfilled in some basic way.

Honey was making little muffled snores at his feet. Scott's leg was stiff, sore. But he was loathe to move. He didn't want to disturb Skye now that she finally slept. He looked down at the smoothness of her face. He tentatively lifted a hand, ran the backs of his fingers softly along her exotic cheekbone, marveled at the way tension had seeped from her features in sleep.

In his arms she was like a vulnerable child who needed protection from the badness of the world. But that child lived in the sinfully sensual body of a strong and infinitely capable woman, one who sent his libido off the Richter scale.

He moved a strand of hair from her face and a strange and unfamiliar ache, warm and liquid, swelled through him, caught in a ball at his throat.

He tried to swallow it down. But it was a tide beyond his control. It crept right up into his eyes. He clenched his jaw, fought to bite it back. He was almost successful, apart from the small wet tear that escaped the corner of his eye. The ball in his throat hurt. He wouldn't let it out. Couldn't. Because it scared the hell out of him. What would happen if he released?

He edged Skye carefully over into the center of the bed, laid her down. She curled into a fetal ball as he covered her with a blanket. He turned, walked to the window. He clenched and unclenched his fists, stared out at the moonlit night, at the silhouettes of heavy brooding pines. By God, he hadn't had that feeling, that sweet painful ache, since he'd held his Leni and their precious, beautiful little Kaitlin.

All these years of hiding out in raw primal jungles and under the naked skies of deserts and it was back. All that running from his pain and it hadn't gone away. It had merely been buried. And now, this woman had unearthed it. She was right. When the numbness started to wear off, it hurt like hell.

He thudded his fist into the windowsill. *Damn her.*

He spun around to look at her. The light of the moon bathed her face, giving it the look of fragile porcelain. Her mouth was parted, breathing gently. As he watched, she muttered something in her sleep. Something foreign. He leaned forward, tried to catch a word.

She murmured again.

He frowned.

It sounded like Greek. He knew the language well. It was one of the many he was fluent in. He leaned even closer. But she said nothing more, just rolled over.

He turned back to the window. Skye dreaming in her native Dutch he could understand. But Greek? His mind went back to the sight of Skye, dressed like a Greek goddess for her wedding. And at dinner she'd tried to brush aside an obvious expertise in Greek mythology. But she said she'd never been to that part of the world. She'd been quick to deny it. Too quick. She'd been nervous. Why?

She held so many secrets. And like him, she seemed to be running from herself. He gave a soft snort at the irony of it. They shared a kinship, a strange pair of outlaws fleeing down the same road. But the very thing that bound them together—their deception—would ultimately tear them apart. They were on a collision course and both would do well to keep their hearts from becoming collateral damage.

Scott bit at the inside of his cheek. He needed to maintain emotional distance. And not just for his sake. He didn't want to hurt her. Whatever she'd done, whatever crime she'd committed, whoever was after her, he believed there was an innate goodness in this woman.

And there *was* someone after her. Someone other than the feds. He checked his watch. Almost four in the morning. He wanted to be gone within the hour. He wanted to leave under the cloak of darkness.

Dawn broke bright over the sea, stealing grays and silver, infusing the world with yellows and greens. Mist rose from the ribbon of tar as dew evaporated under the kiss of morning sun. And steam curled up from their coffee mugs, filling the interior of the car with warm scents of morning.

Skye bit into her cranberry bran muffin, listening halfheartedly to the chatter on the Island radio, meteorologists warning of a storm front that should hit by evening. Hard to believe it, looking at the cloudless blue of the morning sky.

She turned her attention from the weather to the man

driving at her side. He'd woken her before the break of dawn, bundled her and Honey into the SUV. She felt rested.

But he hadn't slept. She'd noticed the untouched covers of the camp cot in their motel room. And she could see the lack of rest in the depth of the lines around his eyes and the ones that bracketed his mouth. What, she wondered, had happened to his wife and child, his family?

She turned back to face the road, sipped her coffee, the warm steam of it moistening her face. They should be at Campbell River within the hour. Another three and they'd be in the wilds near Zeballos. In the middle of nowhere. Where would they all end up when this was over? Would he ever forgive her if he found out who she was?

"Tell me about Charly."

The words sliced into the comfortable silence. He hadn't spoken much in the past two hours since they'd left the motel.

"What do you want to know?"

"What does she do at the Kepplar lab?"

"She's my right hand…my friend."

"She works with you on your assassin bugs?"

"Yes. I was counting on Charly to convince Marshall to halt the beetle project until they could do more research."

His eyes darted to her. "They?"

"I mean 'we.'" She'd slipped up. She didn't want him to know she had no intention of returning to her life in Haven.

He studied her briefly. "You think he'll hold off?"

"No."

"Is that something that worries you?"

"Yes."

"But not enough to go back?"

Was he testing her? "I'll be no use dead," she said bluntly.

He nodded. It surprised her, his acceptance. She had a sense something in him had shifted. Since he'd seen those men in the restaurant. It was as though he was buying into her story.

"What's the worst-case scenario if they release your beetles as scheduled?"

She gave a dry laugh. "That's a tough one. That's why I need more time, to assess the possibilities."

"When you spoke with Marshall on the phone, you mentioned anomalies showing up. What are they?"

"When I checked into the lab, just before we left Haven, I noticed some very slight color differentiations in my core samples."

"Is that serious?"

"Maybe not. But you can't release something foreign into an ecosystem unless you're damn sure what you're dealing with. And, even if you are, there are still always unknown variables, still an element of risk."

"Like the introduction of new pathogens?"

"Yes. My beetles could become a vector for new disease. God, I hope Marshall does the right thing."

"Well, it's his company on the line. I'm sure he'll take that into account."

"I hope you're right, Scott. Because the whitefly epidemic has spread into the States and Marshall wants to be right there behind them. He's had the Canadian government contracts sewn up for several years, but now he's after the big fat carrot—the U.S. Department of Agriculture contracts. And he's in a race with his corporate competition to prove Kepplar can be the best and the fastest."

"So Marshall is ruled by greed over caution?"

"That's putting it mildly. He's so obsessed sometimes I think he'd create a blight just to win a contract to arrest it."

Scott's eyes flashed to hers. "He capable of doing that?"

Skye swallowed the last of her coffee, mulling over the notion. She'd never vocalized it before. Only entertained the idea in the periphery of her brain, almost as a joke.

But now, nothing seemed funny. Now things were deadly serious.

"Yes," she said softly. "I believe he is capable."

"They *lost* them?" He lurched to his feet.

"Only the visual. The tracking device is still working. They're on the move right now. Have been since early morning. The device shows they're headed south. Already nearing the outskirts of Victoria. And we have an ID on the man she's with. He reserved a table under the name Scott McIntyre. We'll have more on him within the hour."

Malik spun around, glared at the portrait. The silver eyes of the woman who was once his stared coolly back at him. And for the first time, worry dug at him. Operation Vector was designed to use her to destroy herself.

Had he been too arrogant, playing her this long? Would she now end up destroying him?

No! He smashed a fist onto his desk.

He'd invested too much in this. For the prephase of Operation Vector he'd paid disenfranchised Soviet scientists handsomely to do the bio work in his Anubis labs.

Then he'd inserted Jozsef, who'd dispersed mosquito eggs infected with Rift Valley fever when he crossed the border into Texas. Then Jozsef had delivered the mutated whitefly to Canada. Armed with this knowledge, his operatives had played the stock markets accordingly, helping to fund the entire project.

Next, details of Skye's travel plans had been carefully leaked to link her to the RVF outbreak. The whitefly links would be divulged later, once her beetles were released.

As expected, the Kepplar labs had picked up the government contract for the whitefly plague. If Kepplar hadn't, Malik would have gone to one of his backup plans.

But it had worked. And that meant sublime justice. Jozsef had interfered with her beetle project, inserted the genetic variants, and now the Canadian government itself was set to unleash a scourge such as North America had never before seen.

The beetles would become a vector for a deadly plague. People would die by the thousands.

And Skye would be blamed. Posthumously, if necessary.

Because the next step would be to release proof of her identity fraud, captured from Jalil's office, along with evidence of her terrorist background. A smile tugged at the corners of Malik's mouth. She even bore his mark on her hip. The world would think she had served him until the very last. A sleeper, activated to unleash a scourge Anubis would take credit for. Thanks to her, fear and terror would shatter the economic monster of the United States. He ran his tongue over his teeth.

The tracking device would lead his men to her.

He'd still triumph.

There was no sign of their tail in his rearview mirror as they drove into Campbell River. Scott breathed a sigh of relief. "Looks like we lost them."

"Thank God. That means we have a clear run to Zeballos, right?"

Scott nodded. "But there's no real town between here and there, apart from Woss. We should stop for supplies. Tell me about the cabin, what's it equipped with?"

"Not much. It's real basic, really. It belongs to Mike Henderson. He's the owner of the general store in Haven. He was to give me away at my nonexistent wedding." She paused. "He's been like a father figure to me. He brought a group of us out this way a couple of years ago, said I could use the cabin anytime."

"Why does he have a cabin out in such a remote area?"

"That's exactly it, remote."

Scott pulled into the parking lot of a mall that boasted a supermarket and a large camping goods store. "I take it any water we might need up there comes from a river?"

"Yes, it's pretty primitive."

"I'll get some water purifiers."

"No need, the water's fresh from heaven."

Scott frowned, motioned with his head toward the car radio. "You heard the forecast. Major storm brewing."

Skye made a face. "Looks clear as glass to me."

"The weather in these parts has a way of sneaking up on you. The kind of precipitation they're predicting could muddy up a river real good. The cabin got a woodstove?"

"Yes."

"Ax and stuff like that?"

"I don't remember."

Scott nodded, mentally checking off equipment he thought they'd need for a stay in the wild. As for how long they'd be there, that was anyone's guess. They'd best be prepared. He opened his wallet, pulled out a wad of cash, handed it to Skye. "Here. Can you handle the grocery supplies?"

"Oh, no." She held up her hands. "I'm not taking that. I don't want your money, McIntyre."

"Just take it."

She shook her head "No way. You've done enough for me. I can handle this."

"Skye—"

She reached for the door handle, swung open the passenger door, slipping out of the car before he could finish his sentence.

"Oh," she said, ducking her head back into the vehicle. "What kind of food you want for Honey?"

He couldn't help but smile as he once again watched her neat rump, her long, sleek legs carrying her determinedly through the parking lot.

"She may be a criminal badass, Honey, but I have to hand it to her, she's got something." He chucked the dog under the chin. "And she's real pretty," he added softly.

* * *

Scott loaded the new gear into the back of the Land Rover, slammed the door shut, made his way around to the driver's side. That's when it caught his eye. The sign. It hung above a small store at the far end of the mall. It drew him, more out of curiosity than anything else. "C'mon, Honey. Let's go take a look."

The golden retriever at his side, Scott hobbled across the parking lot. He stopped outside the store window, looked up at the sign that hung over the door. It was made of wood, old and out of place in this newish mall. It displayed a fish—a trout—leaping for a fly that flicked at the end of a long loop of line.

"Sit, Honey. I won't be long." Scott pushed open the door. The jingle of a little bell announced his presence and he blinked into the gloom.

It was as if he'd stepped back in time.

Even the white-haired man tying flies behind the counter at the rear of the store looked as though he hailed from another era.

The whole scene, right down to the smell of the place, reminded Scott vividly of being a young boy growing up in British Columbia. Of going camping with his dad, stopping off in small rural towns to buy bait and fishing tackle.

The man behind the counter looked up. "Good day, sir. What can I do for you?"

Out of the corner of his eye, Scott could see Honey smearing up the store window with her hot breath and cold snout, her tail whapping to and fro.

The man behind the counter looked at him expectantly. But Scott had lost his tongue. For one brief instant he was eleven again, and his black lab Merlin scratched at the window. His dad stood by his side, talking about tying flies and whether the salmon were running.

Scott swallowed, momentarily shaken.

Then he cleared his throat, stepped forward. "Sorry…about the window."

The man shrugged. ''No problem. I got one of 'em at home. A black lab. Hasn't been able to sit still for the last sixteen years. I've given up hope.'' His smile was broad and genuine, the twinkle in his eyes real. But to Scott, the man was a ghost from the past. A ghost with a black lab.

He fingered the wood of his cane, straining for a sense of present, reminding himself he was all of thirty-nine years old, a battered agent who hadn't cast a fly line for almost a decade.

''So what can I do for you?''

Scott looked down at the fly pinched in the vise on the old man's counter. It was the hackle that caught his eye, made from the ringneck saddle feathers of a pheasant. ''That a Carey Special?'' he asked the old man.

The man raised thick white brows above pale eyes. ''Not many people would recognize that first off. You a keen fly-fisher, then?''

''Haven't cast a line in a while.''

''Well, you still seem to know a thing or two.'' He released the fly from the vise, holding it up for Scott to see. ''My version of the Carey Special. They're what's happening up at Sweetwater Lake about now. Trout are going wild for 'em. I'm going to give this baby a shot this evening. You should come along.''

''I—''

The door bell jingled. Scott swiveled. Skye stood silhouetted against the bright light of the morning.

Again Scott blinked.

''So this is where you two are,'' she said, coming up to join him at the counter. ''Can you bring the car around the other end of the mall so I can load the ton of groceries I just bought?''

The old man chuckled, winked at Scott. ''Missus is callin'.''

''She's not my—'' He bit back his words. The man had shaken him. He didn't have to justify himself, his relationship with Skye to anyone. He straightened his spine and pulled the frayed edges of his memories into check. But he couldn't quite seem to stuff them all back into the box.

Then he felt her cool hand on his arm. "You okay, Scott? You look like you've just seen a ghost."

"It's nothing." He pulled out from under her touch, handed her the keys. "Here, you take the car 'round. I'll be right out."

She studied him with her pewter eyes, reading something. "Sure," she said gently. "Take your time."

He waited for the tinkle of the bell as the door swung shut behind her, then turned his attention back to the storekeeper. "I'll take a couple of those Careys. And one of those rods and line and one of these reels." He pointed them out as he spoke.

"Starter kit?"

"More of a restarter kit, I guess."

The man took a rod from the rack. "So what kept you from the fishing for so long?"

Scott hesitated. How could he tell the old man that shunning the sport that had been so much a part of his youth, part of his dad, part of Leni, the sport that had once given them all so much pleasure, was just a lame attempt at burying the past? "I've been busy. Working."

"Well, this should set you right." He rang up Scott's purchase. "It's always good to see someone get back to old pleasures."

"Thanks." Scott signed the slip, then tucked his card back into his wallet. "Nice place you got here. It looks old school. Doesn't quite fit with the shiny-new-mall image."

The man gave a wry smile. "I used to be down by the water. Then they redeveloped the strip and the high rents squeezed old-timers like myself out." He gestured around the store with a wrinkled hand. "This is my love, but I don't turn over enough stock to pay the big bucks they were demanding. Had to move out here."

"Well, you've brought the old world to the new. You've done a good job."

The old man was quiet for a second. Scott felt as though his eyes were seeing straight into him, right through his alias to the naked boy inside. It was unnerving. Then the man spoke. "You've got to try to take the past with you into the future, you know. That's my philosophy. You stay true to yourself that way." He handed Scott his purchases. "You get lost otherwise. Can take a long time to find that road back home."

Scott stepped out of the store, blinked into the bright sun. He felt a little nauseous. He'd been right. This was turning into a trip down memory lane. He'd known it would be the minute Skye had blurted out the word "Zeballos."

She was physically forcing him down that old road and mentally beyond the memory of his wife. She was making him face himself.

His hand tightened on the bags that held his purchases. He gritted his teeth, limped toward the car.

Fishing gear and food supplies safely loaded into the car, the threesome headed north out of Campbell River as the sun rose in the sky and the warm spring day invited open windows.

Scott hadn't said a word since they'd left the fly-fishing store. Skye figured something back there, in that dim shop, had rattled him. It made her even more curious about him. Because Scott McIntyre struck her as a man not easily shaken by much in life. And the scientist in her couldn't let a curiosity pass without poking at it, without hypothesizing.

She finally let her interest get the better of her. "So what was that about?"

"What?"

"Back there in that store. You looked like you'd seen a ghost."

He said nothing. Just stared ahead at the road. She watched the small muscle at the base of his jaw pulse.

"Sorry. Didn't mean to pry." She should have known better. He'd thrown up new walls since he'd mentioned his wife and child.

He shot her a quick glance. "No. It's okay. That old-timer, he just took me on an unexpected trip down memory lane. That's all."

"Not a happy trip?"

"Made me think of my dad."

"Is he deceased?"

"Lord, no. I just haven't seen my parents for a while. Lost contact."

She smiled. "It's guilt that's eating you, then, McIntyre."

He clenched his teeth, said nothing. She realized she'd angered him.

He turned suddenly on her, his words brusque. "What about you? What about your parents, Skye?"

"I—I don't have any parents." It was close enough to the truth. "They died when I was really young."

"Where?"

Dammit, she didn't want to go there. He'd turned the tables on her. She should have anticipated it, kept her mouth shut. She hesitated. "In Amsterdam. I'm from Holland. I immigrated to Canada when I was twenty-two."

He nodded. "That would explain that hint of an accent you have. I was wondering what it was. You still speak Dutch?"

"I don't have an accent," she snapped. She'd worked hard on erasing it, assimilating.

He raised his brows, said nothing. She felt suddenly wary again.

"Well, do you? Can you still speak Dutch?"

"Of course I can." Dutch was only one of the five languages she was fluent in. Her education at the camp had prepared her for deployment into several countries.

"You speak any other languages?"

"No."

He raised a brow. "I thought most Dutch kids learned several languages at school."

She hesitated. "Well, I—I have a smattering here and there."

"Is Greek one of them?"

Her heart tripped, thumped rapidly against her chest. Her mouth went dry.

Why is he doing this?

Chapter 11

"No," she said as flippantly as she could. "I don't speak Greek."

"You were speaking in your sleep last night. Sounded like Greek."

The blood drained from her head. She turned quickly away so he wouldn't catch her reaction. And she cursed herself. She was slipping. It must be the tension of the last few days getting her. Or the man.

She took a deep breath, swiveled in her seat, faced him square. "You were mistaken. I don't speak Greek. Maybe what you heard was Italian. I speak a little Italian," she offered.

"Sounded Greek."

"What makes you so damned sure of yourself?" she snapped.

His eyes pierced hers. "No need to get snippy, Doctor. I speak Greek myself. I know what it sounds like."

Damn. She'd just dug herself a hole. Tension seeped into her stomach. Neither spoke again until they reached the small town of Woss, the last stop on their road into the wilderness.

But the issue hung heavy and unresolved in the air between them.

"This is where we get more gas. I'd better check oil and tires, as well." Scott pulled into a gas station. "Could you give Honey a run while I see to the vehicle? I bought her a ball at the mall, it's in the back."

"Sure." Skye felt as though she needed a run herself. But it was a knee-jerk reaction. She knew that. Every time it looked as if her secret world was closing in on itself, she ran. She'd promised herself in Chemainus that would stop. That she would trust Scott. But the closer he came to her core, the greater her urge to flee. And to stay.

God, she was a mess.

She took the dog and the ball, made for the small park across the street.

Scott filled the car, checked oil and tires, paid for his purchases, then pulled into a parking lot alongside the pumps. He could see Skye and Honey playing ball in the distance. He activated the code on his sat phone, quickly punched in Rex's number. He didn't have much time before she'd be back.

The Bellona boss was waiting for his call. Rex picked up on the first ring. Scott cut to the chase. "You meet with our RCMP guy?"

"Yeah. Your tail, it's not them. Feds lost you in Haven."

Scott grunted. "Thought as much. Then who the hell is after her?"

"You get a plate?"

Scott gave him the number of the dark green Dodge.

"I'll check into it." There was a new undertone in Rex Logan's voice.

Scott didn't like it. "So what *is* the deal with the RCMP? What do they want from Skye?"

His boss hesitated. ''Agent, this is blowing right open. You need to bring the doctor in.''

Something cold dropped through Scott's gut. ''Whoa, wait just a minute. Why don't you fill me in, let me make that decision.''

Rex cleared his throat but his tone remained crisp. ''Jozsef Danko is not Jozsef Danko.''

''What?''

''Our liaison said the RCMP were investigating him for a money-laundering deal connected with an organized crime syndicate out of Quebec. But the RCMP detectives ran into a bit of a turf issue in Quebec because Canada's Security Intelligence Service was already investigating the syndicate for having possible financial ties to a terrorist organization.''

''Anubis?''

''You got it. It turns out one of the men CSIS has been watching for in connection with this syndicate is—''

''Danko.''

''That's his cover. His real name is Balto Nakiskas. He's a Greek national. And he's a known Anubis operative.''

Scott's stomach tightened. ''Skye's fiancé was a known terrorist?''

''You've got to bring the doctor in, Scott. She's wanted for questioning by just about every agency you can imagine now. RCMP, CSIS and FBI just for starters. *Especially* after they learned of the Bellona angle.''

Scott's mouth went as dry as the Thar desert. He glanced up, saw Skye in the park across the street. He watched her throw the ball for Honey. She moved with the tensile strength, fluidity and grace of a dancer…or a martial arts expert.

She sensed him watching. She stopped, looked up, waved. He waved back, a sick, slow dread crawling low through his gut. She smiled and with a flick of her long hair, picked up the ball, threw it for Honey. The retriever bounded after it in innocent glee.

Scott's brain reeled. A Greek Anubis operative marrying Skye. Her Anubis tattoo. The insects. Her travels.

"Agent, you there?"

"Yeah, I'm here."

"We need you to bring Dr. Van Rijn in ASAP."

He stalled. "*How* do they think she's connected?"

"They believe she's working with Nakiskas."

No. Scott rubbed his brow viciously. *No.* He could *not* believe Skye knew Jozsef was a fake. No way. Her pain had been too honest, too real.

He thought of her Greek mumblings in her sleep.

Or had it?

"They find anything in her house to prove it?" He barked the question.

"No. But they did seize her computer. Turns out it's been accessed remotely for some time. Her system was linked to the Kepplar lab system. There's been an information security breach there, as well."

"So they think she's been feeding Kepplar technology to someone?"

"Maybe. Or it could be a hacker. I've got Scooter working on it. He's following a highly sophisticated electronic trail. The electronic footprints are leading him around the world, being routed and rerouted again. And whoever has had access to her computer has been hitting your McIntyre alias Web site."

"How do you know?"

"Same footprints."

Skye and Honey were leaving the park, starting to cross the street. Scott's fingers curled tight around his sat phone. He felt sick to his stomach. Had she been scamming him all along? Was this wedding thing some kind of elaborate setup? And if it wasn't the cops or CSIS or the FBI tailing them in Duncan…who in hell was it?

And why?

It just wasn't adding up.

And he sure as hell wasn't ready to hand her over. Yet.

"You bringing her in, Agent?"

He cleared his throat. "No."

"Pardon?"

"I said no. Buy me some time. Tell them anything. I can get more out of her this way." He wanted her to tell him herself. He wanted to hear the story from her lips. Because he couldn't believe she was a coldhearted liar. A liar, yes, but coldhearted, no. There had to be some reason, some explanation, something they weren't seeing. Because his deep-down, primal gut instinct told him this woman was too kind, too inherently good.

He trusted his instincts.

Whatever Skye had gotten herself into, it wasn't this. But he couldn't deny the stakes had just been raised.

High.

Real high.

"Agent—"

"I'm getting close to her, Logan. You've got to trust me on this one."

"*How* close, Armstrong?"

Scott read the loaded meaning in Rex Logan's words. "Logan, trust me. I've never let you down before."

"Let's keep it that way." He sounded unsure. "I'll see what I can do. I might be able to buy you a day or so. No more."

"Thanks." He hung up. He knew Rex was going out on a limb here. And, so was he.

Was he throwing away a last shot at getting his old life back? Maybe he *had* fried his brain in the desert sands.

Scott slowly slid his phone into his pocket, watched Skye cross the street, her hand hooked into Honey's collar. She looked as supple and strong as a tall willow branch. Sunshine deflected off the dark gloss of her hair, revealing deep burgundy glints.

He rubbed his aching knee, the knee Anubis rebels had blown out. Could he be wrong about her? Could she be allied, however remotely, to his nemesis, La Sombra?

She came close enough for him to see the bright light of innocent exhilaration in her eyes, the blush of exercise on her cheeks.

Adrenaline, anger and something utterly foreign, spiked in his system, clashed. The cocktail exploded violently in his veins.

He flung open the SUV door, stepped out, swallowed the bolt of pain in his knee, took two strides toward her.

She looked up into his eyes, froze.

He grabbed her shoulders, pulled her aggressively to him. Her lips parted in shock.

He closed his mouth down hard over hers, thrust his tongue between her lips, ran it across the smooth ridge of her teeth, met the slick warmth of her tongue.

She tasted sinfully sweet. Wild. And so female. So alive.

Hot liquid lust spurted through his belly, boiled with anger. Anger at Anubis. At her. For making him feel. At Bellona…the whole bloody world.

He furiously deepened his kiss.

She didn't resist.

He slid his hand down to the small of her back, grasped the firm globe of her behind, yanked her closer, forcing her breasts hard up against his chest, her pelvis up against his groin.

She melted smoothly into him, met his urgency with her mouth. Her own appetite for him drove him near wild.

He *needed* her to be innocent, goddammit.

Because otherwise he had to destroy her. He had to take her down to make his life whole again.

He felt her smooth hand against his cheek, guiding his kiss. His heart pounded hard up against the full, feminine warmth of her breasts. He drank in the scent of her hair, felt the silk of it against his face.

He pulled her pelvis up higher against his thigh. If he didn't stop now—

He jerked back.

Shock, untamed passion, swam through her exotic features. She stared up at him, unfocused eyes as wild and lucid as a silver dawn sky, lips plumped, pink, from the rough force of his kiss.

He held her at arm's length, a hand planted solid on each shoulder, just looked at her. "God, you're beautiful."

"Scott?" Confusion furrowed her brow.

"Come." He slid his arm around her shoulders, ushered her to the car. "Let's get you out of harm's way."

He fired the ignition, set course for the hills.

And he told himself whatever she was hiding, he'd find it. Because now this was personal.

And if she was an innocent victim, a pawn caught in deadly international crossfire, he needed to protect her.

With his life.

And if she was playing him as a pawn, he had to be prepared to take her life.

Before she took his.

Skye moistened her lips. She felt as though a million microscopic bees were buzzing confusedly through her system. A swarm dislodged from a safe hive by a searing hot jab clean through to her core.

It was cousin to panic, but not quite.

Jittery. She felt jittery. But not quite.

She sucked air deep into her lungs, blew it out slowly. She didn't even want to compute how she felt. The volcanic potency of his kiss had left her plain shell-shocked. It had been so proprietary, so male, so dominant…so sudden. It had exploded from somewhere down deep within him like an ancient long-buried force that could no longer be held in check under a shifting surface.

The sheer power of it awed her.

Because it had totally undone her in the most elemental way. She knew if ever confronted with that power again, she would be utterly defenseless in the face of it.

She stole a glance at the man beside her.

What had happened?

What had changed in him?

He seemed imbued with an electric power, determination. It literally vibrated around him. She could feel the crackling silent force of it against the surface of her skin.

Yet his limbs were relaxed, his movements calm, incredibly controlled as he steered their vehicle higher and higher into the mountains, into the wild.

He sensed her looking, flashed his eyes toward her.

Her breath caught. She could not only feel it, she could see it. In those bottle-green eyes, a fierce intensity crackled like sparking flame.

And it ignited the cocktail of panic and sharp, heady anticipation already simmering in her core.

Again she tried to moisten her lips. Her mouth was dry.

She'd felt something like this once before.

In the training camp.

The first time she'd had to leap from the open door of a plane.

Her greatest fear had been that her chute would fail her.

But the parachute had always opened. And the experience had always been beyond words.

But she'd had to make that first jump. She'd had to trust that chute to open.

Skye forced her attention back to the map on her lap.

They were nearing the turnoff to Henderson's place. It was easy to miss. It had no signage. It was just an old, deactivated logging road that would take them the last couple of miles to the isolated cabin.

But as they climbed higher into the mountains, thick dank mist rolled down to engulf them. The drizzle that had started an hour ago turned to hard, spitting sleet.

Skye peered through the windshield, seeking a familiar landmark. But up ahead, the air was even darker, the clouds lower, swollen and puce with their burden. It was impossible to identify anything.

The temperature dropped steadily as they gained elevation. She shivered involuntarily.

"How are we doing?" Scott motioned with his jaw to the map in her hands.

"The road should be just ahead now."

A sharp crack split the air.

Honey and Skye convulsed in unison.

Thunder rumbled around them. The dog whimpered slightly in the back seat.

"I love a good storm. Makes me feel alive." His voice growled low like the thunder. "What about you, Doctor? You like a good storm?"

"I...I've gotten used to the tameness of the weather around Haven."

"Monotonous, predictable."

"Maybe. But safe."

A bolt of light slashed through the blackness ahead of them. Clouds clashed. Snarled. Skye's heart hit like a jackhammer against her rib cage. She rubbed damp palms on her jeans. With every mile into the wilderness, she felt even edgier.

He threw her a look, challenged with his eyes. "Is that what you want, Doctor? Safe?"

"Yeah. Right now I want safe."

The expression on his face changed slightly. "You really do believe these people want to kill you."

It wasn't a question this time.

"I do."

"What makes you think you'll be safe at the cabin?"

"You." She tried to smile. Thunder clapped. Light split the sky.

His face remained dark. Feral. Eyes alive with the energy of the storm. He flicked them at her. And suddenly she wasn't so sure.

"And after the cabin?"

She hadn't managed to think that far. The idea was to come up with a plan while she laid low. "I—I don't know," she whispered.

The hardness lifted slightly from his features. "Skye, you *have* to talk to me. If you want me to help you, you'll have to tell me *exactly* what's going on."

"I—"

Scott slammed on the brakes.

Tires shrieked.

Skye gasped, lurched forward, snapped back against the restraint of her seat belt. The SUV skidded sideways over the slick mountain road. Scott yanked the wheel, fought back.

The Land Rover fishtailed, veered to the edge of the cliff. Nothing below but a sheer drop. Skye held her breath, scrunched her eyes shut. The world spun in sickening gray and screaming tires.

Scott steered deftly into the skid, hit the brakes again, came to a halt—just inches from the edge.

He cut the engine.

The silence inside the car was suddenly deafening.

Just the clack of sleet on their hull, the thud of hearts in chests.

They stared.

It stood in front of them in the middle of the road. A gray wolf. It didn't move. For an instant, Skye thought she was seeing a vision held captive by swirling fingers of cold mist.

Its eyes gleamed yellow. It glared back at them. But in

spite of the ferocity in its stare, it was thin. Frail. Its fur patchy. It favored its hind leg.

It looked so very sad. Alone. Defiant.

Scott wiped his forehead with the back of his hand. It shook slightly.

"It's a wolf," Skye whispered. Behind her a low growl came from deep in Honey's throat. The retriever's eyes were locked with those of the wolf.

"It looks sick." She kept her voice to a whisper.

"He's old. A male."

"He looks so wild."

Scott's voice was rough. "He *is* the wild. The wolf is a symbol, a lone voice of the wilderness." He spoke with such sudden intensity, his eyes locked with those of the spectral apparition on the road in front of them.

"He looks lost," she whispered.

"He was probably the alpha male of his group. But his time has come. Look at his patchy pelt. And he's been injured. He's been kicked out of his pack, the only society he knows. He's been left to fend for himself. Alone. Left to die." Something caught in the gravel of his voice.

"Won't they take him back?"

"No. It's the way of nature."

Skye turned to look at the man. His jaw was clenched, his knuckles white on the wheel of the SUV.

"Maybe the wolf will heal, Scott. Maybe he'll find his way back."

"No. Those who were his allies will turn on him. There's no room in the wild for a broken warrior."

She studied his face. Not once since she had met Scott McIntyre had she seen this kind of emotion etched into his features. Not once had she noticed such tension in his hands. "You...you sound like you know him, Scott."

Her words snapped something in him, hauled him back from wherever it was he'd gone in his mind. He shut down. Instantly.

And the wolf was gone.

As suddenly as he'd appeared out of the gray mists, he vanished. Like a ghost into the storm. Skye blinked, wondering if she'd seen him at all, imagined the whole thing.

Scott reached into the back seat to calm Honey, who was still quivering. "It's okay, girl. Just a distant cousin of yours. One without your domestic sensibilities."

He started the ignition, shifted gears. Both mentally and physically.

But Skye had glimpsed something. For that brief instant, he'd left himself exposed. And she'd seen pain. The same simmering ancient pain reflected in the eyes of the wolf. This hard, weather-beaten man with bewitching green eyes had more than an injured leg. His soul, his spirit, had been somehow damaged. Like the wolf. He, too, had lost his family, perhaps the only real family he'd ever known. And it touched her, more deeply than it should. It made her want to reach out, to touch him. To help him like he was helping her.

But she held back.

Sympathy would only shut him down further.

They drove on in silence, rain coming down in an icy sheet. The road grew more slick. Small rivers formed, gushed along the shoulders of the narrow mountain highway. Trees swayed dangerously in the mounting wind.

But inside their silver cocoon they were dry. It was as though the three of them were bound together on some quest, being buffeted by wild, external elements. A tiny ship on stormy seas. And as they traveled further into the wilderness, they put more and more distance between themselves and the world they were leaving behind.

But they were also traveling inward. Getting closer to each other's secrets. It was a journey that held its own kind of danger.

But there was no turning back now.

"There." She pointed at a gap in the trees, barely visible through the mist. "That's the logging road."

Scott swerved from tar onto muddy dirt track. Rivers of rain chortled down through the ruts. Trees closed them in like a tunnel. Scott switched to four-wheel drive. The going became slow as they negotiated small boulders, branches cast off by the wind. Skye was thankful for the powerful vehicle. And she was grateful to have Scott and Honey at her side. Their company made her feel stronger. It would've been the pits doing this on a bike.

Alone.

She couldn't move. She was dying.

She just didn't know why, didn't understand what was happening. She'd been so happy. She'd left the restaurant in Chemainus to go to her sister's house in Victoria, to give her the little gold beetle that beautiful blond woman insisted she have.

Then the big dark green truck had forced her off the road. Two men had pulled her out of her car. They'd spoken a language she didn't know. But then they'd asked for the gold beetle in English.

She'd given it to them, told them they could have her money, anything, if they'd just let her go. Let her live.

They'd started to hurt her when she couldn't answer questions about the blond woman and the man she'd served at the restaurant.

They'd hurt her bad. Rain dribbled into her eyes.

She couldn't move her broken limbs.

Her breath wheezed out in bubbles. Mud from the ditch seeped into her mouth, down her throat. She had no energy to cough it out. She could see only the gray shapes of the men through her haze of pain. They loomed over her. So big. Fighting about something.

Then they were quiet, a decision reached.

A boot came down on her skull, forced her farther into

the mud, under the ditch water. She squeezed her eyes shut, gagged.

She couldn't die now.

Her family was waiting for her.

With one last burst of effort, she struggled, flailed, against the boot. No use. Her lungs screamed for air. She gasped. One final, desperate, involuntary cry for oxygen. But she took in only mud, grit, water...and knew she'd never take another breath.

Chapter 12

Scott wasn't sure the bridge was safe. It was too dark to see, headlights slicing only a narrow tunnel through the black fury of the storm. He brought the vehicle to a stop, left the lights on, flipped up his collar and stepped out into the driving sheet of rain.

He leaned into the wind, squinted eyes as ice water pummeled his face. He made his way to the river's edge.

Water roared in white froth from a gorge up at his left, plunged down to the narrow wooden bridge. But a logjam had snagged under the structure, forcing water to back up, pressure to build.

Like a bomb ready to blow.

It could be seconds before the bridge gave way.

He yanked his collar higher up around his neck, trudged through the mud back to the SUV, ducked his head in. "Any other way out if that thing blows?" he yelled above the thunder of the river, the roar of the wind in the trees.

"Yeah," she yelled back. "There's another old logging road on the far side of the cabin. It heads further north into the forest but leads out eventually. It'd take a full day or so to get out that way."

Scott climbed into the driver's seat, slammed the door against the weather, shook rain from his sleeves. "Right. At least there's a way out if this baby goes. We'll make a run for it. Ready?"

"As I'll ever be."

Scott shifted gears, drove smoothly through the drag of mud toward the wooden structure.

Water now ran in a glistening black sheet over the surface of the bridge. Scott kept the momentum, felt tires hit slick wood, slip, then bite. He held the pace steady, fought the tug of the current. His wheels hit land on the other side. He accelerated slightly, pulled them up onto the safety of the track.

They made it by seconds.

Behind them a crack and snap of wood was followed by a boom that drowned the sound of the storm.

Scott said nothing, just slowly exhaled. He stopped the car, turned to Skye. "Pass me that flashlight in the glove compartment."

He took it from her, stepped once again out into the driving rain, made his way back to the bridge.

Where it had spanned the river seconds ago there was only a gaping maw with splintered teeth. He shone the flashlight into the boiling river. There was no way they were going to get back that way. He turned, made his way back to the car.

"Well, guys," he said as he slammed his door shut. "We can relax. No one's going to follow us in here. We're well and truly cut off."

He clenched his teeth. Bloody bitch hadn't lost her edge. She'd found the device Nakiskas had placed around her neck, thrown them off her trail by giving it to a waitress.

And this McIntyre...he didn't exist beyond a Web site

and some expertly scattered cyber crap. She was with a professional. And that gnawed at him.

Her last e-mail to Jalil had said something about needing a break from things. Maybe Nakiskas would know where she might go "to think."

He turned to his assistant, his voice deathly calm, belying the madness that swam inside him.

"Fetch Nakiskas," he commanded.

"He's in the sick bay, sir. Doctor thinks he's contracted some kind of pneumonia."

"I don't give a damn how he feels. Get him. *Now.*"

Skye dumped the sleeping bags on the one and only bed. It was big, made of raw pine, covered with a homemade quilt in happy yellows, greens and blues.

The homeyness of it caught her by the throat. It seemed so out of context, so far removed from her plight.

She shook the rain from her hair, wiped water from her face, glanced around the cabin. It seemed smaller than she remembered. Maybe that had something to do with the amount of space Scott McIntyre seemed to swallow with his powerful masculine presence.

He was bent over, feeding logs into the blackened woodstove, coaxing flames to life. Through his rain-dampened shirt his muscles rippled like those of a honed wild animal.

He sensed her scrutiny, turned his head, looked over his shoulder at her.

She swallowed at the sudden dark intimacy in his eyes. And she felt trapped. In this tiny, rustic log structure in the middle of the wilderness, there was no way she could escape the power that thrummed from him, that crackled hot and furious from his green gaze.

There was no way she could run from herself, even.

No way she could deny the elemental desire boiling in her core.

He pushed himself to his feet.

Her heart stuttered.

The room shrank even more around him. His mouth was pulled into a tight line. His eyes tunneled into hers. Her stomach tightened.

He was angry.

Or was he?

She couldn't interpret the emotion etched into the rough sun-weathered planes of his exquisite features.

He inhaled deeply.

She was insanely aware of how the movement made his pecs expand under wet fabric, of how the sculpted muscles of his stomach moved as he took a step toward her.

Her breath hitched in her throat.

She was fully clothed in jeans, T-shirt and rain-sodden jacket. Yet she felt totally naked under his scrutiny, stripped of any form of self-protecting barrier.

She had nowhere to run. Didn't even want to run.

They stood like that, two strangers facing each other, in silence, energy palpable between them. They were clothed yet suddenly bare, suspended from reality in a little haven in the dark woods, a cabin warm with crackling flames in a black woodstove, a homemade quilt on a rustic bed and a rain-dampened dog snoring on a rag rug in front of the fire.

Intimate strangers, she thought.

But suddenly it didn't matter. She felt safe. Here. With him. With rain thrumming on the roof, wind and branches scratching at the windows, the world raging outside. But she was inside, in an oasis of glowing warmth. Hidden from her old world. From Malik and the men who ruled it. She felt as if here she could suspend it all, exist in another sphere.

They'd crossed that bridge to get here and there was no going back.

She stepped closer to him, reached up, felt the rough

stubble on his cheek. His hand snapped to hers, grabbed it. Green fire sparked in his eyes.

She sucked air in sharply. His raw power unnerved her slightly. But it also turned her on.

He tightened his grip on her wrist, jerked her into him. His eyes lanced hers, as if searching for something.

"Scott?" Her voice came out breathy.

He placed a hand over her neck. She had no doubt he could crush the life from her with the latent strength in his fingers. She was at his mercy. The concept was oddly exhilarating. Her stomach flipped, spilling heat through her belly.

He slid his hand up to her chin, lifted her jaw, forced her to look up into the darkening pools of his eyes. She could feel the heightened beat of his heart against her breasts.

"You're angry," she said softly.

"With you," he confirmed. "For making me feel this way." His grip tightened on her jaw. He still held her wrist in a cufflike grasp.

Energy zinged through her blood. She wanted him. Like nothing she'd wanted before. She wanted to open herself to his hard power, to take it in. Draw on it. Feel it pump into her. Become one with it. It made her dizzy. Her breathing became light, irregular.

Her blatant desire only fueled his. She could see it in the shifting shape of his mouth.

"What way?" she asked softly. "What way do I make you feel?"

He ran his hand roughly down her neck, slipped it under the collar of her jacket, slid the jacket down her shoulders. "Don't tell me you can't see it in my eyes, Doctor." His voice was gravel under a turbulent stream. It rolled through her brain, gushed through her core.

She swallowed, lifted her free hand, hesitantly touched his sculpted lips. His lids dipped low.

"Yes, McIntyre. I can see." She explored the firmness

of his lips with her fingertips, increasing the pressure of her touch. "You want to make love to me." Her voice caught on her breath. Her eyes slid up from his mouth, met his. "And I want you to. I want you to lay me down on that bed, open my thighs..."

Her jacket dropped to the floor.

She held his eyes, reached for the hem of her T-shirt, slipped it slowly up over her breasts, over her head, dropped it to the ground.

His eyes moved indolently over her naked torso. His tongue moistened his lips.

Skye fought the weakness in her knees, stood in her jeans, bare-breasted, defying him with her eyes to touch.

She watched his Adam's apple move as he swallowed deeply. She watched as arousal shaped his features into something hard and primal.

She couldn't breathe.

She was acutely aware of her nipples tightening hard under his raw scrutiny.

He moved suddenly, cupped her breast with a rough, calloused hand, found the nub of her nipple, rasped it with the pad of his thumb.

Her world swayed. A shaft of heat snapped clear through from her breast to her groin, spurted liquid warmth through the base of her belly. She pulsed hot and swollen between her legs

He coaxed her nipple to a painful peak. "And...what then, Skye?"

She could barely find her voice. "And...and then, Scott, I want you to touch me, low down. I want you to feel my heat." She leaned into his caress, pressed her breast into his hand.

He moaned, low like the wind.

"I want to feel the hard length of you. I want you inside...I...want..." She slid her hands down over her own naked belly as the words came breathily from her lips.

He followed the movement with hungry eyes.

She found the button of her jeans, undid it, slid the zipper down.

His nostrils flared. He moistened his lips, swallowed hard, all vestiges of civility wiped from his features.

She slipped her hand into her pants, held his eyes, taunted. "Is that what you want, Scott?" she whispered.

His jaw hardened.

He grabbed her shoulder, forced her back onto the bed. He brusquely lowered her jeans over her hips, paused at the sight of her delicate panties.

He ran his hands gently over the white lace. She could feel the heat of his fingers through the sheer fabric.

Then he yanked them off.

She gasped at the swift ferocity of the movement.

He had her now, sprawled out and utterly naked on the comforter. She stared up into the feral set of his features, made all the more primal by the flickering flame light. Her heart tripped in a shallow staccato beat, the fire of desire burning hot and wet between her legs as she watched him remove his clothes.

She swallowed at the sight of him. He was born to be naked. Like an animal. His garments had only served to temper the raw primal power of this man.

With a grunt he straddled her. Her vision swam.

Like a silent beast he held her there, pinned down between massive thighs, brazenly studying her in the flickering gold light, the wind moaning outside, pulling at loose boards, drowning into the sound of the river raging over rocks below.

He lowered himself onto her, his lips almost touching hers. Her body screamed with need at the heat, the male hardness, that brushed her thigh.

"Skye." His voice rolled low and dark through the base of her belly. Lightning cracked outside. Thunder rumbled through the black forest. A new wave of rain blasted against the windows, the roof. She shivered involuntarily.

"I want you to know something, Skye."

She stared up into the fierce green of his smoldering eyes. And she was suddenly petrified of what he was going say. The cocktail of fear and need, heat and cold, shuddered through her.

"I trust you. I need you to know that." His hand slid down her belly, found her hot mound. "And I need you to trust *me*." It was an order. "Do you understand?" His hand clamped firmly over the pulsing heat between her legs.

Her brain reeled, her stomach swooped.

"Yes," she whispered, not recognizing her own voice. She'd give him anything now.

He slid a finger into her.

Her vision swam. Her stomach swooped. She bucked instinctively upward, giving him wider access. He pushed his finger deeper, moaned low at the slickness he found there.

"I'll be here for you," he murmured, hot, into her ear. She shivered at the sensation. "But I need you to be here for me." The meaning of his words roiled like an unseen current under the surface. Thunder rumbled through the black hills.

But before she could open her mouth, he forced his lips down hard on hers. His tongue slid into her mouth. He moved his finger rhythmically up into her.

She swelled hot and tight around it, her tongue tangling with his.

Scott felt a low, throaty growl surge through his chest. She was so wet, so slick, so hot. He probed hungrily with his tongue, tasting her female softness, feeling her molten heat, the damp hair against the palm of his hand. She arched into him. His breath caught as he felt her take him in her hands, massage rhythmically with silk-skinned fingers. She opened her legs wider, guided him to her.

His world spun in a vortex of sensation, snapping the last threads of control. He forced her thighs wide, plunged into her. She bucked, moaned, under him.

It drove him wild, blinded him in scarlet pleasure. He sank deep into her welcoming heat. She lifted her pelvis up to his, opening to him. He felt the skin of her belly against his. Smooth where his was rough with hair. And she tightened around him, milked him with sleek strokes of her muscles.

He could no more halt the instinctive, rhythmic plunge into her core than he could stop breathing. And as he rocked into her, the heat grew, seared, peaked into an exquisite pain.

She moved under him like a lean wild animal, sleek with muscle. Her breaths came short and sharp. Her small sounds grew as he felt himself peak.

They moved harder, faster.

She stilled, every muscle in her body taut. For an instant the night stood still. Then she shattered with a feral cry, wave upon powerful rippling wave sucking at him until he could hold back no more.

He exploded in shuddering release. Both of them toppling in delirious unison into spiraling waves of crimson upon black.

He collapsed, damp, into her arms, the sound of her cry still echoing through his head.

His breathing became regular. Consciousness crept slowly in from the corners of his mind. The sounds of the storm filtered back into his brain. He registered the cabin, the flickering apricot light.

And he blinked. The word she'd cried. It was foreign. Greek.

It stabbed through him.

He remembered why they were here.

He propped himself up onto his elbow, stared at the exquisite woman who lay dusky, naked, sated, in front of him.

She smiled lazily up at him, her cheeks flushed, her silver eyes liquid, haunting.

Something tightened sharp and hard across his chest.

His eyes trailed down her slick body, rested on the small tattoo on her olive-skinned hip.

Her eyes followed his, saw what he was staring at.

They darted back, met his gaze. She looked afraid.

But she said nothing.

A maelstrom of emotion swirled in him. He reached out, stroked the smoothness of her cheek, smiled softly back at her.

Her eyes fluttered closed in what he could only read as relief.

He pulled the comforter over them, lay down beside her, held her. She snuggled against him. Warm. Soft. She fit so perfectly. He felt so stupidly whole.

As much as he wanted answers, he didn't want to lose her.

But he had to ask. Soon.

Because the world was going to come and get her. And he was going to betray her, hand her over to them.

He mentally shook his head. Since when had his mission become a case of betraying Skye?

He held her closer, drank in the musk of her female scent.

Since he'd begun to care.

Since he'd dared tread where he'd promised himself never to go.

The agent who feared no man had been rendered weak by this woman. And this was one wilderness he did not know how to traverse.

He'd known he was in trouble the second she'd stepped over that threshold and into his life only days ago.

Her eyes flickered open.

She blinked into the room, remembered where she was. Henderson's cabin. It was dark.

A finger of ice traced down her spine. She reached out. Cold. He was gone from the bed.

Skye jerked up, clutched the quilt comforter to her breasts. She couldn't say what it was that had woken her with such a jolt.

But something didn't feel right.

The flames in the woodstove had died to glowing embers. And the night had gone deathly still.

The storm was over.

Then she saw him, a hulk of a silhouette by the window, looking out into the black night. He was wearing only his jeans. His dog cowered at his side.

"Scott," she whispered.

He turned.

Then she heard it.

A sound so eerie it raised every fine hair on her body. A howl so primal it reverberated through every cell in her system.

It echoed through the still, dark forest, bounced off the mountains, rising in plaintive pitch upon pitch over the tips of trees.

Honey started a low moan in response. Scott reached his hand down, told her to stay quiet.

"Is it a wolf?"

"Our wolf. The one from the road."

"How do you know?" She climbed out of bed, draped herself in the quilt, joined him at the window.

"Listen."

She did. "What am I hearing?"

"It's a lonesome howl. Hear the pitch?"

She nodded, shivered as the sound once again entered her soul.

"That high pitch, the modulations, it's not an aggressive howl. I think it's our old alpha male."

"He's lonely," she whispered. "The sound…it's so haunting."

He put his arm around her, gathered her close. She could smell the warm maleness of him. She felt ridiculously safe in his hold. Despite all the uncertainty, the fear, a part of her felt oddly at peace in this tiny cabin in the heart of nowhere. And her own heart ached for the male animal alone in the cold woods.

"A wolf separated from its pack sometimes returns to an old rendezvous site," he said softly. "A place where it was once happy, secure. It can howl there for hours."

"Calling out to its past."

"Calling out to its future. Looking for something he'll probably never find again."

Once again the strange and sorrowful sound rose, climbed, echoed into the dark wilderness.

It was immediately followed by another. But this one was different.

Scott went rigid beside her.

"What is it?"

"*That* was a confrontational howl. Can you hear the lower pitch, the coarser tone, especially at the end?"

She listened as the new sound died in low throaty threat. "Our old man has company?"

"Another male. It'll probably kill him."

She moved closer to Scott. "How do you know so much about them?"

He looked down at her. "My dad taught me some stuff. And the wolf has always stolen my imagination. It's the voice of the wilderness. The song of the wild. A symbol of the battle to survive against encroaching civilization." He turned and looked back out into the night. "Not like the jackal."

Skye went stiff.

She felt as if her heart had clean stopped beating.

She said nothing.

"The jackal is associated with evil spirits, death."

The muscles of her throat constricted. She tried to breathe

through them. Why had he brought this up? Was he probing for reaction? She clenched her teeth, pulled the comforter tighter around her.

He threw her a glance.

He *was* watching for reaction.

Or was he?

Was she just reading too much into something that wasn't there? Panic slithered up through her intestines. Cold.

He didn't let it drop. "He's a sly, cunning scavenger, the jackal." His words curled low, dangerous, threatening. "But he's too slimy to step out in the sunlight. He hides his nefarious deeds under the cloak of darkness. You only know he is there because of his eerie howl in the night."

Skye coughed.

He spun to face her. "Did you know, Skye, that the jackal is one of the few mammalian species that mates for life?"

She cleared her throat. "Uh, no. I—I didn't know that."

"You ever been near a jackal, Skye?"

"N-no." She attempted a laugh. It came out awkward. "They don't have jackals in Holland."

"No, I guess they don't."

She scrambled to swing the conversation. "And you? You sound like you've come across this animal."

"I have. I've spent time in Africa, the Middle East...India. All territories of the jackal. And I've crossed his path. I've seen evidence of his presence. But he's the darnedest creature when it comes to cunning and stealth. Can't say I've ever laid eyes on him. Just known he was there. Could smell him in the shadows."

The edge of sheer terror sliced into her stomach. It was as if he was talking of Malik. As though he knew of him, knew of her connection to Anubis.

Malik had business in Africa, the Middle East, India. His cells operated everywhere. "You're...you're personifying the dog,'' she said nervously. ''You're talking about the creature as though he's a man.''

''Am I?''

''You speak as though the dog's a personal foe.''

He laughed suddenly. ''I guess living in the wilds does that to you. You think about yourself on the same terms as the animals that survive…and hunt around you. You personify them, give them identities you can relate to.''

Skye relaxed a little. It made sense. Her own guilt was making her imagine things. She was reading too much into an innocent conversation.

Or was she?

The howl of the wolf snaked once more through her veins. She shivered. She couldn't help wondering if an alpha wolf faced off against a cunning jackal, which of the dogs would win the war.

She reached for his arm. She desperately needed to connect with him, to find that center of comfort again, that sense of warm wholeness. But his muscles were like unyielding rock under her fingers. ''Come back to bed, Scott,'' she urged him. ''The fire's dying. It's getting cold.''

He turned, hooked a knuckle roughly under her chin, jerked her face to his.

''Tell me about the tattoo, Skye.''

Chapter 13

The knife of terror twisted horribly in her gut. *Think, Skye. Think fast. It doesn't mean he suspects anything.* She forced a laugh, kept her voice as light as she could. "It's a symbol of precise, reasoned judgment. At least, that's what I was told when I picked the design out of a book of symbols in an Amsterdam tattoo parlor."

He stared stonily down at her.

She laughed softly. "I was nineteen. It was a lark. They had all sorts of symbols—Celtic, Egyptian, Asian. I liked the Egyptian dog one. I guess the head does look rather jackal-like."

"And the sword?"

"For strength of character. I see it as a symbol of fighting for what you believe in."

She could sense tension increase in his body. Inwardly her stomach jittered.

He couldn't possibly know. No one knew. Only Jalil. She tried to shrug it off. But he'd knocked her off kilter.

Skye peered out the window at the black forest that surrounded them. But all she could see in the drab, mist-shrouded shapes, was the black face of a jackal. Malik.

A shudder shook through her limbs.

"You're right." He broke the silence, took her in his arms. Held her tight. Too tight. As if desperate to hold on to some notion. "It is getting cold out here. Go back to bed. I'll join you as soon as I stoke the fire, get some warmth back into this place."

But the warmth was gone from his voice.

She pulled the comforter tight around her body. It did nothing to chase the inner chill, the sense she'd failed a test.

Oh, God, she had to come clean. She couldn't go on like this. The guilt was eating her, playing tricks with the shadows of her mind.

She had to tell him the truth.

She'd lied again. He was certain of it. She still hadn't trusted him with the truth. And that cut him.

It shouldn't. What in hell had given him the delusion of confidence in the first bloody place? Sex? The way she'd held him? The way she'd made him feel so ridiculously whole for the first time in years?

What a freaking fool he was. Scott jabbed the embers, thrust more wood into the flames. Honey settled once again on the rag rug in front of the stove, her ears flicking, twitching at unfamiliar night noises.

With fire crackling once again in the belly of the stove, Scott climbed back into bed.

Skye took him immediately into her arms.

His heart ached.

He wanted to thrust himself deep into her again, to fill that empty void, to find and hold on to that fleeting sense of center that had slipped like mercury through his fingers.

But more than anything he needed to chase away the lies.

He needed her to trust—to confess.

She moved against him, snuggled into the crooks of his body. Her breasts were warm and soft, heavy against his chest. Her arms were smooth, firm. He felt the silk of her hair, her breath caress his face. She was so essentially female.

His kind of female.

A woman who could be both soft and tender and hard as nails. The kind of woman who'd challenge him, keep him *alive* for the rest of his life. A friend he could take on his wildest adventures. A woman he could take on the next leg of his journey. A woman who might share the passage of life with him.

He shook the notion, tried to focus on the task that had brought him to this point in the first place.

She was a suspected terrorist. Brilliant. Perhaps dangerous.

And he was an agent.

He had no business even entertaining the notion of a future together.

But at the same time, the fact it had even entered his head shook him to his core. Scott Armstrong had not thought about the future. Not for the past nine years. Not since Kaitlin and Leni had died. Not since the Plague Doctor had killed them.

The acrid and familiar anger seeped bitter into his throat.

Was the woman in his arms allied with La Sombra? A man on par with the Plague Doctor?

He stared up at the rafters, watched the flicking light of the flame dance with pagan shadow.

She murmured, pulling him back. He turned, stroked her face. And deep down, a part of him prayed to God he'd find Skye Van Rijn innocent.

He sucked in a breath, filled his lungs to capacity, exhaled slowly.

You really are a fool, Armstrong.

Even if Skye was innocent, it could never work. He was

a Bellona agent. And his job had killed his family. He could never put someone he loved in that position again, endanger them.

Ever.

He closed his eyes, drifted toward sleep. But on the gray fringes of sleep and consciousness, where misty dream toyed with reality, Scott felt at one with the old wolf. Inside, his heart was dark and lonely. He howled to go back to a happy place. He howled for a past to which he'd never return. He howled to a bleak future he'd never fill as he once had the past.

And all around, the wilderness heard him, echoed his baleful sound. On the periphery, a jackal prowled, growing desperate, sensing weakness.

Scott swam up from the dark depths of his dreams, up to the light that he could see above him, shimmering on the surface.

His eyes opened to a cabin filled with the bright yellow warmth of morning sun. He could smell flapjacks, hear coffee percolating on the woodstove. He could feel the warm weight of his dog sleeping on his bed at his feet.

And he felt an old familiar happiness coupled with an odd quirk of excitement. It was the feeling he'd always had as a kid on the first morning he and his dad had woken up on one of their fishing trips.

Scott blinked, momentarily confused.

It wasn't his dog warming his feet. It was Rex's dog. And it wasn't his dad flipping pancakes at the woodstove.

It was the woman he'd made love to.

He nudged at Honey with his foot. "Off. Who said you could sleep on the bed?"

The dog looked up, brown eyes wounded.

Skye spun 'round, frying pan in hand, a smile as warm as the sunshine on her face. "I did—the floor's cold. Morning, handsome."

"Dogs don't sleep on the bed in my house."

"It's not your house. C'mon, grumpy, breakfast is ready and the fish are biting."

"Fish?"

"Don't they bite in the mornings? I've decided you're teaching me how to fly-fish today."

He sat up, rubbed his hands through his hair. "Oh, you have?"

"Yep." She set a plate of flapjacks on the table. "Look at this weather." She waved her hand at the window. "We can't let a day like today slip by."

He smiled in spite of himself. Her energy was infectious. "Come here."

She put her hands on her hips, tilted her chin. "Why?"

"I have a little secret to tell you about fly-fishing."

She walked slowly toward the bed. As she got near, he lunged forward, grabbed her arm.

She squealed.

He yanked her down onto the bed. She wriggled against his hold.

"Want to hear my secret?" he whispered into her ear.

She stilled in his arms, looked up into his eyes. "What's your secret, Scott?"

He bent, spoke softly against her lips. "I can't get enough of you, woman. You've infected me. Whatever you've given to me runs thick in my blood."

He pressed his mouth down onto hers. And he slipped his tongue between her lips as his hands worked to unclothe her body.

"You taste like syrup," he murmured against her mouth as he undid her jeans. "Maple syrup."

She was as hungry for him as he was for her, her arms reaching for him, her tongue dancing with his. Warm. Sweet. Wild. It was as though he was tasting life itself, tapping right into the core of it.

He forced her backward onto the bed and held his breath.

Sunlight pooled warm and gold over her naked body, caught the fine blond hairs on her olive-toned skin. The cool morning air raised tiny goose bumps along her arms, and her nipples were tight, brown nubs.

He pulsed hot, hard with urgent need. He lifted his fingers, gently traced the swell of her breasts, ran his hand firmly down over her belly, found the folds between her thighs.

She wanted him.

She was slick, hot.

He sat back, grasping for a measure of restraint. But she pulled him down onto her and met him with the same raw energy that pounded through him.

The sun changed angles as it rose in the heavens, throwing new shadows across the floor of the cabin. Skye checked her watch—almost noon. They'd spent the better part of the morning in bed, and now she was more than ravenous. "See what you've done," she accused. "The pancakes are cold."

Scott chuckled, stretching like a lazy beast. "I need a shower. We can warm 'em up after." He looked around the cabin. "So where'd the realtor say the en suite was?"

She jabbed him in the ribs. "You got two choices, McIntyre. The river. Or the river."

He sat up. "Coming?"

"The river? You must be nuts. It's like…freezing."

He grinned, a devilish slash across his rough, unshaven jaw. Green sparks of life shot from his eyes.

She hadn't seen him like this. So potently vital. He had a new energy this morning. And it near drove her wild, just looking into those wicked, flashing eyes. She could feel yet another hot little lick of lust unfurl in her belly. She laughed. "Okay. You win. I could handle a cooldown."

They sat on rocks that hung over the river, sipping freshly brewed coffee. Honey explored the bank down below, snuffling in the shallows, trying to bat the shadows of fish with her paws.

Skye felt utterly cleansed after their dip in one of the eddies down below. It was as if the clear, cold mountain water had washed clean through to her soul. As if she'd been reborn and could start with a fresh slate.

She turned to the man beside her. A lock of his brown hair hung over his brow. His green eyes seemed very light out here in the sun, as if he, too, had been unburdened in some way.

He caught her looking, smiled.

She felt her cheeks flush and turned quickly to look at the burbling water, sipped her coffee. It was warm, sweet, tasted only like fresh coffee out in the wilds could taste. "How come stuff always tastes better out in places like this?"

"It's the sex."

She snorted. "Don't flatter yourself."

He laughed. Then his tone turned serious. "Maybe it's just being away from it all. Makes you see and feel things differently. New perspective and all that. My father used to come out to places like this to recharge his batteries."

"And your mom?"

"She enjoyed her own space when we were gone."

Skye shifted on the rock, turned to face him. "Tell me about your dad, Scott."

He shrugged. "Not much to tell."

"Yes, there is. You used to do these amazing things with him when you were a kid. He taught you about nature, wolves, fishing. I saw how you reacted in that tackle shop. Something happened between you and him. What is it that keeps you apart?"

The ledge of his brow dropped low over his eyes. "Why are you asking me this?"

"Because it's eating at you, I can tell. You haven't resolved something. Am I right?"

He studied her face intently, turned away. Nodded. "Yeah."

"Why haven't you seen him in a while? What happened between you?"

He wouldn't look at her. He hesitated. Then he spoke out to the water, to the trees and the sky. "Nothing. The only thing that happened was me. I cut him, my mother, out of my life. My whole goddamn family. Everyone. I just stopped seeing them."

There was a cracked edge to his voice. Low emotion. She reached out, touched his thigh. "Why? Why'd you shut them out?"

He swallowed. "They made me remember. I wanted nothing to do with my old life. Nothing to do with my hometown."

"Remember your wife, your baby?" she asked softly.

"Yes," he replied simply. "They died in a car accident." He lurched up onto his feet, turned his back to her. "It was nine years ago. Sometimes it still feels like yesterday."

Skye set her mug on the rock, stood behind him, put her arms around his waist, rested her cheek against his back. "I'm sorry, Scott. I'm sorry I pressed you on this."

"It's okay. I've tried for so long to run from it. I can't. It's time I faced it. Dealt with it."

He turned slowly around. "You've made me see that."

Her breath caught at the sight of the pain in his eyes, in the set of his features. And she knew in that instant she loved the man. Rough edges and all. Because it all made sense. His distance. His brusque manner. He was in pain. And it wasn't just his leg. His heart had been broken.

And Skye had a desperate desire to mend it. Make it better for him.

And more than anything, she wanted to trust this enigmatic writer. Implicitly.

Because she needed to share, to tell him about her own

baby. About Malik. She needed to tell him who she was. Because hiding from him, lying to him now, when he was opening like this to her, made her feel dirty.

But she was still petrified at how he'd react if she told him she was not Skye Van Rijn. That she was a fake. A liar. An impostor.

A trained terrorist.

She didn't want to lose him now that she'd found him.

She pulled him back to the rock. "Come sit by me. Finish your coffee." They sipped in silence, watching the waters rush by.

It was a new experience for Skye. To sit like this next to a man, to feel such a deep, visceral connection to him, to feel so utterly at peace with him. It was as though she'd found some kind of center to the universe, a place where there was calm.

But she wasn't going to kid herself. She knew she'd have to step back out into the storm eventually and choose a path. Whatever direction she went, the chaos raged one way or the other. She knew that. But maybe this time she could take an ally with her, a friend to hold on to. Maybe. If he didn't hate her for being a liar once he learned the truth. If he didn't detest who she really was.

All she wanted right now was for this quiet, intimate moment to last. But it was now or never. Leave it any later and she'd be breaking their new trust, their tentative bond. It would be betrayal.

She sucked air in deep. "I know how it feels, to cut out your past," she said softly.

"What?"

"And I'm learning that you can't run forever, either."

He shifted on the rock to face her. "Are you running, Skye?"

She gave a soft laugh. "You *know* I'm running, McIntyre."

He leaned forward "Yes. But I'm not sure what you're

running from. I don't understand why you haven't called the police, why you haven't asked for help."

"They haven't been able to help me before. I told you that."

"Are you in trouble with the law, Doctor?" His eyes probed hers. As much as she tried, she couldn't look away. But she couldn't lie to him, either, not anymore.

"I—I don't know if you'd understand."

"Try me."

She tore her eyes from his, looked out over the raging angry waters of the river. Suddenly nervous as all hell.

He reached out, touched her arm. "Skye, we can do this."

She clutched her knees into her chest, rocked slightly. God, she wanted a bond like this. Was her news going to blow this tender connection to smithereens?

He looked suddenly up at the sky, frowned.

She followed his gaze. "What is it?"

"Chopper."

She could hear it. A faint, distant *thuck, thuck, thuck.*

Reality pierced like a blade.

She jumped to her feet, pulled back.

"Relax. It's probably just a helicopter from one of the logging operations in the area."

She nodded. "Yeah."

"Besides, it's miles away."

"Right." But she continued to back into the cover of the trees. It was safer there. "You coming?"

He studied her. "You're terrified."

She nodded.

"All right." She could see he was appraising her, thinking. "I'll join you as soon as I've finished my coffee."

She hesitated. She didn't want him out in the open, on that rock like that. They could see him.

"It's okay, Skye. Relax. If the chopper gets any closer,

I'm gone. Don't worry. No one will see us.'' He whistled for Honey, as if to prove a point.

The dog bounded up the bank, onto the rocks.

''Here, take Honey. Go up to the cabin. I'll be there in a few minutes.''

She bent, hooked her fingers under Honey's collar. ''I'll make us some lunch. Maybe we can still go fishing later?''

''Yeah. Maybe.''

She turned to leave.

Scott watched her walk up the path toward the cabin and listened to the distant chop of the machine in the sky. He figured it was several miles away. But he doubted it was her pursuers. They couldn't have found her. Whoever *they* were. They had no knowledge…unless… ''Skye!''

She spun around at the top of the path.

He yelled out to her. ''When you came up here with Henderson, who else came with you?''

''Charly and her boyfriend, and some of the other guys from the lab.''

''Jozsef?''

''Yes. And Jozsef. Why?''

''Just wondering.''

Skye paused, studying him, then turned and made her way through the trees.

Scott lost sight of her and Honey as they reached the porch. His vantage point on the rock was pretty well screened from the cabin by the towering conifers. He squinted into the bright sky, tried to catch a glimpse of the chopper. He couldn't. But the sound of it had taken on a new tone to his ears. An ominous one. If Jozsef, alias Balto Nakiskas, had come here with Skye, there was a chance their location was compromised.

He fished out his satellite phone, dialed Rex.

He needed answers. Quick.

''Armstrong, we've been waiting for your call.'' Scott

noted the use of the word "we." This was bigger than just Bellona now.

"Rex, any word on that plate I gave you?"

"Yeah, we ran the number. A rental. Paid for by a company that ships gourmet foods from Europe."

"What's the name of the company?"

"KTS Global. They're held by a parent company in Belgium, which in turn seems to be a shell for another numbered company in Athens. It's one of the companies Danko invested for. Made a killing from the beef embargo."

Scott's pulse spiked. Everything was circling in. Everything kept coming back to Greece.

"Any further word on Nakiskas?"

"No. But Scooter's guys have narrowed down the search for the system that has been hacking into Dr. Van Rijn's computer. Pretty complicated setup. He followed the trail from the doctor's computer to a server in Amsterdam. That server tapped into the computer of an Iranian refugee who went by the name of Jalil."

"He the hacker?"

"No. Appears he was another victim of the hacker. Looks like this Jalil was a confidant of Dr. Van Rijn's. She's been e-mailing him for some time. She told him in her most recent correspondence that she was taking time out to think. It's dated the night before you two left Haven."

"Christ. Have our guys spoken to this Jalil?"

"He's dead."

"What?"

"Unsolved homicide. Killed almost a year ago. The Dutch authorities say he'd been tortured."

His stomach swooped. "Skye's been e-mailing a *dead* guy for this past year?"

Someone tortured for information?

"He may be dead, but his computer's not. We traced it to a room in an Amsterdam building. The room is rented by Ergo. It's a subsidiary of the same Belgium operation that owns KTS Global."

"We've opened a bloody can of worms."

"It gets even more interesting. The e-mails to Jalil's computer are being routed through two different hubs. Scooter's European guy has finally tracked it all back to one key server in northern Greece."

The muscles across his neck strapped tight. Greece again. "An Anubis cell?"

"We think so. We're zeroing in on the location as we speak. We have Greek authorities and U.S. military standing by. They'll move in as soon as it's confirmed."

Scott said nothing. Ice coursed through his veins. He glanced up at the cabin. How in hell was Skye connected to all this? And who in hell was after her? If Nakiskas *was* Anubis, and if his company had rented the car the goons were tracking them in.... That could mean Anubis itself was after the doctor. But why? What was she hiding from him? What did Anubis want from her?

Rex's voice sliced into his tumbling thoughts. "There's something else. Specialists at Vancouver General have identified the illness contracted by Charly Sheldon, Dr. Van Rijn's assistant."

"And?"

"It's Q-20. Incredibly rare. Never before seen outside of Central Africa. Docs reckon she must have inhaled the virus somehow. It first manifested in her lungs. But the thing is, Sheldon hasn't been out of the country, let alone to Africa."

"And Skye Van Rijn has."

"She's key in all this." He paused. "Bring her in."

The leaden surge of ice in his blood thickened. His gut clenched. He wasn't ready to hand Skye over to the bureaucratic machine. She *had* to be a victim.

"That was an order, Agent."

"Give me till morning."

"Scott."

"I'll have her story by morning. More than you'll ever get in an interrogation chamber."

"I can't do—"

Scott held the phone out toward the roar of the river. "What's that...Logan? You're breaking up...Logan, I can't hear you..."

He flipped the phone shut. The bitterness of bile crept up into his mouth. He'd finally gone over the edge. He'd let his goddamn heart win out over his head. He was laying his career on the line for a woman. And all the while, a dark little thought circled his brain. What if she really was guilty? What if she was a supreme con artist who'd played him for a jackass? What if he really was totally washed up?

He buried his face in his hands, rubbed at his skin till it burned. "Don't let me down, Skye." He whispered. "Don't let me down."

Scott lifted his head, stared out over the roiling river, pulled himself back into focus. A bubble of anger erupted in his belly. Then another.

Yes. He'd have her story by dawn.

And God help the woman if the worst was confirmed. Because she'd given him hope.

She'd dared to let him look to the future.

And if she took that from him now...

He pushed himself to his feet, faced the path up to the cabin, forced cool, calculated calm on the bitter cocktail simmering inside.

This was his very last shot.

Chapter 14

The cabin door crashed open. Scott loomed in the doorway, his eyes glittering. Angry energy crackled sharply around him.

Skye stepped back. "Scott, I—I was just coming to get you. I've packed a lunch." She held up the pack, tried to smile. "I thought I'd show you where Henderson catches his trout. It's about a mile down the river where a small tributary feeds into a little lake."

His features were implacable granite. "Sure." He limped over to where he'd stacked the fly rod and tackle. He grabbed his backpack, dumped his clothes out onto the floor, replaced the first-aid kit that had tumbled out with his gear. He stuffed his fishing tackle into the bag, slung it over his shoulders, reached for his cane and his rod.

"Let's go, then."

"Scott, what is it?"

His eyes flicked up, met hers, held. "Nothing."

She opened her mouth, thought better of it. But his switch in mood made her edgy. Real edgy.

She led the way from the cabin along a narrow trail spongy and fragrant with pine needles. It wound through the forest and down to the lake. Honey ran ahead, snuffling in rich loam under the trees, releasing the scent of resin and warm, fecund earth.

But Scott remained stonily silent behind her.

The forest understory was thicker down by the water. Brush scrambled to cover the path. Much of it was swollen with the buds of berries, the promise of a rich fall harvest. Skye crouched low through the dense undergrowth. They were almost at the lake. She moved the brambles aside, revealed a still body of water and a microcosm of life.

Electric-blue damsels and big brown dragonflies pinged and darted over the surface of the lake. Beetles crawled across the pads of lilies. Small birds clung from reeds that poked out from the water. The air was warm and full of sound.

A fish leaped, greedy for the insects that skimmed the surface of its world. It plopped back, rippling the surface.

Still Scott said nothing. He crouched on the bank, studied the insect life. Then he opened his fly box, tied a tiny fly to the end of his leader.

"What's that?" she asked in an effort to break the thick silence that hung around him.

"Damsel fly."

She nodded. He was going to fool the fish who were already leaping for the real damsels. She watched as he fed the line out with his left hand, flicked the rod deftly, delicately with his right. His little damsel mimicked the real thing, just flecking the surface before being yanked back. Droplets of water flicked off the line as it looped, danced back and forth. They caught the sunlight like jewels. Here one minute. Gone the next.

He got a bite, lifted the rod lightly up, set the hook. He started to play his catch. The fish fought back, leaped, spraying water jewels and a shimmer of rainbow scales.

But he reeled it in easily. It was small. He crouched as he pulled it closer to the shoreline. He stopped short of lifting it from the sanctuary of its pond.

He turned to Skye. "Take it," he said. "Careful. Don't damage the scales. Open the mouth, release the hook."

Crouching, she reached into the water. It was cool against her skin. She grasped the little fish. It slipped from her fingers. She tried again, this time clasping it gently. It flopped like a slippery little heart in her hands. Its mouth gasped in stress. With her fingers she reached into its mouth, pinched the tiny hook buried in the flesh, slipped it out. It came out easily. The barb had been pressed back.

"Good," he said. "Now hold it under its belly. Careful. Keep it in the water, let it revive. It'll go on its own."

And it did, with a soft flick of its tail, it made a choice and swam back to the safety of its pond.

Skye rested back on her haunches, staring into the water where the fish had disappeared. It gave her a strange kind of elation mixed with awe, having had the privilege of holding a creature from a different element, setting it free.

He was watching her.

She looked up. His face was still hard as stone. But something in his eyes said different.

"You never keep them?" she asked.

"Not unless I need food."

She nodded. "I like the idea of setting it free." And as she spoke, she, too, craved release. She'd been like that little fish. On a line too long, gasping for life. And Scott had shown it to her, dangled it in front of her like a dazzling damsel fly. Could she take the bait? Would she, too, be ultimately set free? Or would the system hook her, reel her in, swallow her for supper?

She had a choice to make. A momentous decision. And in taking that bait, in coming clean, she might lose the man. This man who'd sharpened her yearning for freedom, for the richness of an open and honest life.

She searched his eyes as if for guidance. Something in them softened, almost imperceptibly. He crouched slowly beside her. "It's good to fish again," he said quietly. "Thanks."

She couldn't read the message under his words, interpret the strange look in his eyes. "Why thanks?" she asked.

"You brought me out here, set me back on this road. I'd forgotten the taste of it." He looked away, out over the lake. "Whatever these past few days have been about, at least I'll take that away."

Her chest tightened. There was a sense of finality about his words. She tried to laugh, make light of it. "You're not planning on leaving me here, are you?"

"Skye, what do you hope to achieve, hiding in this cabin? How long do you plan on staying out here?"

She took air deep into her lungs. Nervous. But she wanted to do this. Tell him. Everything. And he was forcing it. Right now. Pushing her right up to the edge. She looked over and felt a sickening wave of dizziness. Like she'd felt in the plane when she'd had a chute strapped to her back. But she had to leap. Or she'd never know the feeling that awaited. She'd never know the brilliance of the life that may lie on the other side. She prayed her chute would open. And she jumped.

"I…thought it would be a safe place to think. I need to make some decisions, a plan." She swallowed, waited for his reaction. Over the buzz of dragonflies and clicking noise of bugs, she could hear the chopper hovering in the distance.

"What kind of decisions?"

"I needed to know if I could trust you. Totally, because I—I don't think I can do this alone."

His brow lowered over his eyes. The sound of the chopper died. It had landed somewhere. Somewhere not far away.

"Do what alone? Talk to me, Skye."

"I'm—My name is not Skye."

He went rigid. Something shuttered instantly in his eyes.

"I'm not from Holland."

The muscle in his jaw jumped wildly, but he said nothing.

Terror leached into her chest. "Say something, Scott."

Don't let me lose you.

He jerked his eyes away, took a bottle of water out of his pack and swigged, wiping his mouth with the back of his hand. "I'm listening." His voice was hoarse.

But she couldn't talk. She couldn't do it. Her mouth was dry like crumbled bone. The sides of her throat stuck together. With a trembling hand she reached for his water bottle, took it from him, drank deep.

He watched her carefully. "You're scared."

She nodded her head.

"Of me?"

A lump caught at the base of her throat. "No." She closed her eyes, gathering her thoughts. Then she opened them and looked directly into his. "I'm scared of losing you."

"Pardon?"

"I'm afraid that after I tell you my story, you'll hate me for what I've done. For who I am."

Something unbelievably tender flashed through his features. But it was fleeting. There. Then gone. Replaced with a hard set of his jaw, a sharp glint in his eyes. He reminded her of an animal poised to leap on its prey, tear its throat. "Everything. Tell me everything, Skye."

She wanted to hear him say that whatever she told him, it would be okay, that he'd understand. But he didn't. He was glaring at her. Eyes angry. But she was committed now.

"All right. This is my story. And by God I hope you understand. I *need* you to understand." She could feel the hot wetness of emotion in her eyes. She swallowed it back.

But the edge of it cracked through her voice. "I need *you,* Scott," she whispered.

He raised his hand, as if to reach out, touch her. Then pulled it back.

"Everything, Skye." His voice was thick. "Now."

She bit down on the pang of hurt, threw back her head, looked up at the evening sky. Birds played on currents of air.

"When I was a child, I always envied them." She motioned with her chin to where the birds soared above. "They always seemed so free. They could go where they wanted…I couldn't." She choked over the ball of pain that blocked her throat. This was even harder than she'd thought, putting into words for the first time what she'd always kept buried deep in her soul.

This time he did touch her; his hand rested warm on her arm. It fed her courage.

"Start at the beginning," he said softly.

"Okay." She nodded, sucked in her breath. "I'm not Skye Van Rijn. I assumed the identity of a dead child with that name. I was not born in Holland. I was born in northern Greece, near the Albanian border. I don't know who my father is. My mother was a soldier of the communist movement, a member of a terrorist cell tolerated by the Greek government because of its commitment to act against Turkey."

He was dead silent, a muscle pulsing at his temple. Then he spoke. "Like the Greeks tolerate the Kurdistan Workers Party?"

"Yes. But this has little to do with the PKK. It masquerades as a splinter of the old PKK. But it's something far more dangerous."

"What group is it?" He barked the question. Her stomach jumped.

"It's…it's the heart of Anubis, Scott."

Every muscle in his body tensed. The muscle pulsed faster. His brows dropped down like a hawk. His eyes scorched.

"They...they have a training camp. I was born in that camp. Raised there. Schooled there. I never knew about the real world—"

"The leader?" His fingers dug into her arm. "Who runs this camp?"

"They call him La Sombra."

Scott's fingers bit harder. "You *know* La Sombra?" His voice was ominous, foreign.

She nodded, afraid at the depth of hate in his face.

"What is his name? His *real* name?"

"Malik Leandros. It means Master. And if he finds me, he will kill me for telling you."

Scott dropped her arm like something gone bad.

She winced.

He dragged his fingers hard though his hair, pulling at the roots. "That tattoo on your hip—"

"Malik's idea."

"He *branded* you?" There was disgust in his voice.

"In a way."

"What about the sword?" He spat the question.

"I am the sword. The Sword of Anubis. I was christened Zeva, which means sword."

He lurched suddenly to his feet, turned his back on her, stared out over the lake to where Honey was chasing bugs. He clenched, unclenched, fists at his sides.

He swung abruptly back to face her. "You were his lover," he said simply. "You're a terrorist."

She leaped up, tried to take his hand. He wrenched free. Something ripped in her heart. Her chute. It wasn't going to open for her this time. She'd made a mistake. She flailed wildly. "Scott, *please,* let me explain."

He stared at her, his face all hard planes devoid of any emotion whatsoever. "Yes. Explain."

"I can't talk to you, standing like this. Please, sit."

Slowly he lowered himself back down to the bank. She joined him. "I escaped, Scott. I've been running, hiding from Malik for thirteen years. I am no more a terrorist than you. All I want is an honest life. All I want is to be free."

Scott rubbed his hands brutally over his face. "What happened? How did you end up here?"

"I never had a choice, Scott. Remember that. I was born into Malik's camp. I was taught he was Master. Then, when I turned eighteen, I caught his attention. He wanted me. In the way a man wants a woman."

His body stiffened. His obvious distaste shot pain into her heart. She swallowed. "Malik always got what he wanted. A part of me was even flattered. I was young, insulated, schooled in the dogma he preached. And he was like a god, beautiful, dark and powerful like Zeus. He took me into his private residence and personally taught me the art of sex and languages. He taught me to fight. He wanted to deploy me to other countries. To seduce secrets from men."

Scott winced again. Pain sliced through his features. He looked away.

"But I got pregnant when I was nineteen. He said I must get rid of my baby. He said a child would make a warrior weak. He said there were lesser women for the task. But I couldn't do it. I felt this new life growing inside me and I began to question everything. Him…the camp…my ideals…. I wanted another way for me, for my baby. It made him furious. I told him I was leaving. We had a terrible fight. I used all my skills, but he hurt me. Badly. I was bleeding." Skye choked back a sob.

Scott turned back to face her. "What then?"

"An older woman from the camp took pity on me, got some other women from the nearby village to smuggle me over the Albanian border. They knew people there who helped me get to Amsterdam. But I—" Her voice cracked. "I…lost my baby." Pain spilled wet from her eyes. She clutched her knees tight into her chest, rocked as the sky began to darken.

Scott's mouth was set in a tight line. "What happened then?"

"I was put in touch with an Iranian refugee named Jalil."

His eyes snapped to hers. "Jalil?"

"Yes. He became my one friend, still is. He helped me get to Canada. He made me Skye Van Rijn. Gave me papers, a new life." She took a deep breath, shuddering as she exhaled. "I owe him my life."

Something new crossed his features. Confusion pulled at his brow. He opened his mouth to speak. Shut it. Looked away. "And the degrees? Your doctorate?"

"Those are mine." She snapped. "They are *me*. The real me. I earned them."

"And now La Sombra has found you."

"Who else could have sent those men?"

Scott blew out a long stream of breath. The sun was sinking behind distant mountains. Cold shadows crawled out from under crevices, crept toward them.

The haunting cry of a loon echoed.

He felt smacked in the gut, couldn't breathe. He didn't know if he should believe her. He had to tell her about Jalil. But he had to be sure she wasn't playing him.

"Scott, I'm…I'm sorry."

He nodded. That's all he could do. And he searched her eyes, tried to see. Was she lying again? Playing the victim when in fact she still might be working with La Sombra, with Nakiskas. She could still be responsible for the RVF outbreak in the States. She could be telling him this now in a desperate attempt to keep him on side, until she no longer needed him. She was brilliant. He'd seen that from the information in her dossier. He'd be a fool to think she wasn't capable. He'd been a fool once already.

She laid her hand on his arm. "Can you find it in yourself

to try to understand?'' A forlorn desperation snaked through her voice.

He tore his eyes from hers. Stared instead at the livid orange strips of cloud streaking the evening sky, catching the last rays of sun as the day died. ''You have to turn yourself in, Skye. You have to come forward.''

''I know. Can you help me? You said you'd be there for me. Can you, now that you know? Can you go all the way?''

He forced himself to look at her. And his gut clenched. His heart, his instincts, screamed at him. Deafened him. She wasn't Skye Van Rijn. She was Zeva, a Greek warrior. But still—Skye or Zeva or Sword of Anubis, whatever name she bore—deep down he believed he knew this woman. He'd felt a connection.

Skye. Zeva. They were just names. It was the woman inside that he'd glimpsed, touched. Who'd touched him. It was the person inside he cared about. That strong fighter. That vulnerable woman. That inner beauty.

His brain may be trying to tell him different. But his heart told him she was true. He struggled to suck in air.

Right here, right now, he stood at a cusp. Like the Janus Creek. And he was Janus himself, with two faces. He could see one road one way and another leading the other way. He lurched to his feet, bit back the pain that exploded into his knee, clenched his teeth. His nails dug into his palms. He could no longer stand in the middle of nowhere. No longer teeter on the cusp. No longer wear a mask of two faces. Screw Janus. He had to pick a road. He couldn't hide anymore.

''I will.''

Her gasp of relief was audible.

''I'll be there for you.'' He reached a hand down, pulled her gently to her feet, held her at arm's length. ''But, Skye, we have to talk.'' Because he had to tell her, too. Everything. Like her, he had to come clean before they could move forward and face the world. Before they could fight La Sombra. Together. But it was getting dark. And he'd heard the helicopter land somewhere in the forest. It would be safer to move inside, to talk in the cabin.

"It's getting cold out here. Come. We'll go back to the cabin, make a fire. We can talk there."

"Thank you, Scott," she whispered, tears slipping down her cheeks. "Thank you. Oh, God, thank you."

Her words twisted like a dagger in him. Telling her he was not McIntyre was going to be a killer. So would telling her about Nakiskas, about Charly…about Jalil.

He whistled for Honey, turned, leaned heavily on his cane, started up the trail. It led steeply uphill from the lake. He felt drained. Going down hadn't been too much of a problem for his knee. Going up felt like hell. He slipped, caught himself, doubled over his cane as he swallowed the pain.

"Here, lean on me. Put your arm around me. Let me help you."

He bit back pride, put his arm around her slender, strong shoulders. And something slipped in his stomach. Not in nine years had he had someone to lean on.

"You have to rest that knee or you'll never mend."

"I know."

But as they neared the cabin, Honey froze in her tracks, the hackles on her neck rising. A low growl emanated from her throat. Scott felt the fine hairs on his own neck rise. He could smell it.

Danger.

He laid a hand on Skye's arm, stilled her as they listened. It was dark under the trees, but silent. Only the roar of the nearby river could be heard.

Still, it didn't feel right. The road was closed because of the bridge. But they'd heard the chopper land in the distance. And he knew the stakes now. La Sombra would stop at nothing.

"Come," he whispered. "Let's get into the cabin. I'll get backup."

"*Backup?* How?"

"I have a phone."

"There's no cell reception here."

"It's satellite."

She halted. "Who would give you backup? Why do you have a sat phone?" A wary edge crept into her voice.

"I'll explain in the cabin. Move. Quick." He felt in his pack, withdrew his gun.

She stared at the weapon, her eyes huge.

"Move, Skye. Come on."

She peered up at his face in the dark shadows, but she didn't move.

"Now."

That's when he heard the crack. He whirled around. Scott saw the dim shape in the trees the same time Honey did. The dog snarled, exploded into a charge. Metal glinted as a man in the shadows whirled, raised a gun. Honey lunged for his arm, tore flesh. Scott aimed, yelled at Skye to get in the cabin.

He fired. The man reeled under the impact, pulling the trigger as he went down.

The slug tore through Scott's upper left arm. He wheeled back from the force.

An utterly eerie shriek sliced the air behind him. The battle cry of a warrior. Scott clutched his arm, staggered around. *Skye.* Through a haze of pain he saw a second man lurch out of the cabin toward her. He wielded a knife low, aimed straight at her belly. But she braced, swiveled the instant he slashed at her. The knife swiped air. He flailed forward with the momentum. Before he could regain balance, Skye unleashed another scream, a kick. Her heel caught him under his throat. The man's head cracked back.

For an instant he was still.

A grotesque frieze in the dusk air.

Then he slid slowly into a limp pile on the porch. Skye lunged for the knife.

Scott felt the wet warmth of his own blood seeping through his fingers, his legs giving out under him. He heard Honey snarl. Another shadow. Behind the canoe stacked up on the far side of the porch. Going for Skye.

Scott opened his mouth to scream a warning. But Honey had already alerted her.

Skye whirled, flexed. Before Scott could blink, the knife left her hand, flew true. The man bellowed as metal sunk deep into his jugular. His hands flew to his throat, clutched. Blood pumped through his fingers. He slumped back against the canoe, leaving a fat trail of gleaming black ooze as he went down.

Scott stumbled toward the deck, toward her. He'd been right. From the instant he'd first laid eyes on Skye, he knew she'd been trained to kill. "Skye—"

"Look out! Behind you!" Skye yelled, diving for cover on the porch.

Scott whirled just in time to catch another glint of metal. In a last-ditch attempt, the man he'd left for dead under the trees raised his arm and fired.

Scott flung himself sideways, tearing his knee. But the bullet slammed the sat phone in his chest pocket and glanced to the side. He sank to the ground.

"Scott. Oh, God, are you all right?" Skye was at his side. "Your arm, you've been shot."

"Flesh wound," he gasped, coughed.

"Your chest?"

"Phone...saved my life."

"Can you get your arm around me?"

He struggled into a sitting position. He couldn't breathe. A vortex of nausea swallowed him. He felt as if his knee joint had been ripped apart, as if a mallet had smashed his ribs. He wheezed, trying to suck in air. She grabbed his arm, pulled him up, shifted her shoulder into his armpit.

"Steady," she said. "We can do this."

He held tight on to her. "This…isn't…right." The words rasped from his lungs. "I'm…supposed to be the hero… saving you…"

"Shh. You have saved me," she whispered. "In more ways than you'll ever know." She edged him slowly into the dark cabin, helped him across the room, eased him onto the bed. He slumped back, vision narrowing into a dark tunnel of pain. He fought it, holding on to the pinpricks of light.

Skye lit a lantern, fingers moving fast. She had to stop the bleeding. "Where's the first-aid kit?"

"My pack…dropped it outside."

Skye wadded a small towel and pressed it firmly to Scott's arm. "Hold that tight. Keep the pressure. I'll be right back." She could see he was wobbling on the edge of consciousness. She grabbed the flashlight and ducked back out into the dark.

A quick check told her two men were dead. The third was unconscious. Black blood dribbled from his ear. She held back his lids, shone light into his eyes. They were filling with blood. Signs of brain damage. And his neck was broken. He wasn't going to make it.

She retrieved the Smith and Wesson that Scott had dropped, took the Glock from the man under the trees, slipped it into the back of her jeans. She felt in his pockets. They must have had some form of communication. Then she found it. A stubby satellite phone. Damaged, of no use. She held it in her hand, stared at it under the gleam of the flashlight.

Her hand begin to tremble.

He'd found her.

Malik's men had found her.

And between her and Scott, with the help of Honey, they'd wiped out three of his assassins. Just snuffed out their lives.

A wave of anguish crashed in her chest.

Malik had done this to her.

He'd trained her to kill. And he'd sent the men. He'd forced her. He'd made her into something she despised.

She detested him. More than anything on this earth.

And now the person she cared most about in the world was bleeding in the cabin. And she'd brought him here. He'd gotten himself hurt for her.

Her fault.

She dropped the phone to the forest floor, grabbed the backpack and ducked back into the cabin.

She lit a second lantern, set it on the table, fumbled in the pack. The first-aid kit was at the bottom. She felt it with her fingers, yanked at it. It was stuck. Hooked on a piece of nylon or something. She turned the pack upside down, shook out the contents. It was still stuck. She reached in, groped around, found the strap that was holding it, pulled.

The bottom of the pack came loose, releasing the first-aid kit. She turned it upside down again, shook it free.

The kit fell with a clunk onto the table.

His wallet thudded after it, bounced open, spilling contents.

A slip of paper wafted after it, settled like a feather on top.

A credit card slip.

For a meal at Mumbai airport. Only a week ago.

Skye stared at the strange name on the bottom. Scott *Armstrong.*

She felt her jaw drop and turned her head slowly to look at her companion.

He lay on the bed, eyes closed, pain etched into his features. He clutched the wound on his arm, pale as death. Blood seeped through the cracks between his fingers.

She turned, rummaged quickly through his wallet, found two credit cards. One for Scott McIntyre. One for Scott Armstrong.

Her hand began to tremble. Her eyes flicked to the bed.

Backup.

He was going to call for backup.

With a sat phone.

He had a gun.

No ordinary civilian in Canada carried a handgun.

The tremor spread to her limbs. She forced herself to her feet.

Tiny beads of perspiration broke out above her lip. She wiped them away with trembling fingers, stared at the man on the bed. He was no innocent writer.

Then who the hell is he?

Chapter 15

The bitter bile of betrayal leached acid into Skye's stomach. Her brain spun in a dizzying kaleidoscope. Maybe the name on the slip meant nothing. Maybe McIntyre was his writer's alias. He said he'd been traveling.

Who was she kidding? He had to be working for someone. His moving in next door must have been orchestrated.

Oh, God. Her hand flew to her forehead. He'd befriended her. Seduced her. Made love to her. Deceived her. He had stolen into her heart… For her secrets? Had everything been a lie?

No. She couldn't believe it. Panic danced through her blood, skittered through her gut.

Who is he?

All those things, those little hints that should have alerted her, they crashed now like a tsunami through her brain. The knife at his ankle. His wary moves. The professional way he'd escaped their tail. The way he'd disguised her with that wig. The way he'd picked up on her Greek connections. She should've seen it coming.

No. She *had* seen it coming. Only she'd refused to acknowledge it. Refused to act on it. Because he had made her feel.

But it was all a lie.

Terror clawed through her stomach. She'd told him everything. Oh, God. And he'd just sat there. Listening. Had he known all along? Her eyes shot to the door.

She could run. Her eyes flicked back to the pile of contents on the table. The car keys lay among them. She glanced at the man on the bed. He needed help. He was bleeding badly. Honey whimpered at his side.

The sight of those pleading doggy eyes tugged at her soul. She couldn't just leave Scott to die like that. A maelstrom of confusion crashed through her. Whoever he was, this man had gotten hurt trying to save her life. She had to fix him up, stop the bleeding.

Then she'd run.

"It's okay, girl," she whispered. "I'll take care of him."

She lugged the heavy wood table over to the bedside. Steadying her hands, she took the scissors from the first-aid kit and cut into his sleeve. She tore it open and set about cleaning away blood so she could get a good look at the wound. He groaned softly at her touch, winced as disinfectant stung. His lids fluttered open and he looked up at her with those hauntingly beautiful bottle-green eyes. Those eyes that had lied to her. She halted, caught by what she saw there.

She forced her attention back to his injury, willed herself to focus on his injury.

He'd been right—it was a surface wound. The bullet had ripped through his flesh. It was a mess but it wasn't life-threatening. Not if she stopped the blood. She worked quickly, efficiently, as she'd been trained to do. She taped the edges of the wound tightly with the adhesive butterfly sutures she found in the kit. They would serve until he could get it sewn up properly. She found analgesics and antibiotics in the first-aid bag. It was a comprehensive back-country kit he carried. But she wasn't surprised at his survival skills.

Not now.

He was someone sent to spy on her. Someone trained to betray her. She could no longer control the tremor in her limbs. With unsteady hands she unscrewed the cap of a water bottle, gave him the pain relievers. "Here, drink."

He did. "Thanks, nurse." He motioned with his chin to the neatly bandaged wound on his arm. "You learn to do that in the camp?"

"Yes. Let me look at your chest."

She peeled off the remainder of his shirt, found the smashed wreckage of his phone in his pocket, set it on the table. The impact of the bullet glancing off the phone had caused the myriad of blood vessels under his skin to rupture. The blood was spreading, pooling into what was going to be a devil of a bruise. She pressed tentatively with her fingers. He gasped in pain.

"I don't think your ribs are cracked." She was concerned, however, about other internal bleeding. "How does it feel? You got a sense there's any serious damage in there?"

He shook his head. "Nah. I think I got lucky."

She helped prop him up. He groaned in pain.

"Knee?"

"Blown it. Probably for good now."

She said nothing, started to remove his pants. He helped by lifting his butt as she edged the jeans carefully down his legs. His knee was a balloon of wobbly mass. She swallowed her shock, averted her eyes. "It needs ice, but I haven't got any. Maybe these anti-inflammatories will help. I'll splint it, bandage it." She set the pills on the table and got to work splinting his knee with two pieces of wood from the woodpile. Job complete, she stood back, stared down at him.

He frowned. "I look that bad?"

"You'll live." But he sure as hell wasn't going to be able to follow her.

She shut her eyes, tried to marshal her thoughts. She should go. Now. But she couldn't just leave him like this. She spun on her heels, marched out the door and stepped once again into the dark. She scanned the ground with the flashlight, located his wooden cane.

She propped it against the wall beside the bed where he could reach it, then filled his water bottle, set it next to the pills. She filled Honey's water bowl, poured dog biscuits into another. And she placed his gun carefully on the table within his reach. The Glock she tucked into the back of her jeans. Grabbing the car keys, she started throwing her things into her pack.

He watched in silence.

"You going somewhere?"

Her eyes snapped to his. "I am."

"Where?" He struggled to pull himself up into a sitting position.

"I'm taking your vehicle."

"What're you talking about?"

She held up the sales slip, credit card. "These. They say your name is Scott Armstrong."

He blanched.

"Who *are* you?"

"Skye—"

"Nothing about us was true, was it? You slept with me, made me care for you." She fought the quavering edge in her voice, grasping for a tone of confidence, authority. "Dammit, you made me care. You didn't have to go that far."

"Skye, sit down. I can explain."

"Lie to me some more?" Her whole body shook uncontrollably now. "I don't think so." A deep ache swelled in her chest as she looked into his eyes, his face, saw his hurt. It threatened to suck her up, drown her. Obliterate her.

"Sit. I'll tell you everything. I was going to before we were attacked."

"Right." She remained standing.

He pushed himself into a full sitting position, grimacing as he moved, eyes flashing in spite of his pain. Or because of it.

"Sit."

She backed closer to the door. "You said nothing, down at the lake, while I spilled my guts. You knew all along, didn't you? And you didn't say a goddamn thing. You watched me bleed. You're no better than a filthy, scheming jackal."

"Skye, hear me out." His voice was laced with pain but he spoke with urgent force. "I *needed* you to tell me. You have to understand that. It *had* to come from you."

Uncertain, unsteady, she lowered herself onto the chair nearest the door, well across the room from him, still clutching the keys. "Why?"

"Because in my heart I believe in you."

Her heart gave a sickening lurch. She swayed momentarily from dizziness.

"I wanted to know you were a victim in this. I had to be certain. I couldn't turn you in without giving you a chance to tell me...everything." He coughed. Agony twisted his features as the spasm racked his injured chest. He caught his breath. "I had to be sure. I *need* you to be innocent, Skye. Goddammit, I need *you.*"

He slumped back, face bloodless.

Lord, she wanted to believe him. More than life, she wanted to believe him. Her chest ached. She half rose to go to him. Held back. "Who are you? Who do you work for?"

"My name is Scott Armstrong. I'm an agent with the Bellona Channel."

She felt her mouth drop open. "You...you were sent to spy on me," she whispered. "Why?"

"I'm going to give it to you straight. I may live to eat my words, but I believe in you, Skye. Remember that."

"Tell me," she said quietly. The yellow light of the lanterns flickered and shadows shivered as she spoke.

"Bellona thought you might be connected to the Rift Valley Fever outbreak in the States."

Her mind reeled. "Why?"

"You were there at the right time. You'd come via Africa. You have the expertise."

"And *that's* what you were going on?"

"You are also on record as having expressed the opinion that an ecological attack would be an ideal anti-imperialist ploy to undermine the American economy."

"It's true."

"It's *that* kind of sentiment that alerted authorities. Our intelligence indicated you'd expressed revolutionary views. It was my mission to sound you out."

"And that included making love to me?"

"Skye—"

She gave a soft, wry laugh. "Don't even try to explain. I know of these things. That's what Malik trained me to do."

"This was different, Skye."

She ignored the hurt in his eyes. "Since when do you put people under surveillance for a theory, *Agent* Armstrong? Is that what the world has come to?"

"It's what men like Malik Leandros have reduced the world to. And checking you out was Bellona mandate. We keep an eye on things government sometimes overlooks. If it proves serious, we involve various law-enforcement agencies where necessary."

Skye rubbed one hand over her face. She felt tired. Very, very tired. But she had to know. "How long have I been watched?"

Scott's head flopped back on the pillow. Drained, he stared up at the ceiling, took a deep, shaky breath, blew it out slowly. "You weren't exactly a high priority until the *invalid* rolled into town."

Skye leaned forward. "What do you mean?"

"Bellona was looking to keep me busy and out of their hair while I recuperated." He gave a dry little laugh, coughed, winced. "I think my boss thought once I laid eyes on you, you'd help keep my mind off other things."

"Like your wife and child, like your injury," she said softly.

"Yeah." He closed his eyes, gathered his thoughts, opened them. "I figure Rex thought you'd help dig me out of my morose pit. He even threw in the dog for good measure."

Confusion spiraled through her brain, clashed with anger, empathy, pain. The whirling force of mixed emotions held her immobile in its vortex. She could only stare at the powerful, injured male that lay on the pine bed.

He struggled to sit again. "Rex was right. You did distract me, in more ways than one. But he was wrong about one thing, Skye. This was no lame mission. This is a major coup. This could net us La Sombra, the world's most wanted man."

Reality smacked her sharply up the back of the head.

The injured Bellona agent thought netting Malik would redeem him, show his organization he was still strong. She could see it all now, how he was using her. She tasted bitterness. "So I played right into your hands when I asked for your help."

Scott nodded.

"You fed off my need. You fed off my fear of Malik's men."

"Skye, those guys in the brown car, they weren't La Sombra's. They were feds."

"What...what feds?"

"Come here, closer, sit on the bed. What I'm going to tell you isn't going to be easy."

She clamped her teeth together. "I'll stay here, *Agent.*" She was afraid to go near him. Terrified he'd capture her in another elegant web of lies, hold her heart prisoner with false words, render her immobile with a warm, caring touch. "Just spit it out. All of it."

He hesitated.

"All of it," she demanded.

"The feds were after a guy who is now known to be Balto Nakiskas. An Anubis operative."

"What has that got to do with me?"

"Skye...Jozsef Danko *is* Balto Nakiskas."

The world tilted under her chair. Her head swam. She felt sick. Couldn't breathe. She pulled at her shirt, tried to loosen its grip on her neck, tried to harness her thoughts. But the blood was draining from her brain, leaving her numb, stupid. "Jozsef?" The word came out a soft croak.

"Please, come sit here."

"No," she snapped. She didn't know where to turn. She had to keep her distance from him. "I don't believe you." But she did. She was just having trouble computing it. "He...he was going to marry me."

"Yes."

She shook her head. "W-why?"

"We're not sure."

"If Jozsef works for Malik, that means Malik has known where I am for more than a year. Why...why didn't he just kill me?"

"He must have a purpose for you."

"But *how* did he find me?"

"Jalil."

"Jalil? You know about Jalil?"

"He's dead, Skye. Has been for over a year."

Blood drained instantly from her head. "Oh my God," she said softly.

"A system from northern Greece has been tapping into Jalil's computer."

"Northern Greece? *Malik?*"

"That's our guess. Except we thought it was just another cell. Authorities are closing in on it as we speak."

"But Jalil was e-mailing me."

"They set it up so you thought you were still corresponding with him. They got into your computer through Jalil's system. My guess is they got to know you that way. They learned what buttons "Jozsef" needed to press in order to insinuate himself into your life, in order to woo you."

She tried to swallow. Her mouth was like sawdust. Tears welled hot, spilled silently down her face. She jerked up from her chair, spun to face the window, clutched arms tight to her stomach. "How...how could I let this happen?"

"Don't blame yourself, Skye. I've seen this kind of thing done before. A hacker who gets into a personal computer can learn a lot about that person. He can make you think you are his soul mate. Like you told me, you thought he was almost too perfect."

"No...how could I let this happen to Jalil."

"It was beyond your control—"

"No!" She jerked around to face him. "He died because of *me!*"

"That's the assumption."

"Did they torture him?" She glared at him, defying him to tell the truth.

Scott hesitated. "Yes."

She stared at the stranger on the bed. "Jalil was my friend."

Skye took a step, then another. She paced the room quickly, back and forth, her boots clonking on the wood floor. She had to think. Why had Malik sent Jozsef into her life? What purpose could he have had for her? She froze.

Oh, God. The blights. She whirled, faced Scott. "That

trip to Texas, and to Africa, they were for Jozsef's business. It was at his insistence that I joined him."

"He insisted?"

"Yes. He was doing work for an import-export company out of Europe."

"Don't tell me—KTS Global?"

"How do you know?"

"It's the company that paid for the rental of the truck that was tailing us. KTS Global is held by a parent company in Belgium, which in turn seems to be a shell for another numbered company in Athens."

"Malik?"

"It's a good bet."

She sucked in a shaky breath. "Jozsef took sample tins of Belgian foie gras on those trips. He had opportunity to introduce pathogens. He could have contained it in those tins." Then it hit her. Skye's stomach heaved, dry. "Jozsef also insisted I go with him to Ontario, just before the whitefly outbreak." She turned slowly to face Scott. "Oh, my God. It was him. And they wanted to blame *me*. They've been setting me up all this time. They probably leaked the information about my travels."

Scott struggled to sit up again. "It's possible." His mouth pulled sideways in a grimace. "In fact, I'd bet my life on it." He held his hand out to her. "I just knew you hadn't done it, Skye. I knew it," he said softly. "Come here."

She felt the primal tug of his gentle words at her very soul. But she held her ground. Stood steady on the floor in the middle of the cabin. It was her only way to maintain any kind of mental order. Because everything else was spinning out of control. It was too much to absorb at once. She forced her thoughts into coherency. Jozsef, alias Nakiskas. The man had demonstrated an unhealthy interest in her beetle project. Her brain reeled. *Had Jozsef meddled with her beetles, too?*

Was it possible that he'd introduced something that could make them a vector for yet another disastrous outbreak, one she'd be held liable for? One the Canadian government would itself spread across the country?

Was it all part of a diabolical plan? First to introduce genetically altered whitefly. Then to infect whatever assassin bug was sent after it?

Jozsef had opportunity. He'd been in her lab at odd times. He'd had access to her computer.

It was vintage Malik. The master strategist had found her, and he was using her to do his dirty work. And he'd filtered intelligence out, making it look like she was to blame. No one would believe she was innocent once they knew of her background. She'd go down as his soldier, after all these years. He'd get the notoriety. The credit would go to Anubis. And she'd be reviled. *If* he let her live long enough.

"Scott, Jozsef meddled with my beetle project. I'm sure of it now. That's why the core group showed those strange variations."

"Did Charly handle those beetles?"

"Charly is *not* involved in this."

"Skye, she *is* involved, against her will. She's been diagnosed with Q-20. They believe she inhaled the virus somehow."

Skye's knees sagged. She groped for the table edge. "Inhaled?"

"That's their best guess. The illness manifested first in her lungs."

It *couldn't* be. Yet the subtle changes she'd seen in her adult beetles and grubs were certainly more indicative of the African cousin of her little Asian beetle. When researching a predator, she'd ruled out the African beetle. Although it had a voracious appetite for whitefly, it had a propensity to carry a cotton-like fungus that could end up doing more damage to crops than the whitefly it was sent to destroy.

And, it was suspected, that in very, very rare cases, the

dung of the tiny African beetle could host the deadly Q-20 virus. It hadn't been proven. But it had been a major factor in her decision not to use the African beetle.

Jozsef would have seen her notes. Malik must have used the information, gotten Jozsef to introduce the African beetle or an infected genetic variation into her core group. He *wanted* her beetles to spread the cotton-like fungus across North America. And that meant Charly must have contracted Q-20 in her lab.

As far as she could recall, Q-20 first attacked the lungs of its human host. The first sign in victims was pneumonia-like symptoms. If the patient was old, or very young or immunocompromised, it would kill them at this stage. If the human host was strong, medication *might* save them. If not, the virus would move next to attack internal organs. At this point, it was almost always fatal. She prayed they'd diagnosed Charly early enough.

Skye's heart pounded. She had to get back to the lab, to check her beetles. If she was right, if Jozsef *had* infected them, they would end up killing millions.

And they were due to be released across the country in one week.

Skye spun around, grabbed her backpack. If she took the SUV, she could make it out through the backcountry and be back in Haven by tomorrow afternoon.

Determined, single-minded, she marched for the door.

"Skye, where are you going?"

She halted, hand on the doorknob, turned to faced him. "I have a job to finish, *Agent.*"

"You can't run anymore, you said so yourself. You have to turn yourself in."

"I'm not running. I'm fighting. I will stop him. Myself. I will not be deceived anymore. Not by Malik. Not by Nakiskas. Not by *you.* I will *not* let him win. Not this time."

"Where are you going?"

"To stop those beetles."

"Let Bellona help. Turn yourself in, dammit."

"Right. Then your job will be done. You'll be the redeemed hero, and I'll go to prison. You can wash your hands of me. Is that how it goes?"

"Dammit, Skye, I said I'd be there for you, and I meant it!" He struggled to get his legs over the side of the bed, to stand, but he crumpled under a wave of pain.

She winced inside. He'd be fine if he only lay still. "I'll send someone for you."

"We can do this, Skye. We can defeat La Sombra together."

"Sorry, Scott," she whispered. "I thought we were a team. I was wrong."

She pulled open the cabin door, stepped out into the dark wilderness night. Alone.

Scott tried to force himself to his feet, to go after her, but his knee failed. He collapsed against the side of the bed, slid down to the cold floor and clamped down on a scream of pain. A sickening wave, spinning with dots of light, swirled in his brain.

The lantern light flickered, mocking in the tiny room that had become his prison. Honey quivered, whimpered, licked his face. He was too weak to push her away. "We lost her, girl. Goddammit, we lost her." He stared at the closed door, heard the roar of the SUV engine out in the dark.

Blackness swallowed him.

Skye clenched her jaw, curled fingers tight around the wheel. All around her the dark shapes of conifers stabbed into the night sky like secret soldiers closing in on her.

She blew out a shaky breath of relief as the dirt track finally started to descend. Dawn was a distant peach-and-violet hint along the tops of the mountains. It wouldn't be much longer now until the logging road intersected with the highway. She could be at the Kepplar labs in another six hours. Once she got to her beetles and quarantined them, she'd turn herself in, tell the authorities where to find Scott.

Malik stared, mesmerized by the little pulsing red dot on the computer screen. It emanated from the GPS device in Dimitri's satellite phone. It had been motionless, just pulsing in the same spot for hours.

They should have reported in by now. Had Dimitri's attack failed?

It was all going wrong.

The virus had matured too quickly—that Sheldon woman should not have gotten sick. Now the authorities had been alerted by her mysterious illness. Nakiskas was infected, too. His doctor said he'd be dead in days, if not sooner.

Suddenly, the emergency alarm shrilled from the far computer. Malik spun around to see his assistant's face, deadly white. "The base. In Greece. It's being raided."

His heart stalled. This was not possible. "By who?"

"Greek military. U.S. forces."

"Cut all communication from the ship! Blackout!" He grabbed a jacket. "Prepare the chopper. I'm releasing those beetles. Now!"

His assistant's eyes flared in shock. "You? You will risk it?"

"Operation Vector will *not* be compromised." He would *not* let that bitch beat him at his game. Ever.

Chapter 16

It was daylight when he woke.

Scott winced against the sunlight that cut across his face as Honey's cool snout prodded him.

He moved his arm but stilled immediately as pain burst, radiated, into his neck, chest, leg.

God, he was a mess. He fought his way out of the pain-induced stupor, fumbled for the analgesics Skye had left on the table for him, swallowed with gulps from the bottle she'd set next to them. The water hurt his dehydrated throat as it went down.

What was left of his shirt was stiff with crusted blood. He was cold. He forced his eyes open, peered at his watch, pulling the figures into focus. Noon. Damn—he'd lost more than twelve hours. He had to move. But his body was stiff as a board, rigid as the splint Skye had fashioned to hold his leg together. He reached down, touched his knee, flinched. It was a bloody mess. The bone that anchored his knee joint must have cracked. The worst case scenario Dr.

Singh had warned him about. All he had to worry about now was a blood clot.

But he didn't have time to worry.

He tightened the bandage Skye had bound around his leg, strangling the pain. If he lost his goddamn limb, so be it. That wouldn't make him a cripple. He knew now being injured was a state of mind. He'd be crippled if he failed this woman. This woman who had the heart, the guts, to take on a formidable foe. This woman who'd snagged his soul and shown him where the road lay.

The road home.

He couldn't imagine a future if he failed her, couldn't imagine one without her.

He clawed himself up, fumbled among the belongings spread across the table. He located the map. With his finger he followed the line of the river, recalling where he'd last heard the sound of the chopper landing.

Their attackers had been neutralized. The chopper would still be there. If he could just get there, just reach that helicopter, he might still get to her before Malik did.

Tires screeching, Skye roared into the Kepplar compound. The afternoon weather had turned foul. A wind howled off the ocean. Clouds roiled black on the horizon. Fat drops spat at her windshield.

There were no cars out front, and she remembered then it was Sunday. The labs would be empty. She rammed on the brakes, lurched out of the vehicle.

And halted.

The front doors were open. This was highly unusual. She hesitated. But she didn't have time—she had to get those beetles. She bolted down the corridor toward her lab, her boots resounding on the floors of the dark, empty building.

She shoved open the door of her lab. It crashed back against the wall.

She stopped dead.

Her beetles. Everything. Gone. Her stomach swooped.

A muffled groan sounded behind her.

She spun around. "Marshall!"

He was slumped on the floor against the wall, his face fish-belly white. He clutched his stomach. Thick black blood welled between white knuckles.

"Oh, God, Marshall." She dropped down beside him. "What happened?"

"The beetles," he croaked. "They…took the beetles…shot me…"

Panic surged through her chest. "Who? Who shot you?"

"Two men… Friends of Jozsef's."

She grasped his face between her hands. "Marshall, Jozsef is a terrorist."

"He…he was going to help me broker a contract. With…with the Americans. He was helping…me."

"No, Marshall. He works for the Anubis network. He infected the beetles. They will kill millions. Where are these men?"

His eyes rolled back.

Panic kicked at her ribs. "Marshall, stay with me."

He pulled into focus. "I—I'm…so sorry, Skye…" His chin slumped onto his chest. She felt his pulse. He was gone.

Desperate she shook his limp body. "Marshall. Oh, God, who took the beetles?"

"I did."

She froze.

It came from behind her. The voice that lurked in her darkest nightmares.

Her mind went gray and blank as the Arctic. Ice gripped her throat. Her limbs lost sensation.

"Stand up and drop your weapon." His Greek-accented words ground through her brain. Neither time nor distance had dulled its raw command.

Her stomach turned to water.

She was suddenly eighteen again, unable to move, to think. Powerless in the face of this black force.

After all this time, all these years, she could do nothing in the face of her nemesis. A thick viscosity oozed cold through her brain, swamping, suffocating rational thought.

All she could think of was Scott and Honey and their golden warmth. But they were gone—she was alone.

"Turn."

She couldn't not obey.

She dropped her gun with a loud clatter to the floor, forced herself to her feet, made her leaden body turn slowly around.

She looked first at his feet. Then up the length of his faded jeans, the bulging muscles of his powerful thighs, up the solid torso and into the sharp, striking face of the dark and obscenely powerful man.

Her brain screamed.

But she was compelled to look deep into the inky void of his eyes.

He smiled, teeth stark against olive skin. The teeth of a jackal.

God help me.

"I have waited for this moment, Zeva." His voice curled cold and black through her veins. "Come to me." He stepped forward, held out an olive-skinned hand. The dark, seductive power of his voice reached through time, curled around her throat.

Then she heard the sound of chopper blades gaining momentum. Dread pooled cold in her stomach. He was going to take her away.

He grabbed her arm, yanked it up behind her back. She couldn't even flinch at the pain. She could smell him, his male strength. He jerked her arm higher, forced her forward, in front of him. She felt the barrel of the cold gun at the base of her neck.

And suddenly there was no energy, no life left in her. No will even to live.

She'd failed to make it on her own. The beetles were gone. She'd lost Scott.

She walked with Malik Leandros to the waiting helicopter outside, feeling his breath hot and humid at her neck.

She walked to certain death…and worse before it, she knew.

He'd won.

Scott left the chopper beyond the fence of the compound, Honey locked safely inside. He was spent from the effort it had taken to get this far. With rasping lungs, he dragged his useless splinted leg behind him, worked his way through the Kepplar parking lot. Sweat drenched his aching torso. He could hear rotor blades warming up on the far side of the compound.

He reached the wall, let a wave of blackness pass, found focus again. He dug his nails into the brick as his world swayed. He gagged, steadied himself, waited again for the wave to pass, his vision to return. He hugged the edge of the building, used it to prop himself up, pull himself up along through the dizzying pain.

He could see the small chopper now, near the hangar at the far end of the compound. The doors had been removed. Perfect for shooting anyone who dared give chase.

The pilot, stocky, dark-skinned, wearing an orange flight suit, was loading sealed boxes from the shed. Alone.

The pilot ducked into the chopper with a box. Scott swiped the rain, the cold sweat from his eyes, felt for the gun that Skye had left him. He held his breath, dragged himself around to the loading bay while the pilot was out of sight.

There was one last box. He lifted the lid carefully. Beetles! In sealed jars.

He dropped the lid back into position and waited for the pilot.

From behind a packing crate, he could see another man exit the far end of the Kepplar building. Very tall. Dark. He had Skye. A gun to her head. Even from this distance she looked lifeless, crumpled, pale as a porcelain doll. Hair, soaked by the downpour, clung to her face like paint.

La Sombra?

He tensed. It *had* to be him. Because Skye had no fight left. It was not like her. She'd been defeated in some very elemental way.

Anger exploded violently in him. He struggled for breath, willed his fury down. She'd be okay. He'd make it so. He watched as the man forced Skye toward the chopper. They would have to go around the hangar to get here. He waited until they disappeared from sight.

And he braced as the pilot came back for the final box.

Malik forced Skye's head low under the lethal blades. The deafening downdraft slapped wet hair painfully around her face. She didn't care. She had nothing left to fight for.

He shoved her up into the cabin. A pilot waited at the controls, helmeted head turned away from them.

Malik began to climb in after her.

But the pilot touched the controls, lifted the mechanical beast sharply into the air.

Skye gasped, groped for purchase, missed, fell sideways.

Malik flailed backward, as his leg slipped out the door. He cursed, grasped the edge of the seat, pulled himself back up into the cockpit with one hand, gun still clutched in the other.

"Niko!" He barked.

The pilot's head turned. Malik gasped.

Scott! Skye's stomach swooped. Sweet Lord! He'd come for her. Her heart stuttered, beat back to life. Warmth flushed into her cheeks.

Then she saw the gray pallor of his skin. The black holes of his eyes. The sunken hollows in his cheeks. The sheen of fever. Oh, God, he must be in terrible pain.

She scrambled to pull herself up.

The chopper lurched higher into the air as Scott tried again to dislodge Malik.

Malik cursed and slid back toward the open door. Again his foot slipped, dangled over air. With awesome strength, he hauled himself up into the cockpit, raised the gun to Scott's head. His finger curled around the trigger, squeezed.

Skye jerked into action. The heel of her boot cracked up against Malik's jaw. His head flew back, spewing drops of blood. His shot went wild, piercing the Plexiglas window.

Skye unleashed another kick, connected the side of his face. His neck cracked sideways, his skin split open, blood gushed. He growled in pain.

The gun clattered to the floor.

Skye lunged for it.

Malik checked her with a shoulder of rock, cracked his elbow up into her cheekbone and lurched for Scott at the controls.

Skye slumped back, momentarily dazed. Blood oozed down her face, warm and thick. She watched, as if in distant slow motion, Malik grab Scott around the neck, tear him off the controls.

The chopper veered sideways.

Skye instantly found her focus, swung forward, seized the controls. The chopper swooped. In terror she saw they were over the ocean. She pulled on the controls, guided them out of a nosedive, then steered the buffeted craft into a violent, mounting wind.

Beside her Malik forced Scott to the ground, tightened fingers around his throat, a bestial growl rumbled in his own. Scott, on the brink of consciousness, flailed back at him. Then Malik leaned on his torn-up knee.

A terrible howl of pain filled the air, melded with the deafening roar of blades.

Images of a wolf and jackal tearing at throats sparked through Skye's mind. He was not going to make it, she had to help him. This was her fault.

She lunged over to pull Malik off.

"Just fly the damn thing!" Scott growled. "Focus!"

Malik's fist connected with his jaw. Scott slumped back in a grunt of pain. Malik pulled himself up, reached for the gun. But Scott dug into a final reservoir of strength, kicked up at him with his good leg. Skye took the cue, veered the craft sharply sideways. Gravity, the force of Scott's kick, spun Malik and the gun toward the gaping maw of the door.

The gray sea lurched hungry far below.

Scott moaned, kicked one last time. Malik went over, grasping vainly at the door in a last desperate attempt to escape the churning orifice below. He missed.

But he caught the skids.

The chopper lurched.

Malik swayed below, attached by one hand.

Skye struggled to steady the craft.

Scott found the knife at his ankle, hooked his good foot in the bottom of the seat, leaned out the door, slicing wildly at La Sombra.

The skin split over his knuckles. In a scream of pain he fell, spinning, wheeling wildly down to the waiting sea, the wind sucking a terrible sound from him.

Scott clawed his way up into the passenger seat. He slumped back. Limp.

"Scott. Oh, my God, Scott—"

"Fly, girl." His voice was like sandpaper. "Keep flying. Thank God you can fly."

He'd lost too much moisture, blood. He wasn't going to make it. The wind tore at them. Rain lashed at their craft. She had to get him to medical attention. But she tensed suddenly as another chopper loomed large out of the gray, closed in on them. "There's someone on our tail."

He struggled to look up. "Bellona."

"Bellona?"

"Yeah." Scott eased the helmet off, let his head flop back in the seat. His face was gray, damp with pain. His brown hair was matted with sweat. A muscle pulsed wildly in his neck. "Bellona and CSIS, RCMP, FBI...the whole freaking world. They're after me, too, now."

She stared, blank.

"For not handing you over." He coughed, wheezed, clutched his chest. "I'm...on their Wanted list. Wouldn't stand down when ordered. I took that helicopter in the forest, came after you." He struggled for another wheezing breath. "I'm done for, baby. It's you and me. In it together for the long haul." He gasped when he tried to move his knee. It was at an awful angle. He tried to pull his leg back into alignment.

Oh, God. He'd compromised his job—his life—for her. She was overwhelmed with emotion. Tears pricked hot, spilled down her face in cathartic release. She wiped them away, realized she was still bleeding.

"Can you land this thing?"

"Yes."

"Good. Take her in. They can have us now. The beetles are in back. Sealed jars."

She stared at him. A sob jerked though her body. She wanted to fly forever. She didn't want to go back to reality. To risk losing him. She wanted to fly them into the storm where they would never be separated.

He reached out, held her hand over the controls. It was ice cold. "Take her back, Skye," he said softly. "I'll be there...for you. Always. I promised you that."

She swallowed the aching balled lump in her throat.

"Why? Why, Scott?" she whispered.

"Because I love you, Skye—I *love* you."

Tears blurred her vision.

''Fly this damn thing, will you? Focus.'' He slumped back, slid into unconsciousness, overcome by his injuries, his fight.

And with new courage and fierce determination, she turned for the shore, rode the wind, flew the beast in.

To face her future. With him.

Chapter 17

Skye paused, took a deep breath, clutched the bouquet close to her chest and pushed open the door to the hospital ward.

"Hey, beautiful." Scott's eyes twinkled deep green. His voice was rich, welcoming. It rolled right through her, infused her with warmth.

She smiled at the rugged man in the white hospital bed. Not even hospital sheets could tame the wild look of him.

But inside, her heart ached.

This was going to be one of the toughest things she'd ever done in her messed-up life.

"Is that my cue to say, 'Hello, handsome'?" She set the flowers on the table at the bottom of his hospital bed.

A large grin slashed his face. "Daisies. I like daisies."

"I do, too." She fussed with the blooms, not looking at him. "They're happy flowers."

"Skye."

Her eyes flicked up.

"What is it, Skye?" Concern creased his brow.

She forced another smile. "Nothing." She came around to his side, took his hand. It was big and rough in her own. "I've just been to see Charly and she's doing great. They caught the virus in time. She's going to be fine. How's the leg?"

He pulled a face. "It'll do. I'll be in a cast for a couple of months. But they figure if I listen to the doctors this time around, I could eventually come close to being as good as new."

She reached out, laid the palm of her hand on his cheek, felt the rough male stubble against her skin. "I want to thank you, Scott. For everything. You were true to your word. You were there for me. I don't know how you did it, but you came through. You're one hell of a man."

His brow dropped low. "You winding up for something?"

"I couldn't fight him without you. I lost it…when I saw him. I simply lost my strength. I needed you there, your spirit. You risked everything to be there for me. I want to thank you for that." She swallowed. She was choking on the words. But she had to get it all out. She wouldn't have another chance.

He struggled into a sitting position, his eyes glinted fierce. He grabbed her wrist, powerful fingers encircling like a metal cuff.

"Skye, what are you telling me here?"

"I'm leaving. I came to say goodbye."

His features slackened with shock. He pulled himself sharply back. His grip tightened. "Why?"

"I must."

He lurched up, snagged his hand behind her head, tugged her face down inches from his. His eyes bored into hers. Hot. Furious. "Don't you dare! I love you, Skye. You're not going anywhere."

She tried to pull back, couldn't breathe. Lurking below the glint of his eye, she saw raw pain. It ripped through her heart. ''Scott, you don't know me. Everything about me was a lie. You still call me Skye. You think I'm someone I'm not. I'm facing criminal charges...I don't even belong in this country. I'm an illegal alien. I'll be deported before you walk again.''

She *had* to give him this out.

As much as it rent her apart. She had to show him a back door. But, Lord, she prayed he wouldn't take it, step right out of her life. Because she had nothing else in this world. Nothing she wanted more than him.

''That's bull and you know it,'' he snapped. ''I know you better than anyone else on this planet. To me you *are* Skye. Always will be. I didn't fall in love with Zeva the Greek fighter. I didn't fall in love with Van Rijn the bug doctor. I fell in love with *you,* dammit. The person underneath it all. The dear, gentle, strong woman who reached deep inside my heart and stole my very soul.'' Sparks of wet, livid life shot from his green eyes. ''Stay with me,'' he pleaded, his voice rough. ''Stay with me always.''

Her heart lurched, swooped. It was as though the bottom of her world had fallen out from under her. And she was light. Flying free, silvery bonds of love linking her to a voluminous chute. This man. She blinked back the tears stinging behind her eyes.

She couldn't speak, couldn't breathe with relief.

''You will always be Skye. It's the name that gave you freedom to come to this country. The one Jalil found for you. And it's the name that will give you the freedom to stay.''

''W-what do you mean?''

''That's what your new papers will say. *Skye.* You belong in this country. You performed a heroic act for this land, and you brought La Sombra's empire down. Canada is honored to make you a citizen.''

She felt her jaw drop.

''Yeah.'' A wicked slash of a grin cut his face. Small

lines fanned sharply out from the brilliant green of his eyes. "Bellona organized it with Immigration. You're legal. But...there are two catches."

"Catches?"

"Conditions. Number one—you marry me." His eyes bored hot into hers as he said the words, stared her down. Waited.

That odd ache in her chest cracked, exploded. She choked on the sensation. Her hand flew to her mouth. Hot warmth swelled, radiated, through her body. It spilled out in tears. Sweet, hot tears that slid down her cheeks. She had no voice.

He watched her intently. Then he dropped his voice to a rough gravel whisper. "The citizenship papers, they'll read Skye Armstrong. *Agent* Skye Armstrong."

She opened her mouth. Still no words came out.

"Can't have Van Rijn on those papers. That name belonged to someone else. So you're just gonna have to marry me and get legit. I want your hand. I want us to marry in that little Haven chapel. And I want you in the dress of a Greek goddess."

He pulled her slowly to him, whispered in her ear, "Will you marry me, Skye? Can you forgive me?"

"Yes," she whispered. "Oh, God, yes. If you can ever forgive me."

He pulled her mouth down onto his.

And she melted into him. Breathed in the male scent of him, tasted the wild strength of him. Tasted life.

He wrapped his arms around her. Tight.

And she felt whole. Loved. Wanted. Needed. As never before.

She'd found a home. A country. A name. A place she'd always be welcome. A place she belonged. A man she loved more than anything in this universe.

She pulled back slightly as his words registered. "Did you say *Agent* Skye Armstrong?

"Ah, yeah. That's condition number two."

"I don't understand."

"Condition number two is you go to work for the Bellona Channel."

"Me?"

"We don't usually recruit from the ranks of trained terrorists, but you come ideally equipped with the science background *and* the ability to do undercover detective work for Bellona when needed. Rex wants you to help me head up our new island lab facility. Bellona has been wanting to get that lab operational for a while now. It'll serve as a highly specialized division focused on developing antidotes and vaccines for pathogens with a potential to be weaponized. We'll do fieldwork as needed."

Skye felt dizzy. She could not have dreamed this up in her wildest fantasy. "Scott...I—I don't know what to say."

"Say yes."

"We'll be a team?"

Moisture filled his green eyes. "Yes, a real team."

Skye choked back the tears in her throat, strained for some focus. "Before I accept, Agent, I need to ask you something. I need you to tell me about your wife and child. I need to know what really happened."

He didn't hesitate. "Leni and Kaitlin were killed in a suspicious car accident after I was warned to stay away from a man we called the Plague Doctor. My boss, Rex Logan, and I were on his case some years ago. Rex heeded the warning, walked away to save the woman he loved and their son. And they live to this day. They're a family." His voice cracked slightly.

"And you, Scott, you couldn't walk from your wife, your baby. And they were killed?"

"I—I've never been able to come to terms with it. With my guilt."

She smoothed his cheek. "And you've been running ever since. Like me."

He stroked her arm. ''But you helped me come back, Skye. You showed me how to get home.''

''And you can be with me? You aren't afraid anymore?''

He shook his head. ''No. We're a team. We're in this thing together. We both understand the game...don't we?''

''Yes,'' she whispered. ''We do. And I accept. Both conditions.''

Scott steered the SUV onto the Lion's Gate Bridge. Bright shafts of sun cut through cloud. It made the cruise ships and tiny fishing boats below seem like bright shining toys on the glittering waters of the Burrard Inlet.

Ahead mountains loomed green and imposing clear through to Alaska. They held rivers, adventure, a potential lifetime of discovery.

His home.

It had never looked more beautiful, more promising. And it seemed like ages ago, another life, that he had flown in here, fighting every step of the way, only to be handed a dossier on Skye Van Rijn, a yellow dog and a key to the future.

He glanced at the woman sitting beside him holding the black bundle of fur. He smiled—couldn't help himself—couldn't contain the raw, elemental joy that emanated from his very core. She returned his smile. And he felt ridiculously whole.

It had been one hell of a passage. But he'd finally made it. He finally felt he could say goodbye to Leni and Kaitlin. Lay them properly and honourably to rest in his mind. Stop beating himself up over it all.

Skye had helped him face it. Deal with it. She'd taken his hand and shown him the road through the wilderness. And like two crazy pilgrims in a hellish landscape, they had traveled it together, faced the demons, faced each other along the way. And found their treasure. Found trust... and love.

He reached over, squeezed her hand.

"How much longer to the ferry?" she asked. "I think Merlin has to pee."

Scott chuckled. Ah, the glories of owning a dog. "We'll stop on the other side of the bridge."

At the sound of their voices, Merlin lifted glistening black puppy eyes, wiggled her plump little body. Scott reached over, ruffled her silky fur. He was looking forward to training her. Working with her. It had been hell giving Honey back. It had been Skye's idea to get a puppy of their own. And once the seed had been sown, nothing but a black lab would do. And she was named Merlin in honor of his childhood canine friend. The one who'd accompanied him and his dad on their fishing trips.

He'd asked his father and mother to help pick out the puppy. They'd been delighted. And they had welcomed Skye warmly into their home.

Skye was watching his face. He was sure she could see straight into him at times.

"I love your mom and dad, Scott. I feel like I'm finally getting the parents I never had in my life."

"You read my mind? I was just thinking about them."

She chuckled.

"They like you, too, Skye. They figure you brought their prodigal son back to life."

She reached over, laid a hand on his knee, stared out over the glittering water. "Maybe one day I'll try to find out what happened to my own birth mother."

"Well, you better wait. Mom wouldn't want to share you or the wedding planning with anyone else on this earth right now."

The sun was sinking in a fiery orange ball over the island mountains as Scott drove the three of them onto the ferry for the last leg of their trip to Haven.

With their vehicle parked in the ship's bowels, they made

their way up to the top deck, stepped out into the bracing sea air, and worked their way to the back of the boat. The water below churned white and green as the ferry vibrated with the rumble of engines firing up.

Scott had Merlin tucked into his jacket. Skye poked his bulging belly. "You're not supposed to bring dogs to the upper deck," she whispered.

He winked. "I won't tell if you don't."

She grinned. "You're incorrigible, Armstrong. Don't you ever play by the rules?"

He slipped his arm around her, pulled her in close. She smelled like citrus and sunshine. "Nope," he said. "But I have a feeling rules are not your thing, either."

She snuggled into him. "I just have one rule. No more secrets."

"No more secrets," he whispered into her hair.

Skye stared out over the expanse of ocean and couldn't help but wonder what secrets lurked in its depths. "They never found his body," she said.

He leaned in close to her. "He's gone, Skye. Even if he made it out of that fall alive, even if he didn't drown, everything he built has been crushed. It would take decades for him to ever amass that kind of power again."

She nodded. "Thank God you got to those beetles in time." She turned to him. "The test results came back. They weren't sterile. They would've reproduced. He would have released a deadly scourge like nothing seen before."

He stroked her cheek. "Not now."

"You're right." She smiled, hooked her arm into his. "Enough of the past. Now we look to the future."

And they watched gold sovereigns of sunshine shimmer on the evening water as the wake of the ferry grew in a wide and frothing vee behind them. They watched the shining towers of Vancouver grow small in the distance.

But ahead there was hope. Promise. Because the three of them were going home.

Together.

* * * * *

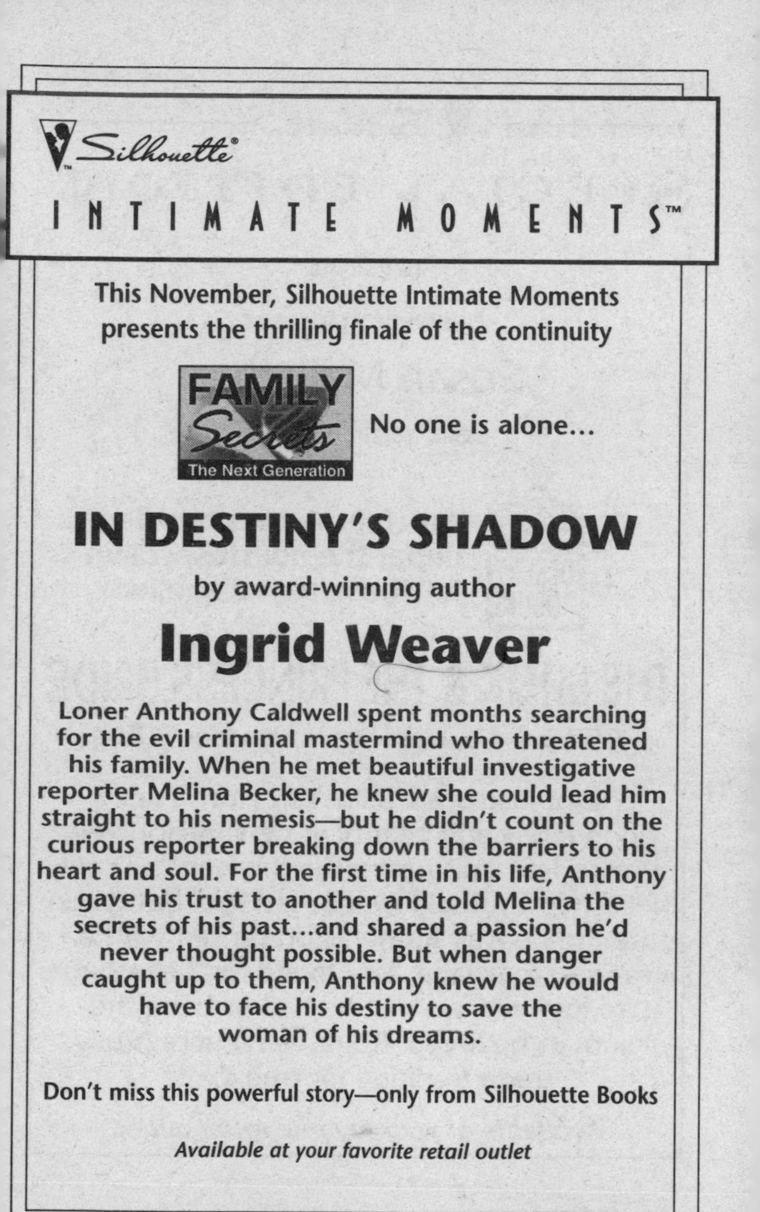
Silhouette®
INTIMATE MOMENTS™
This November, Silhouette Intimate Moments
presents the thrilling finale of the continuity
FAMILY Secrets
The Next Generation
No one is alone...
IN DESTINY'S SHADOW
by award-winning author
Ingrid Weaver
Loner Anthony Caldwell spent months searching for the evil criminal mastermind who threatened his family. When he met beautiful investigative reporter Melina Becker, he knew she could lead him straight to his nemesis—but he didn't count on the curious reporter breaking down the barriers to his heart and soul. For the first time in his life, Anthony gave his trust to another and told Melina the secrets of his past...and shared a passion he'd never thought possible. But when danger caught up to them, Anthony knew he would have to face his destiny to save the woman of his dreams.
Don't miss this powerful story—only from Silhouette Books
Available at your favorite retail outlet
Visit Silhouette Books at www.eHarlequin.com
SIMIDS

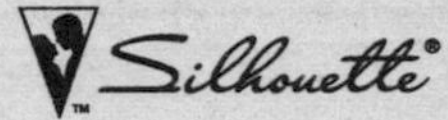

SPECIAL EDITION™

presents

bestselling author

Susan Mallery's

next installment of

Watch how passions flare under the hot desert sun for these rogue sheiks!

THE SHEIK & THE PRINCESS BRIDE

(SSE #1647, available November 2004)

Flight instructor Billie Van Horn's sexy good looks and charming personality blew Prince Jefri away from the moment he met her. Their mutual love burned hot, but when the Prince was suddenly presented with an arranged marriage, Jefri found himself unable to love the woman he had or have the woman he loved. Could Jefri successfully trade tradition for true love?

Available at your favorite retail outlet.

Visit Silhouette Books at www.eHarlequin.com SSETSATPB

Silhouette®

SPECIAL EDITION™

Coming in November to
Silhouette Special Edition
The fifth book in the exciting continuity

THE PARKS EMPIRE

DARK SECRETS. OLD LIES. NEW LOVES.

THE MARRIAGE ACT

(Silhouette Special Edition #1646)

by

Elissa Ambrose

Plain-Jane accountant Linda Mailer had never done anything shocking in her life—until she had a one-night stand with a sexy detective and found herself pregnant! *Then* she discovered that her anonymous Romeo was none other than Tyler Carlton, the man spearheading the investigation of her beleaguered boss, Walter Parks. Tyler wanted to give his child a real family, and convinced Linda to marry him. Their passion sparked in close quarters, but Linda was wary of Tyler's motives and afraid of losing her heart. Was he using her to get to Walter—or had they found the true love they'd both longed for?

Available at your favorite retail outlet.

Visit Silhouette Books at www.eHarlequin.com SSETMA

Clip this page and mail it to Silhouette Reader Service™

IN U.S.A.
3010 Walden Ave.
P.O. Box 1867
Buffalo, N.Y. 14240-1867

IN CANADA
P.O. Box 609
Fort Erie, Ontario
L2A 5X3

YES! Please send me 2 free Silhouette Intimate Moments® novels and my free surprise gift. After receiving them, if I don't wish to receive anymore, I can return the shipping statement marked cancel. If I don't cancel, I will receive 6 brand-new novels every month, before they're available in stores! In the U.S.A., bill me at the bargain price of $4.24 plus 25¢ shipping and handling per book and applicable sales tax, if any*. In Canada, bill me at the bargain price of $4.99 plus 25¢ shipping and handling per book and applicable taxes**. That's the complete price and a savings of at least 10% off the cover prices—what a great deal! I understand that accepting the 2 free books and gift places me under no obligation ever to buy any books. I can always return a shipment and cancel at any time. Even if I never buy another book from Silhouette, the 2 free books and gift are mine to keep forever.

245 SDN DZ9A
345 SDN DZ9C

Name (PLEASE PRINT)

Address Apt.#

City State/Prov. Zip/Postal Code

Not valid to current Silhouette Intimate Moments® subscribers.

Want to try two free books from another series?
Call 1-800-873-8635 or visit www.morefreebooks.com.

* Terms and prices subject to change without notice. Sales tax applicable in N.Y.
** Canadian residents will be charged applicable provincial taxes and GST.
All orders subject to approval. Offer limited to one per household].
® are registered trademarks owned and used by the trademark owner and or its licensee.

INMOM04R

©2004 Harlequin Enterprises Limited

Coming in November 2004 from

Silhouette Desire

Author **Peggy Moreland** presents

Sins of a Tanner

Melissa Jacobs dreaded asking her ex-lover Whit Tanner for help, but when the smashingly sexy rancher came to her aid, hours spent at her home turned into hours of intimacy. Yet Melissa was hiding a sinful secret that could either tear them apart, or bring them together forever.

The TANNERS of TEXAS

Born to a legacy of scandal— destined for love as deep as their Texas roots!

Available at your favorite retail outlet.

Visit Silhouette Books at www.eHarlequin.com

SDSOAT

eHARLEQUIN.com

The Ultimate Destination for Women's Fiction

For **FREE online reading,** visit
www.eHarlequin.com now and enjoy:

Online Reads
Read **Daily** and **Weekly** chapters from our Internet-exclusive stories by your favorite authors.

Interactive Novels
Cast your vote to help decide how these stories unfold…then stay tuned!

Quick Reads
For shorter romantic reads, try our collection of Poems, Toasts, & More!

Online Read Library
Miss one of our online reads?
Come here to catch up!

Reading Groups
Discuss, share and rave with other community members!

For great reading online,
visit www.eHarlequin.com today!

INTONL04R

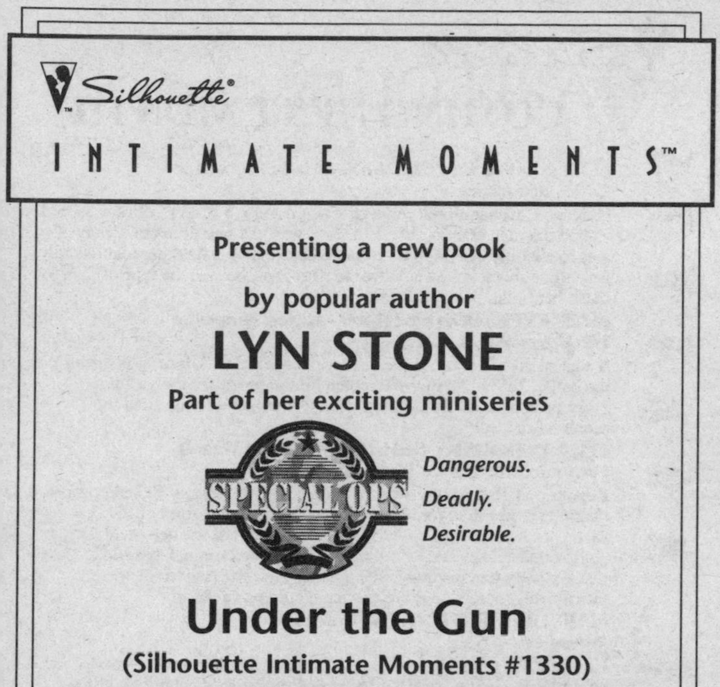

After escaping the bullet that killed his twin, Special Agent Will Griffin awakens from a coma to discover the killer at his bedside. Thanks to some quick action, he's on the run again. But this time it's with the one woman—Special Ops Agent Holly Amberson—whose very proximity makes him feel like he's under the gun. Because once the assassin is caught, Will knows his life won't mean a damn without Holly in it.

Available in November 2004 at your favourite retail outlet

Be sure to look for these earlier titles in the Special Ops miniseries:

Down to the Wire (Silhouette Intimate Moments #1281)
Against the Wall (Silhouette Intimate Moments #1295)

Visit Silhouette Books at www.eHarlequin.com

SIMUTG

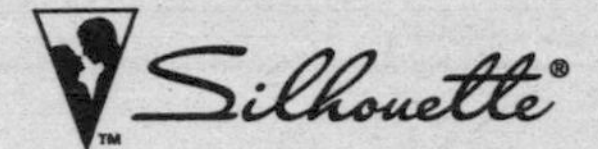

INTIMATE MOMENTS®

COMING NEXT MONTH

#1327 ALONE IN THE DARK—Marie Ferrarella
Cavanaugh Justice
Patience Cavanaugh felt relieved when detective Brady Coltrane agreed to find the man stalking her. But there was just one problem. Brady was irresistibly sexy—and he wanted more than a working relationship. Even though she'd vowed never to date cops, he was the type of man to make her break her own rules....

#1328 EVERYBODY'S HERO—Karen Templeton
The Men of Mayes County
It was an all-out war between the sexes—and Joe Salazar was losing the battle. Taylor McIntyre tempted him to yearn for things he'd given up long ago. Would their need to be together withstand the secret he carried?

#1329 IN DESTINY'S SHADOW—Ingrid Weaver
Family Secrets: The Next Generation
Reporter Melina Becker was 100 percent sure Anthony Benedict was too potent and secretive for his own good. His psychic ability had saved her from a criminal who was determined to see her—and her story—dead. They were hunting for that same criminal, but Melina knew that Anthony had his own risky agenda. And she *had* to uncover his secrets—before danger caught up to them!

#1330 UNDER THE GUN—Lyn Stone
Special Ops
He could see things before they happened...but that hadn't saved soldier Will Griffin from the bullet that had killed his brother. Now he and fellow operative Holly Amberson were under the gun. With his life—and hers—on the line, Will would risk everything to stop a terrorist attack and protect the woman he was falling in love with....

#1331 NOT A MOMENT TOO SOON—Linda O. Johnston
Shauna O'Leary's ability to write stories that somehow became reality had driven a wedge into her relationship with private investigator Hunter Strahm. But after a madman kidnapped his daughter, he could no longer deny Shauna's ability could save his child. Yet how could he expect her to trust and love him again when he was putting her in jeopardy for the sake of his child?

#1332 VIRGIN IN DISGUISE—Rosemary Heim
Bounty hunter Angel Donovan was a driven woman—driven to distraction by her latest quarry. Personal involvement was not an option in her life—until she captured Frank Cabrini, and suddenly the tables were turned. The closer she came to understanding her sexy captive, the less certain she was of who had captured whom... and whether the real culprit was within her grasp.